THE
BONES OF
BARRY
KNIGHT

EMMA MUSTY

Legend Press Ltd, 51 Gower Street, London, WC1E 6HJ
info@legendpress.co.uk | www.legendpress.co.uk

Contents © Emma Musty 2022
The right of the above author to be identified as the author of this work has
been asserted in accordance with the Copyright, Designs and Patents Act
1988. British Library Cataloguing in Publication Data available.

Print ISBN 978-1-91505-4-722
Ebook ISBN 978-1-91505-4-739
Set in Times. Printed by CPI Print
Cover design by Kari Brownlie | www.karibrownlie.co.uk

Printed and bound by CPI Group (UK) Ltd, Croydon CR0 4YY

Emma Musty is a writer and editor with the Are You Syrious? Daily Digest, which chronicles news from the ground regarding the refugee situation in Europe, and a long term member of Khora Community Centre which works with marginalised groups in Athens. She is also a freelance Human Rights report writer, previously for Refugee Rights Europe. She found her writing legs in Wales and has a PhD from Aberystwyth University. Emma's first novel, *The Exile and The Mapmaker*, was published by Legend Press in June 2021.

Follow Emma on Twitter
@EmmaMusty

and on Instagram
@emmamusty_author

In memory of Angus Petrie, you are missed.

For all the parents, children, siblings and friends who will never be found.

You'll die at sea.
Your head rocked by the roaring waves,
your body swaying in the water,
like a perforated boat.
In the prime of youth you'll go,
shy of your 30th birthday.

– Abdel Wahab Yousif (aka Latinos)

PROLOGUE

One day in the year of my birth, a man I'd never meet finally decided that he'd had enough of the situation in our country. Maybe this happened as he sipped his tea that morning or as he kissed his wife, or maybe it was his wife who said it first: 'It's time, darling, we must change the world together.' However it started, the repercussions of this decision would lead to me fleeing seven years later, would force the hot breath out of my mouth as I ran – for my mother's life, for the memory of my brother and father – through a city that seemed to be roaring, whose bones creaked under the weight of the rest of the world. We would cross multiple countries and traverse borders that existed only in the depths of the sea. We would survive for just long enough to die for real.

Of course, you could trace the beginning of this war back further. Right now I'm in the perfect place to do it; my bones one small part of a museum exhibit. I could speak of the origin of walls, of the rising and falling of empires as regular as the tide, wiping everything clean, over and over again. Maybe you've studied history already, maybe not, but I guess you sense its presence on this page. It's all I am, after all. To help you understand it, I could tell you the name of my country, the nature of my war, so you could pick apart my story, tell me how it really happened – but I don't know the modern name anyway and, besides, it doesn't matter.

Now I lie scattered, broken up into fractions of what I once was, no more than pieces of bone encased in glass and wood. The story of human evolution is right next door: Homo ergaster with her strong face and solid posture, hominid confidently strolling through the plains with no idea of what is about to befall him, Homo antecessor merrily spurring a porcelain fish from a dry river bed, and finally Homo sapiens, the interim victor. Yet we were not the only weavers of ritual, not the only ones to love and question, to mourn our dead. Homo neanderthalensis was right there with us, along with the elephants of course.

At night, as I hover through the galleries, I stare into the glassy eyes of animals I never saw alive, and, from what I hear from the chatter of my guests, can no longer be seen. Monkeys scream at me silently as I pass them on the staircase. They're upset about the extinctions, right from the very first one up until now. In the case of the woolly mammoths, it was the warming temperatures in the south that forced them to flee, the first humans hunting the remaining refugees. Even the survivors of the Pleistocene transition are now gone. Here in the museum, the common-spotted cuscus, the bush-tailed rock wallaby and the rabbit-eared bandicoot stare out blind-eyed, nailed down as they are to wooden plinths, and call out a mute protest at their annihilation to a moth-eaten giraffe killed and stuffed in 1909. I wonder if they also inhabit this space as I do, trapped and unseen. Sometimes I wait, listening for their voices. Occasionally I hear a distant howl or hoot – and then, nothing.

There are other people with me, speaking a language that I know, though it's not my own. Some of them I knew in life; some not, though I had at least seen their faces in the refugee camp where I lived. Now, we are all part of the same spectacle. Their voices surround me as do their bones; it is all we have left, half-lives and memories. We are displayed as we were found, our last moment preserved for eternity, lived relationships enacted still through entangled limbs held in place by the once sun-warmed earth that surrounds us.

I've tried to filter out our stories, our difficult truths and complicated lies. Sneaking around the darkened corridors of the museum and the archive room that the curators think is locked, I've managed to piece together an account of how we ended up here. We want to be understood. We are a lesson, and I hope that when it has finally been learnt, we will be free.

1

APATHY: A BEGINNER'S GUIDE

BARRY

If I were to write a book about my life, I'd cut out all the shit bits. This bit here, for example, would definitely not be in it. This bit here is terrible: the waking up in the morning and not knowing what the fuck is going on, again, the opening of your eyes to the colour beige, the knowledge that you are somehow living a beige life and that this means that at some point, you clearly stopped paying attention. My precious guitar lies broken-stringed in the corner and there's a stranger in my bed. I can hear her breathing, but have to acknowledge that I am only guessing at the gender of this person, which, along with their name, escapes me.

Outside, the close-cut grass of the lawn leading to the offensively bright blues of the sea and sky reminds me I'm in Florida and there's a small sense of comfort in this knowledge. The gig last night went well, I think, although the second half is a little hazy. A touch too much of the good stuff might have been imbibed in the interval, but the crowd seemed to like it, they certainly made a lot of noise. This is usually a good thing, apart from that one time in Berlin when it was definitely a bad thing. Something else that would be left out of the book.

Tonight there'll be a different venue, another few lines and a new stranger. This one is waking up. It's time to be brave, to investigate, so I turn on my side and there she is, her blonde hair falling over her unlined face, a dried crust at the corners of her otherwise perfect mouth. A few freckles scattered along her cheeks. It's tempting to rouse her, but suddenly she looks a little too innocent, and maybe a little too young, so instead I clamber out of bed naked and leave the room.

'Sam!' I shout as I approach the kitchen, 'Coffee!'

Sam appears from his bedroom, his face crumpled. He's not aging that well, our Sam.

'Give me a minute, you bastard,' he replies and he goes to the bathroom and pisses with the door open.

When he re-emerges, I ask if he knows the name of the stranger; we settle on Jade, though neither of us is a hundred percent sure. Sam clatters around the kitchen making far too much noise for this time in the morning. It makes me want to go straight back to bed but the stranger is there and I can't cope with looking at her face again until I've had coffee. All the air wheezes out of the leatherette-covered stool by the breakfast island when I sit on it and makes me think of an old man's lungs searching for air, and failing to find it.

Sam's talking at me, telling me to put clothes on, asking me not to put my naked arse on the stools – my stools, I think, but don't say. The person potentially called Jade enters wearing the shirt I wore on stage last night. They often do this, then forget to take it off when they leave and, the next thing you know, your favourite shirt's on bloody eBay. Once I even had to bid to get my own jacket back.

I offer her coffee, a necessary courtesy, but Sam's the one who actually pours it while giving me his I'm-trying-not-to-head-butt-you look, which I have, over the years, decided to take as a form of affection. In retribution he disappears, dresses, and leaves the house. I hate this bit and so try to get it over with as quickly as possible by asking if she needs a lift home, which I can give her on the way to the sound check. Chivalry is not dead.

The driver drops Jade – I'm now feeling quite confident about the name – off at the small apartment building where she says she lives alone. It's two storeys, blindingly white, and has a neat little lawn all around it with a complex sprinkler system ejaculating water into the air at regular intervals. She kisses me on the cheek as she leaves and whispers her goodbye. It's too much, this vision of another life, a life where you meet someone, get to know them, move into a little white house together, purchase a cat, etc. I turn away and pay attention to the passing traffic instead.

I arrive far too early for the sound check, but relieved to be there. When the band finally turns up, they make their way straight to the stage, nodding to me casually as they pass. They're alright guys, but they've only been hired for the tour and, however much I concentrate, I can't remember their names. Twenty-odd years ago I was in a real band. That's how this whole gig got started. Steve, Gaz and Martin. The boys. We thought we'd be together for ever, but it didn't last, of course, nothing does. Sam arrived just at the end, a fixer, and he stuck with me after the split.

I climb the stairs to the stage last, find my X, stand on it and test my mic. The arena is cavernous. I can't see the outer reaches – it could be Dante's inferno out there for all I know. With the edges of this universe unknown and the blinding stage lights I can't see anything at all. I turn around to smile-squint at the guy on lead guitar. He nods at me in a way that reminds me he is paid to do it. I try not to show that this physically hurts me, a pain in my chest that grows outward, grabbing at my ribcage, constricting my breathing.

Back in the day it was Steve who was right there next to me every night, with his ridiculous moustache and fucking beautiful big blue eyes. Gaz was on drums, best drummer on planet Earth, couldn't even see his hands move. And then

Martin, sweet, mysterious Martin. As quiet as a mouse until you placed a bass guitar in his hands and then a sweating, pulsating, machine of a man exploded through his skin taking his T-shirt with him. Girls didn't know what to do with him when they met him off stage. They expected the animal they'd seen playing these rough bass lines; instead, they met the mouse.

Being on stage now is like being surrounded by ghosts, reverberations from other gigs, in different countries, with better people, in happier times. Even that time in Berlin was better than this shit. These people are just strangers, fucking strangers everywhere, strangers without names and names without friends attached to them. Steve died of a heroin overdose six years ago, although what actually killed him, was choking on his own vomit. Death by vomit; one of the few moments when heroin overdose is the preferable statement to come out in the press, which is how I heard about it because Steve hadn't talked to me for two years, after I slept with his wife, who I'm pretty sure neither of us actually liked very much anyway. Fuck. The pain in my chest is continuing to expand, I can feel it in my fingers, in my toes, pain is all around me, it's everywhere I go. The knowledge that I will soon pass out or be sick or both is causing me to sweat.

Sam is walking towards me. He is the only person here who knows exactly what is happening to me at this precise moment, the only person in the whole goddamn world who even cares. He'll lead me away, we'll kill the ghosts together. The guy on drums is staring at me as I take Sam's hand and clutch it tight while he helps me off stage. This bit is also not going in the book.

'Come on, mate. You're all right, everything's gonna be fine,' he coos at me and it's almost too much, the softness of his voice, the fact that he's the only person that knows me anymore.

In the corridor outside the dressing room I crack right down the middle. All I can do is curl into him and let myself be held. He guides me into the room and sits me down on the small suede sofa, placing himself on the chair opposite. He puts his hands on my face.

'Look at me.'

'No.'

'Come on, you got to.'

I slowly raise my head and briefly manage to look him in the eye, but all the things we don't, can't, talk about are sat there between us, this is the problem with knowing each other, this is the risk that comes with knowing anyone at all.

'No, mate. Not now and not here,' he says, and I know I have to pull myself together, because Berlin was one thing, but by this point there are far worse things than bad gigs that I have to make myself forget. I take a deep breath, give myself a few sharp slaps and stand up.

'You're right. Pass me the stuff,' the good stuff, the one true friend.

The gig passes in a blur of dizzying lights and smoke machines. Dreamlike, ecstatic, entirely forgettable. As the last song finishes, I experience a brief moment of actual euphoria, which ends as soon as the lights go out.

'I love you Miami,' I scream into the darkness, pondering the meaning of this. What is it about Miami that I love? I can't think of a single thing.

After a deep bow I walk off the stage. Sam is there, just at the edge, waiting as he always does, but as I reach out to give him our customary hug, the craziness before the gig once again forgotten, forgiven, tucked away until tomorrow, he pulls back.

'We've got a problem, mate,' he says as he places a hand on my shoulder, 'that girl from last night.'

Jade.

'She was underage, mate. Where you dropped her off, that wasn't her flat, it was her parents'.'

That thing about feeling like a shit tonne of bricks is falling on you? It's happening to me right now.

'What do they want?'

'They're already talking to lawyers, mate, they saw you. It was our lawyer that called me.'

More bricks, big, heavy, fucking bricks. The book doesn't even exist anymore, nobody would read a book written by this person.

'But?'

'There is no but this time.'

'But last time…'

'Last time we fucked up this bad, we were on home turf, we had room to negotiate.'

'Money? Surely they'd take money?'

Sam's just shaking his head by this point, like the conversation is over, like there's nothing we can do. Part of me is still waiting to hear that this is a joke, but the other part of me knows it's not, and that part of me is shitting itself.

'The New York lawyer is flying down to meet us. She'll be here first thing tomorrow. We'll have to cancel Atlanta, maybe the rest of the tour.'

The strangers, the band, and all the rest of them, will hate me. I need to get home – preferably to one of the homes in another country, best of all, the one in London, the first one, the real one, the one where my cat would live if I had one – but Sam says I'm not allowed to leave. The driver takes us to the Miami home, the beige home, and my hands only stop shaking when I've downed three shots of vodka.

The doorbell rings and we both jump.

'That'll be the police.'

I know, by the way he says it, that he was expecting them.

'What? They can't arrest me, can they?'

'Yes, mate, you've been accused of a crime, this is what happens. The lawyer held them off from coming to the concert, but now you have to go willingly.'

The bricks are stacked so high now that a guy's turned up with cement to make sure his handiwork stays in place, he's blocking up all the air holes.

'Why didn't you tell me?'

'I didn't want you legging it and making it worse,' says Sam as he walks to the door.

I can hear them walking down the corridor towards me and Sam's right, I have an overwhelming urge to leg it, but instead I hold out my wrists like I've seen them do on TV. This will be the night when my career finally, inevitably, dies, and with this knowledge also comes a sense of relief.

They walk me outside and I raise my head just enough to check the press aren't here yet. One of the cops puts a hand on my head to stop me hitting it on my way into the car and I have the overpowering sensation that I'm living someone else's life, that there's been some terrible fucking confusion but that in a minute it'll all be alright again and I'll be at home with my fourth vodka, Sam and an old movie.

But it's not stopping and the pain is growing in my chest again. There's no Sam and no comfort. I'm pretty sure the cop car is expanding and contracting with my breathing and each time it contracts there's less and less room. I keep my head down. Some last part of my admittedly gigantic ego is refusing to die, or at least if it does die it's refusing to be seen dying. I crouch lower. If just one person recognises me it's all over, and, even if they don't, the papers will find out anyway, they always do – well, most of the time. I might have got out of a scrape before, but back then Sam had had a plan. There'd been no problem, in the end, to get rid of – at least not the sort of problem that puts you in prison, just the sort that keeps you up at night and makes you think twice about standing on high ledges unsupervised.

2

RITES OF PASSAGE

ANA

I'm still holding Catherine's hand even though it's now cold to the touch. I rub her skin gently between my fingers, as if I might bring back the warmth that was once there, and look around the room. This is the last moment in which this space will truly be hers. The dresser at which she would brusquely comb her short hair. The mirror, flecked with liver spots. The ink-stained wood of her desk, because in this house everything was constantly written on. The books on childhood development, various aspects of human rights law and a scatter of academic journals that lie piled with newspaper clippings about human migration. The unlikely floral curtains that must have come with the house thirty years ago. The cardigan slung across the back of the chair.

I look again at her face; her eyes still open but clouded. She was a force that moved within this world, and she is no longer. She was my mother, my other mother, and she is gone. I release her hand, leaving it on top of the bedspread, also floral and probably from a charity shop. She was a re-user of things. She did not believe in waste.

I make the phone call that must be made and can no longer be avoided. In the hallway I move my hastily discarded airport-tagged holdalls to make way, then go to wait outside the front of the cottage with the dogs. But I reconsider and instead take them upstairs with me one last time. They too must say goodbye. They sniff the air of the room and sense the change. One whimpers quietly, the other licks the hand I so recently let go of.

'They will come to take her away from us,' I tell the dogs, to prove to myself that I am still alive and have a voice. They clamber onto the bed and will not be moved until the ambulance arrives, when they greet the technicians by barking at their garish yellow and green suits.

A woman around my own age, with her hair tied up in a ponytail, tells me what I already know. With her colleagues she loads this body which I have loved for as long as I can remember into the back of the ambulance and drives away with it. I feel the loss of her physical presence instantly.

In the kitchen I take the bottle of good whisky from the cupboard and raise a glass to her. She does not respond, and I know that she will be quiet for ever now. She will not be coming back. I will not wake up in the morning and discover that this was all a dream.

The landline phone sits mutely on the kitchen table asking me to pick it up and find company, but instead I pour another glass. There will be plenty of time for talking. Other people would call their father at this point, but I have never had one. I pour another glass. I can hear Catherine telling me that I cannot go using her death as an excuse to fall apart, and then I give myself one night off from being sensible and knock back the whole shot. Just one night on my own with a bottle of whisky in an empty house that once held a family, even if it was only a family of two.

This is when the tears come in a rage of grief and self-pity; a great wide-open expanse of loneliness, so vast that nothing else is visible at the edges. All my horizons blur into the sky. The earth and the heavens become one. I find myself on the floor with my fists in my eyes choking back a scream buried deep inside me, like an ancient reservoir of oil waiting to bubble up through a well. The lone metal structure in the desert, rusty and creaking and unable to stop, is me.

Some hours later I wake up, momentarily confused as to which country I'm in, only to discover I am under the kitchen table, like the survivor of an earthquake. My throat is sore, and my eyes clogged and burning. The dogs are curled around me, trying to cushion me from myself.

I roll onto my back and stare up into the blackness of the table's underside. Of course, I know, I will get through this, everyone does, or at least most people do. I drag myself up, hitting my head as I do, and bring the roaring pain in my skull to my attention. I go to make toast, which I will force myself to eat, and tea, which I will force myself to drink.

Behind the kettle, in the moonlit semi-darkness, is the framed and faded press clipping that announced my arrival into Catherine's life. I take it out of the frame to hold it closer.

BABY BOMB

Bomb Squad Finds Baby on Tube

Last night an abandoned black suitcase was reported by passengers on a Bakerloo line train. The station was evacuated and the bomb squad was called. In the words of mission commander Detective Superintendent Bhalla, "nobody expected what happened next". The unmistakable sound of a baby crying came directly from the suitcase. "We just couldn't believe it!" Bhalla said. Officers approached carefully and found not a bomb, but a baby girl. The infant is thought to have been born outside of a hospital environment but evidence suggests she has been well cared for. She was found wearing a striped baby grow and blanket. She is now under the care of a local social worker. Police are urging the mother or anyone with knowledge of the child to come forward.

Catherine had been the social worker. When nobody came to claim me, she adopted me. Reading the cutting brings the tears back and I forget about the toast. I can't bring myself to put the scrap of paper back in its frame, so I tuck it in my shirt pocket to keep it safe.

At some point I realise that dawn is approaching; the toast is long cold, and the trees at the bottom of the garden are silhouetted against the grey-blue of morning. I take myself upstairs and tuck myself in. Sleep has finally become inevitable and I do not wake until the full light of day attacks me. My body feels so heavy I wonder if I will ever move again. The headache is still there. I grope around in the bedside table drawer until I find painkillers. The dogs hear me and come upstairs to jump on the bed and nudge me to life with their wet noses.

I finally get up and make my way to the top of the stairs, avoiding looking towards Catherine's room. Her door is open, her bed empty. The indentation of her head will still be on the pillow. The shape of her body will remain in the dips of the mattress.

It is time to call someone real. But still I hesitate. I let the dogs into the garden and make coffee. I drink it leaning up against the counter, like she used to, looking out of the window down the length of the lawn towards the woods and their darkness.

Today she will not feed the dogs. I will. She will not be here, though her notes and lists are still stuck to the fridge with magnets. She will remain unfinished, halfway through some things and yet to start others; a person who liked to be so efficient. Did she ever email the council about the recycling collection days? Did she order new ink for the printer or take her old winter clothes to the charity shop? Had she started the article whose scrawl of a title I can't quite make out? Her handwriting had become spidery, like that of an old person, because without either of us noticing, that is what she had become. I try to make out the country the title refers to. I think the second line is the name of a charity she was investigating, but the last line is a mystery that I will not be able to ask her about later.

When she reached retirement, she took up writing to keep herself busy.

'I can't just stop,' she'd said, 'I'm not one of those people.'

It was supposed to be a hobby, but it turned out she wasn't one of those people either.

'I must take after my daughter,' she'd say, laughing, as she sat down to pen some reply for the reader's section in the nationals on immigration, or Brexit, or infringement into the green belt. 'I have a lot of time to be opinionated.'

She even started a blog called Angry Old Woman Rants.

I sit at the kitchen table to call her brother in Seattle. Technically he's my uncle, but I've never really known him. Uncle seems too close a family tie for the relationship we have. He says he'll book his flights as soon as I have made the arrangements and, for some reason, this is the first time I've thought of this. Her funeral will be my job. This is what you inherit first. Familial duty. Burial rites. I call her lawyer. She gave me the number a few weeks ago for just this moment. I'm surprised now that she didn't just hand me the will and tell me her wishes outright. This would have been the practical thing to do, but even practical people fear death I suppose. Even practical people think there might be some small cause for hope. The lawyer says she'll call me back when she's looked through the will and as I put the phone down I catch sight of Catherine's bulging address book and realise that I haven't even started yet.

Next, to put off everything else, I call work. Pete, my editor, gives his condolences. He thanks me for filing my copy on the famine in Yemen and tells me to take some time.

'We're here for you if you need anything,' he says, and I nod and hang up, the memory of the dark eyes of children gone beyond hunger momentarily obscuring my grief. Their fragile bones. The powerlessness you feel when confronted by such an enormity of pain.

I look at the whisky bottle on the table, stop myself from reaching for it and instead pick up the address book. I open it by accident at my own name and see the neat rows of my university addresses and all the phone numbers I have had over the years. A few additional numbers from my ex-partners are squeezed into the corners. It's a tiny biro map of my life drawn by the only person who knew me well enough to do so.

For my bedtime stories while I was growing up, at least once a week we would tell a new version of my origin myth. I'd cut out pictures from magazines and assemble a thousand different lives in what we called my "memory book". We wrote down version after version, each illustrated by my own childish hand. I never imagined my birth parents as exiled royalty or foreign diplomats; I wanted them to be as real as I was, though I did believe they could be from anywhere. So one day I would be the daughter of an Indian carpenter, the next of a South American tribe. On another day my parents would be out-of-work Londoners struggling to make their way in the world, an ex-shop assistant and an unpopular novelist. Or a Bosnian bus driver and an office cleaner with no legal status. I could have had a DNA test to narrow it down a little, but I never did. I didn't feel it would truly explain where I came from – only my birth parents could have done that and nobody knew who they were. On the up side, if I was from nowhere, I was also from everywhere. I was free. The world belonged to me.

Catherine was my only anchor to a geographic place. This house, this garden, these lanes and fields. This green, green land. Those long summers that seem, from the perspective of adulthood, the biggest myth of all. The only disruption to our quiet lives were the foster children who passed through for short stays between families, on their journeys between two lives. They were often distant, sometimes violent and always confused by the turns their stories were taking. I never held their anger against them. They were in pain, but without all the boundaries that we put in place as adults to protect ourselves.

Catherine protected me during my teenage years, when identity suddenly matters the most and the questions you have only ever asked in private begin to be asked by strangers, outsiders to your inner world, with no knowledge of the damage they can wreak.

'Don't you want to know?' they'd ask.

'Go back to where you came from,' they'd shout.

At home, after the tears, we'd laugh at their stupidity and their narrow understanding of the world. They would never understand the freedom I had. In the end, we often decided that we felt sorry for them because they only had one story, one view, and no ability to see the many choices laid out before them. Of course, they also had a mum and a dad and a history they could claim as their own, but recognising this just made me cling to Catherine all the more fiercely.

My memory book became my diary and my only true confidant, allowing me to scrawl the feelings I couldn't voice even to Catherine. My first love, a boy who passed through our house for only a few days, my second love, a girl at school who was so beautiful I couldn't even form sentences in her presence. I stopped asking where I came from and concentrated on where I was going.

And then, two years ago, at the same time as Catherine was having her first tests and just before she started her first treatment, we finally found out. A call from the police station, another article in the paper. Twenty-five people had been found starved of oxygen in a truck outside Dover. Two of them, believed to be married, were thought to be my parents.

They had been carrying a photo of me and a copy of the same newspaper clipping we have in the kitchen.

They had died trying to breathe.

When they left me it was likely because they were being deported and all these years later, they had been trying to come back. I was asked if I wanted to see their bodies. I said no. It was too much, it still is. They were not my parents. I did not know them. Having craved them for so long, having given them up with the rest of my childhood things, I rejected them. Their bodies were repatriated to their relatives in Afghanistan. I was no longer from nowhere, but neither was I from there.

Catherine tried to speak to me about it, but I refused. I went to work. I came here on weekends to look after her. I refused some more. Eventually, she dropped it. I told no one else apart from Callum, my only remaining friend from school. It was easier that way.

And one day, these press clippings, my memory book with my imagined lives and teenage romances, the handful of articles I've published which are good enough to survive a news cycle, will be all that is left of me. Just like Catherine's lists and notes, her half-done things, I will never be finished.

I reach for the whisky after all.

3

YOUR DEATH WILL
BE TELEVISED

AMANDA

The truth is – and I hate myself for thinking this, but there's really no getting away from it – that what the world really needs right now, the only wakeup call that could possibly work, is a really impactful photo of a dead kid. And impactful in this context is difficult. There are dead kids everywhere, quite literally, and it's very easy to find their photos. But the world doesn't want mounds of dead kids covered in dust, or headless dead kids washed up on beaches. It wants the perfect kid, the could-just-be-sleeping kid, the looks-just-like-my-nephew-when-he-was-three kid. Now, that kid is hard to come by.

This kid, the right kid, represents all the others neatly – doesn't force you to ask too many questions, doesn't come with wordy leftist explanations as to why the kid is dead (even if they're right, even if I agree with them), does not make you question your lifestyle or your country's past, does not make you look too deeply into the roots of it all. This picture is perfect because it makes everyone pause for just long enough to dig their hands into their pockets, or to make a quick bank transfer. And then they can carry on with their lives and we can carry on with ours.

This is where I'm at. This is where twenty-three years in the charity sector has led me. If a picture of the CEO of an NGO lying face down on the pavement would have the same impact, then I'd do it. I'd jump out the bloody window right now. In fact, I might do it anyway. This, however, is not an argument I can make in a board meeting. Several words will have to be replaced with the phrase media strategy. And the backup, if no perfect picture miraculously emerges? It's even worse: it's Barry bloody Knight, and even he's not a definite.

I unbutton my jacket to let some air in and allow for breathing. I'm currently wearing a suit and I never wear a suit, but it's to impress all the men I'm about to talk to. And now here's Sophie, and she's leaning on my office door in that way she does when she's about to make my day worse.

'It's about Barry Knight,' she says, and I want to throw something at the wall.

She holds her tablet right in front of my face, the headline of a British tabloid taking up the entirety of my vision.

A KNIGHT OF SHAME!

Barry Knight accused of statutory rape
under Florida law

I close my eyes and let out a long, 'Oh.'

I manage not to swear, because it'll sound angry, and obviously I'm not angry with Sophie. This is not her fault. She did not feed Barry drugs or beckon him towards the teenager, and I never wanted to be one of those bosses that took shit out on their workers. In fact, I never wanted to be a boss, at all.

'Well?' she asks, with her eyes all big. She has one

of those faces that makes you just want to die from the innocence of it.

'We'll have to see if they intend to press charges.'

Back in my office I sit down at the computer and try to pay attention to the budget in front of me, a breakdown of Portaloo hire costs – installation, maintenance, cleaning, associated supplies – that's been flagged as one of our over-expenditures. I have to work out which bit to cut – the number of units, the frequency of cleaning, the amount of supplies, whether or not to bother maintaining them at all or just let them become the giant pile of shit they are destined to become anyway. I think about one of the endless emails I've recently received from volunteer groups, this from an environmental charity offering to come and dig compost toilets. And despite the fact that this breaks numerous regulations, despite the fact that many camps are on rocky plateaus in the middle of nowhere or covered in tarmac, or both, suddenly it's tempting – mostly because I like the idea of handing over this entire problem to someone else and having them say, 'Don't worry, we'll deal with it.' I am no longer sure that I want to be held responsible for whether someone living over 10,000 miles away – sometimes much further, sometimes a lot closer than most people realise – has a place to take a shit or not. I want the world to be a place where everyone who needs to take a shit can do so in a way that feels culturally and hygienically appropriate to them. It's a simple enough wish, isn't it? Well, not according to the board.

The computer's gone to sleep and I wish I could too but instead I walk to the window. Outside the streets are slicked with rain water. Autumn sun glitters the trees in the park opposite, drenching the golden leaves in honey, reminding me of Greek food, of good meals and laughter.

I've been with the charity since the start and remain as hands-on as I can. I arrived when it was still a minor enterprise, a small group of well-organised, passionate people trying to do their best in difficult circumstances. We were like a family, but better, because we actually liked each other. We worked tirelessly on our campaigns, travelled to the countries where help was needed and worked there ourselves, facilitated the set-up of grassroots projects, supported communities to care for the children of their towns and villages who had been made orphans by war, even dug a few compost toilets. And I loved it. I loved the work and loved the people I worked with. But that was a long time ago. Now I'm the only one left. Alex had kids and moved to Dorset. Ruhi went on to work in banking. Jem died of lung cancer. Omar left the charity, and me, after we finished up a project in the Gaza strip. I should have stayed with him. But against all advice, even the drunken words screamed at my own bathroom mirror, I stuck it out with the charity we started together. I learnt to compromise, a little more each day, to keep this whole thing going. Barry Knight was already a low point and I should have seen this coming. Why couldn't the stupid bastard just keep his cock in his pants for five minutes?

The camp he's supposed to visit has been entirely forgotten by the authorities. The occupants – many of whom have already tried to cross the Mediterranean, before being dragged back – have also survived war, or climate crisis, or gender-based violence, or homophobia, or economic collapse, or political upheaval, or some deranged and damaging aspect of Western foreign policy – anything from the appropriation of fishing rights, to the industrial poisoning of farmland, to shoot-on-sight orders at our external borders – and now they're stuck with less food than they had at home and the possibility of yet another war. A group of women who have lost their own children, and some who just want to give their time, are trying to look after the orphans. But they have next to no resources and now there are nearly five hundred bloody kids, five hundred kids who are about to have even fewer toilets. The only compensation they will receive are two tiny classrooms built by one of the overenthusiastic volunteer groups, though with these numbers they'll be lucky if they get even one class a week. But if Barry is seen to be paying attention, then the public will do the same. It's just that simple. Although it's not, obviously – it never is – but it's something.

Of course, at some point during the development of the charity, the fact that not all the children we worked with were specifically fleeing war, even though this is indeed what our name suggests, had to be discussed. The first time we talked about expanding our remit to climate refugees, for example, there'd been an argument.

'It is a form of violence to carry on doing things that you know will negatively impact others, and it is our violence. It is people like us who are doing it,' Alex had said, holding her pregnant belly, mindlessly eating one of those giant packets of crisps designed for a group of hungry teenagers. I had always thought people were supposed to crave healthy things, or strange things, or things they didn't usually eat, but Alex had always loved crisps and pregnancy was a great reason to eat them constantly.

'You're right, it lands at our door, but governments and corporations have to act. We're stretched already. How would we even get the funds? And if we did, how would we dish them out? There's not enough of us as it is, Alex, and you're leaving.' Omar had shrugged his shoulders in that way he did, his hands raised up to the sky as if he was asking the universe itself about our collective sanity. 'It's crazy; we should concentrate on advocacy, on getting the word out.'

Omar. His photo is still on my desk, the two of us together. It was taken on the beach in Gaza a few months before he left. He has his arm around me; I remember the feeling of it, the feeling of safety and of warmth and of love. Our eyes are screwed up against the sun. There's a candy floss seller in the background handing over a little pink cloud to a kid with rolled-up trousers wet from the sea. It seems like a long time ago now, and still the very thought of that day makes me shiver, as if I haven't been warm since. But then it's also just cold in here, the way it is in old, badly insulated buildings, and I pull my jacket sleeves down to cover my hands to warm them. It doesn't help, so I reach down to touch the radiator under the window to see if it's working. A weak heat is emanating from it. There is another office; the 'central office' which has proper heating and dimmer switches. But this is the building we started out in, graduating from the basement to the fifth floor. Despite the fact it can be bloody cold, has the feel of an abandoned public hospital and is on the opposite side of the river to where I actually live, I'm not quite ready to leave it. How long the board will let me get away with this, I do not know. They like to use words like consolidation and maximisation, and other words that end in 'ation'.

Sophie's back at the door again and is doing the sorry-to-bother-you quiet knock thing which I can't stand because it's pointless, and also because it underlines the fact that she's not disturbing me anyway as I'm not actually doing anything useful.

'Have you replied to that woman yet? Catherine Something, the one with cancer, the one who says she knows you? Only you asked me to remind you before I left.'

Of course I haven't, further proof that I am useless. I can't even remember who this woman is. I stare at Sophie until she continues.

'The one that said she was dying and that she'd take us down with her if it was the last thing she did.'

Oh yes, how could I forget? How does she know me?

'I'll do it right now.'

The problem with investigative journalists, or writers, or dying women, or whoever this person is, is that they often fail to see the bigger picture. Okay, I get that the dead kid rant was strong and that maybe it should give me pause for thought as to where I'm at and, as a consequence, where this charity is at, but I'm a realist, I have to be. Being a realist is essentially my job, and in the real world compromises have to be made. So, this woman, Catherine Whatever-her-name-is, is probably worried about the conditions in the camps we work in, where the money comes from and where it goes, etc. Well, she's not the only one; most national governments are worried, the board of this charity is worried, hell, even I'm worried. The only problem is that we're all worried for different reasons. The board thinks that there are too many toilets, the journalist woman probably thinks conditions should be better and that there should be more toilets (although I still haven't actually read her email), and the governments think that the camps should be worse, potentially with no toilets at all, so they don't create a pull factor, as if having an adequate number of toilets will bring thousands running – 'Have you heard, in the camp a little further north they have loads of toilets!' 'Praise be to God, we must leave everything and go there now!' So, to be allowed to be there – to have access to these humans, to provide them with any services at all – we have to compromise, and that's just life. That's the bottom line.

4

RIGHTS OF PASSAGE

SALEEMA

From this high place where I'm sitting – way above the camp, in a hollow made by the wind, hidden in the towering rocks – I can see everything. The dust trails of the vans of charity workers driving out to us. The broken walls and fences that surround the camp. The low buildings with the tarps slung over their roofs. The office where the government man works. The security guards cradling their guns and picking their teeth. The dirty white tents lined up in rows in the centre. The washing strung up between them. The roofs of the wooden and tin shelters people have built to expand their living space, the blanket-wrapped bamboo lean-tos. The construction site that they say will be classrooms. I can see the younger kids, some of whom I know, running through it all. A couple of their mothers are waving at them to stop, probably shouting, but I am too far away to hear. The men are huddled in one of the few shady corners to the side of the charity cabins, bent over into their conversations, smoking.

That's why I like it up here, I can see it all laid out before me, a living map. And it's quiet. And I can read. There's no library here, but one of the security guards brings books for me. He's not so bad, though my mum says I shouldn't talk to him. She says nothing in this life is free. I hide them so she doesn't make me give them back.

I lean up against the rock and pretend it's my father's lap I'm sitting on. I close my eyes for a moment and imagine his embrace, the strength of it and the feeling of safety. Sometimes, when I read, I imagine it's his voice reading to me, telling me tales of far-off countries, of wizards and children who can perform magic. I whisper the spells to myself. 'Expelliarmus,' I say under my breath when the security guards are shouting at someone, and once I think maybe it worked because they stopped and walked away.

Noor is climbing up to me. I can hear her scrabbling at the rocks. She is the only other person that knows about this place.

'Hi,' she says and her face and hands are dusty from the climb, but her cheeks are shining red like apples underneath.

'What was all the fuss about down there?' I ask her.

'Ahmad stole rice again.'

'He's going to get us all in trouble.'

'He's just hungry.'

'Well, so are we and we don't steal rice.'

'Only because we're not brave enough.'

'Who are you saying isn't brave?'

'Us, both of us.'

'I'll prove you wrong, I'll get us both rice and for our families.'

'Saleema…' she begins, as if she's going to tell me off, but she stops.

'It doesn't matter, come on, let's go. I'll get the rice and I won't get caught like that stupid boy,' I tell her.

We are sliding down through all the little rocks and spiky plants, kicking up dust like the cars do when they're going fast. It feels so good that I could squeal with delight, but I don't in case anyone in the camp hears me and yells at us. It's still light when we get to the wall and climb through a break in it, but the sun is starting to set over the rocks and dunes and the world is turning pink. We sneak up to the building where the charity people put the new rice. It came days ago, but no one's given us any yet. Noor sticks with me. She won't leave me now, even though this was my idea and she doesn't really approve.

The door is padlocked, but that's stupid because the building doesn't have a proper roof, and with Noor's help I scramble up the back wall, wriggle under the tarp, and drop down on the inside straight on top of the sacks. I find an open one and sniff it before putting my hands into it and lifting handfuls into my skirt which I bundle up like a bowl. I'm half done when I hear Noor whispering my name. I grab one more handful and start towards the back of the room where I got in, wondering if I'll be able to climb with all this rice, but then the door starts to open and I have to leap behind a sack right at the back.

Two men I don't recognise come in; one looks like a security guard, the other looks like he lives here in the camp. I can see them but they can't see me. I hold my breath so they can't possibly hear me. One of them opens another sack and I'm thinking that we're not the only people that steal rice and that they have no right to tell us off if they're doing it as well, but it's not rice that they pull out, it's something long, black and shiny. I can't see it very well, but I know it's a gun. I have to put my hand over my own mouth to stop any noise from coming out and when I do this some of the rice spills and makes a quiet rushing sound. The men look up for a moment and stare towards my corner.

'Probably just rats,' says the security guard.

'British?'

'The rats or the gun?'

They both laugh about this and the man who looks like he lives here gives the other man money.

'A bit more of that and you and your family can leave this shithole,' says the security guard, waving the money around.

'And go where?'

The security guard shrugs. 'Let me know if you change your mind. Things are hotting up out there.'

'That's why I got the gun.'

'Might not be enough. Think about it.'

I worry that they will see my eyes shining through the gap in the sacks so I shut them tight and when I hear one of them walking towards me I bite down on my hand. I don't breathe, and I don't move, and I'm crying, but it's okay because that doesn't make any noise.

'I'll take a bit of this rice while I'm here.'

'No you won't. This rice is going to market, it's paying for the roof over your head.'

I open my eyes again. I can't believe they are going to sell our rice. The man who lives here can't believe it either. I can see it in the way he looks at the security guard. And all I want is for them both to go away, which, finally, they do. The problem is that even though they've gone, I'm still too scared to move. My body's gone stiff. But Noor is still outside and she whispers my name.

'I'm coming,' I tell her, 'and I spilt the rice a bit, but I didn't get caught.'

'Didn't you?' says my mother, standing next to Noor, her arms folded.

'Well, we can't put it back, we have it now, and they're going to sell the rest.'

My mother is as strong as a tree and sways just as easily. I wait to see which way the wind is blowing.

'You can never do this again. These people are dangerous,' she says, taking me by the shoulders, and looking straight into my eyes.

I nod. She's scaring me a little, and I don't know what she'll decide about the rice.

'Okay, we're all hungry, let's eat,' she finally says. 'Fetch your mother and sister, Noor.'

I relax when I hear this pronouncement. We walk home and I watch my mother light the little fire outside our shelter and then I go to fetch the water from the tap. There's still a few people queuing so it takes a while and you can see that everyone is wondering what everybody else is using the water for and if they're going to make it hot and, if they are, how they got the fuel and if they're eating or drinking tea, and if that's the case then where did it come from? I keep my head down so as not to face these questions. I wouldn't be able to give a very straight answer right now and suddenly I feel ashamed that I have stolen from these people. If only there was more I would offer it to them, but there is not, so I stay quiet. Either way, soon even the rice in the store will all be gone.

It's warm by our little fire and the rice is delicious, hot and salty. I must have fallen asleep from the weight of it in my stomach because the next thing I know, it's morning and my mother is shaking me awake in the half light. The UNHCR people are coming, she says, we have to go now to have a chance.

I stretch and yawn. I do not have to dress because I am still wearing my clothes. It's cold in the desert at night. My mother holds my hand as we walk to the other side of the camp, as if she's scared of losing me. When we reach the Portakabins, there are already others waiting and it looks like they slept there with their blankets all night. There are little mounds of families, different sized legs and heads sticking out.

If we're lucky, my mother says, they will take us away from here to a place where we will live in a house and I will go to school again, but she's been saying this since we left our home and since long before then too. We applied with my father and my brother. My mother keeps having to take names off the list. I think they must only have a very small amount of room. They couldn't take four, but maybe they can take two, or maybe they don't want us at all, so they are waiting for us to die, one by one.

It's cold while we stand in line and it takes forever for the sun to get up and do her dance across the sky until finally she shares her warmth. We wait for hours. My legs hurt, my throat is dry, and I wonder if by waiting here we have lost all chance of breakfast. They only give it out when the UNHCR are here, or the charity. I stare at the red, orange, brown all around us. The sun makes the desert even redder, but in the shadows it's pretty much black. I stare until my eyes hurt. I hang on to my mother's arm, acting like a kid. I know I'm dragging her down, but I do it anyway until she tells me off so I stand and kick the dirt instead, making little clouds like the charity vans.

We finally get to the front. The man wearing a UNHCR waistcoat lets us in and the beautiful woman in the nice clean clothes tells us there is no news. She tells us to come back next week. She smiles when she says it and moves a strand of her perfectly blonde hair from her face to behind her ear and even this is beautiful. I want to ask her if we can stay here, in this Portakabin with its electric kettle and stove. It seems solid, and clean, and I imagine it standing here empty all night. But I've spent too long staring at it all and a man gives me a small shove to move me on. Now I feel very sorry about breakfast; the UNHCR are leaving and they definitely won't give it out after they've gone. I feel almost like I might cry about it so instead I start running. I run to the shelter. I get my book. I run from the camp up the cliff path with it. I sit down. My stomach is screaming and growling like a monster I carry with me and then I do cry, because every time we go to the UNHCR lady I remember all the times we went with my father and my brother. I remember a time when I was small and one of them carried me, or when it was my father who held my hand. I remember how happy he looked and how much faith he had. I remember how it felt when he smiled at me with his hope all over his face and I knew I didn't have to worry about anything and that he would keep me safe. And then they took him away and put him in prison, and then they killed him, and then he was dead, and that is how sudden life is, and how sudden death is.

5

PURGATORY FOR LOSERS

BARRY

I'm stuck in some shitty cell with all the other losers. The police have already tried to question me and I've already told them I'm waiting for my lawyer. If I could go back in time and take back yesterday, I would. I can think of a thousand things I should have done differently, not just last night, but during the entirety of my stupid existence. And now there's mumbling coming from all around me. If the press don't already know then they'll definitely get a heads up when this lot gets released.

'Aren't you that guy?' asks the spotty kid to my left.

And I shake my head and try to tuck my own chin into my own neck. Spontaneous combustion would be preferable to this shit, or any other form of instant death. I should have jumped off one of those tall buildings when I had the chance.

'You are! You're that guy. Hey, everyone, it's him, the famous guy.'

In the far reaches of my consciousness the brick guy with the cement is back, but this time he's just laughing, and if it wouldn't make me look crazy I'd scream at him to fuck off.

'What famous guy?' someone else is asking and by now it's all fucking pointless anyway unless I can find a way of turning invisible or of convincing them they haven't really seen me. Yet, no matter how much I concentrate, neither of these things are happening. The force is not strong with this one.

'The singer, what's his name again? I can't think, it's on the tip of my tongue. Hey, what's your name?'

For fuck's sake, I close my eyes, I imagine I'm somewhere else, somewhere far fucking away, but there's no point.

'Barry, that's it, Barry Knight.'

'Barry Knight?'

'Yeah, that's it, Barry Knight.'

'Wait till I tell the old lady that I spent a night in a cell with "the Knight". Amazing. Hey, Barry, what did you do to end up in here with us lot?'

'Just fuck off, will you? Fuck off, all of you,' is what I manage, because I've never been particularly good at making friends, hence the hire band etc.

'Alright, Jesus,' the guy says, 'just trying to make conversation.'

I figure if I can just keep my eyes closed for long enough then eventually I will fall asleep, but what actually happens is I find myself replaying the last time I was in a cop station, because some kid saw me do something even I only barely remembered, and then – once we'd wrapped a few lies around it – even I forgot. The truth, you know, is complicated. I convinced myself of the lie – I stayed at the party, I hadn't been driving, what the kid said was impossible – and because all my mates are wasters too, when they said to the officers that I'd definitely been there the whole time, they actually believed it themselves. So, you see, it became the truth. Not even my fault really, I'd believed one thing, Sam told me to believe another, so I did.

And now it's daylight, and I'm sober for the first time in a while, I can see exactly whose fault this is. A copper turns up and I expect something dramatic to happen like it does to the black kids in films. I expect him to beat me up or to throw me in solitary or to say something like, you're going down for a long time, son. But instead he says:

'Your lawyer's here, you've got bail.'

So I stand up and brush my clothes down and remind myself that I'm about to meet a woman who hates me. She's always hated me as far as I can tell, but Sam says she's the best at what she does, which seems to be getting people she really dislikes off charges they should be sent down for.

'How do I look?' I ask the officer, for something to say, to give him a little of the showman.

'Like you could use a shower.'

And that's not going in the book either.

He says she's waiting for me by the front desk, and there she is, but Sam's not and my hands shake with the questions of why he's not and where he is.

'Mr Knight,' my lawyer says coolly. And when I take her hand, even though she held it out for me to shake, I can already feel her pulling it away.

Constance. A name I have always thought stood for 'constantly on your back'. But now I need her and it's difficult ground to negotiate. I excuse myself and run to the bathroom unsure if I'll throw up, shit myself, or cry. In the end I do none of it. I wash my face and take a moment to soak up my reflection. My hair is greying at the temples and thinning on top. Lines extend in radials from my eyes. I am a man in his fifties who does not look after himself. There is no getting away from it. The press are going to hang me.

I walk out of the building with Constance at my side, suddenly glad of her imposing presence and the fact she does human rights cases for free on the side. I face the cameras without turning away; anything else will look like guilt, and if Constance is here, maybe that's not the line we're going for.

'Say nothing,' she whispers as we descend the stairs, and it's not like I was going to anyway.

In the car I ask where Sam is, but she doesn't know and I can't understand how it's possible. After all, it was him that called her. The next question I want to ask is sticking in my throat, but I have to get it out there, I have to know the depth of the shit I'm in.

'How old is she?'

'Seventeen. Technically she is not underage in terms of the federal law, but her parents are saying she was under the influence, that you took advantage of her.'

'Maybe I did.' I mean, I guess I definitely did.

'Well, that's not what you'll say in court.'

'In court?'

Brick guy's brought in a second cement guy to help out with the extra work, and by this point they're both literally pissing themselves, and I know they're not real, that they're some fucked up part of my psyche, but it still hurts.

'It looks that way.'

'Fuck.'

The car drops me off and she nods her I-wish-I-never-had-to-see you-again-but-you-pay-me-loads-of-money goodbye after pencilling me into her diary for some future date I didn't listen to. The media still aren't outside, which must be some kind of miracle. Maybe there's a terrorist attack down the road I haven't heard about. I half run to the front door and, realising I don't have my keys, knock, feeling bollock naked even though I'm fully clothed. There's no answer. I try again, but nothing, so I knock on the windows to the kitchen and the sitting room, still nothing. I can't believe I can't get into my own bloody house. Where the fuck is Sam? There is no way round to the back from here unless I climb over the security wall. I can just imagine the image of my arse in the air, scaling my own garden wall, on the front page of every newspaper by morning. I want to shout Sam's name, but I don't want the neighbours to hear. I don't want anyone to hear. I try the door again.

'Sam, you bastard, open the fucking door,' I say in a growling whisper.

I'm standing, staring at the front door like it's some complex fucking puzzle, when Sam appears behind me.

'They let you out,' he says flatly.

'Why weren't you there?'

'Nobody told me.'

Really. Sam has always been great at lying in general but pretty shit at lying to me, at least when I'm sober.

'I don't believe you.'

'Look, let's get inside and get some coffee on. You look like shit.'

I stand aside while he opens the door, a bag of groceries tucked under one arm, far too calm. We walk through to the kitchen in silence.

'Why weren't you there?' I ask again, conscious that I sound like an abandoned wife, but I don't care, because that's exactly how I feel.

'I told you, nobody told me they were letting you out,' he says, just like the terrible, lying husband that he is.

'The lawyers called you as soon as they'd been contacted by the girl's family. I don't believe that they would then fail to mention my release. I think you were planning a nice little vacation in Miami at my expense.' I'm just being mean now, and it feels good on the face of it, but it makes my chest hurt at the same time.

'Barry, stop it, okay?'

'No, not until you tell me why.'

He's silent for a moment while he puts the groceries away. 'Okay,' he says and turns to me once again. 'It's Emily.'

'And?'

'She's been asking me to give this up, stay in London. If she saw the pair of us splattered all over the front pages of the tabloids that'd be it, especially considering the circumstances.'

'She's never liked me.'

'That might well be true, but it's not like you've ever done anything to help the situation.'

Well, fuck it.

I go to the window and close all the blinds at the front of the house, bunker mode, and take myself off for a shower. I need to digest the last couple of days, and potentially to hit my head against something hard, in a room where no one can see me.

I try to nap in the beige bedroom, but all I can see is Jade that morning, in the moments just before everything turned to shit. Young, innocent, and about to ruin my fucking life. I get up and stand for a moment in the doorway, taking in the frilled curtains, the white carpet, the cut-glass chandelier. None of it is really mine. I go back to the kitchen.

'I want to go home,' I say to Sam who's sitting on one of the high stools fiddling on his phone.

'This is your home. I mean, it's one of them,' he says as he looks up at me. His expression tells me I'm disturbing him from something important, or at least something more interesting than me and my problems.

'I want to go to London,' I reply, my voice a little shaky now.

'Well, right now you can't, mate,' he says as he finally comes to put his arms around me. 'I'm sorry I wasn't there.'

I feel tears coming but I'm trying to hold them back, because the question I'm about to ask is stupid, and so is the fact that I care what the response is.

'What about that time I bought her a potted plant?'

'It was a lovely gesture.'

'But?'

'She's allergic.'

It's too much. I let the tears come, and wish I was the sort of man who didn't hate himself for doing it. I pull away from Sam and go to sit down, leaning my elbows on the counter. Sam comes to sit opposite me.

'I've fucked up haven't I? I've really fucked up,' I say to him through the tears.

I'm on the point of letting go completely when I look up again and see his face. It's not what I'd call a picture of compassion, and of course the grown-up in me knows I'm being a dick, but I can't seem to stop myself.

'Screw you, Sam. If you want out, just go.'

'Out?'

'Yes, mate, out. This isn't the fucking mafia, I won't kill you if you leave. If you don't want to be here I would rather be hung, drawn and quartered in my own good company.'

'You wouldn't last two fucking seconds without me.'

'Really, just watch me.'

'Yeah? Well how about this. I am sick and tired of you ordering me around like some sort of skivvy and cleaning up after you. We've been in this gig a long time now and I've kept you in the game, but have you ever, one single time, thanked me? No, the fuck you have. And now "the Knight" has fucked up again and who does he want to fix it? Me. Well, fuck you, Barry. If you think you can survive this alone, then good luck to you.'

I take a deep breath. The tears have stopped, but my hands are still shaking.

'You're right, Sam, you're right as always. I'm sorry. You're the last friend I have left. You're the only one that stuck it out. Without you I'd be in a ditch somewhere drinking my own piss. Please don't go.'

'And?'

'And, thank you. Thank you for everything you've done for this useless old bastard.'

'And?'

He's pushing it now, but I love him.

'I wouldn't be able to do it without you. Without you there is no fucking point anyway.'

'Okay, then let's make a plan.'

Finally, I can start breathing evenly again. My hands stop shaking. 'Yes, please, Sam. Can we make a plan?' I'm no longer the wife, I'm the kid that doesn't want Daddy to go out for cigarettes and never come back, but with the distinct advantage of also being the person who pays Daddy the big fat wage packet. Without me, Sam would have to get a real job to maintain the lifestyle I've got him and Emily oh so accustomed to.

'We can always make a plan, mate. We've got out of worse before, haven't we?'

'We have.'

'So, we say yes to the war orphans.'

'But I thought I couldn't travel?'

'You can't, not right now, but we still have a little time before this goes crazy in the press and to get ahead of the narrative. We say yes now, counter story, yeah?'

'Yeah.'

'I'll go see Jade, she's a good girl, young, but she seems nice. The sort of girl that cares about the world.'

'Okay?'

'I'll explain that you're a bit of a philanthropist, say you don't like to talk about it, but that actually you spend tonnes of your time doing charity stuff. I'll admit that you fucked up. I mean, this girl's already on our side, it's her parents doing all the talking. I'll give her a new angle to argue from.'

'The war orphans?'

'Yes, the war orphans can save us.'

'When will you go?'

'Right now, mate. See, if I go to the house, having not been seen anywhere in the media yet, the parents don't know me. I can say I'm the, I don't know, the lawyer, for example, or a journo covering the story, or anything really that gets me access. It'll all start to blow over by morning, mate.'

'Really?' Thank all the gods I don't believe in. I could kiss this man, but instead I tell him I love him.

'I fucking love you too, you old bastard,' he says, before he leaves the house to start his mission, and suddenly I'm all on my own and my sober mind is trying to drag me back to all the things I must forget, like the feeling of London's night air on my face, the car windows down, the way everything blurred into one, like a giant streaming ribbon of street lights and neon kebab signs. There had been a bump, like when you hit a fox, and Sam had said, Drive, drive, drive. I'd felt upset about the fox. Only it wasn't a bloody fox, was it.

I bring my hands up to my face, to my throat, and squeeze, but I know it doesn't work, I've tried it before. My hands move to my hair and tug. The tears are back. I know I've always been a fucking fuck-up, pretty much from birth on.

A roar is growing in me, taking me over. I let out a deep and wretched scream, pick up the bar stool next to me and crash it into the marble worktop. It doesn't make a dent so I try it on the coffee machine which cracks and splinters and spills the last of the cold coffee. I raise it above the drinks cabinet and then think better of it. I put the bar stool down.

I drink vodka from the bottle, surrounded by shattered glass, until the world begins to fuzz around the edges and my mind goes quiet.

6

MUDDY LEGGED BOY

SOL

Everything is fucked. You can put a nice face on it, go to a demo, prance around in the streets dressed like a tree talking about whales, but all you're really doing is passing the time until your inevitable demise. I get why people do it. At moments I even admire them. They can still feel something. They can actually care. They haven't let themselves be beaten down by all the lies and the fake news. The tweets, which should be offences in themselves. If politicians can't manage to say something nice, which doesn't start a race war, in 280 characters or less, they just should stay quiet, and if they can't stop themselves, then Twitter itself should be banned. It's not even a proper form of communication. It's just an excuse for the stupid and vacuous to scream into the void, in the hope that they will hear their own voice coming back to them.

In this town, cynicism is a way of life. We've made a sort of art out of it, and now it's the only art form we truly respect; everything else has been tarnished. If you look back, it's colonial. If you look at the present, it's killing the planet, or it's overtly not killing the planet which is almost worse. If you look to the future there's just a giant black hole in the shape of a gravestone with humanity written across its width, spanning the void left by one of the innumerable apocalypses.

This is my truth. Or at least it would be, if truth still existed.

Anyway, enough, enough, because despite it all I'm in a lecture by Naomi Klein, and I'm taking notes – like a deranged Muppet, because what good will notes do during the apocalypse/s. And she's good, she draws you in. She's thought a lot. She means what she says, but I can't help but criticise her passion. It makes me uncomfortable. She seems so sure, too sure. And what is there to be sure of, what is there to hold on to? As far as I can see from the cheap seats, absolutely shit all.

So I leave five minutes early and I don't try to meet her, or to make conversation with any of the other hopeful cunts that made their way here in the rain. Instead I go to a bar I don't work at and order a cold, cold beer to wash down the small wedge of hope she's managed to implant in me, the only thing that aches more than pain itself. I promise myself I'll thank the bar staff for every single drink, and I plan to give myself a lot of opportunities to do so, but before I know it there's this guy standing right there in front of me and it's one of those moments when you just know.

Several hours later I wake up in my own bed with him lying next to me. In the half-light he looks just like Leila. It's the red hair, the shape of his eyes, the way he looked at me in the bar earlier. I pull him close, pull her close, as if they are one and the same, as if I can call her back through his body.

I don't explain this to him, this ghost-fucking I'm doing, that I've been doing ever since I lost her. I don't know if he'd get it, or if I'd want him to, or if I could explain it to him even if I realised that I wanted him to understand. And either way, he'll be gone in a few hours.

When I wake again to weak sunlight, he has, as predicted,

left. There's a note on the pillow. A number. A name. I crumple it up in my sweaty palms and throw it at the wall and then pick it up again, unfurl it and stare at it. His handwriting is not hers, but I kiss the note anyway and place it on my chest like a plaster to hold my heart in, but it's all too much so I crawl out of bed to confront the day.

There's no tea in the house so I go out into the world to hunt for it. In the corner shop I see the newspaper and stop in the doorway, only coming to when an old guy barges past me mumbling about "the youth round here" and "manners".

BARRY KNIGHT'S MERCY MISSION

**The singer Barry Knight is due to
visit the refugee camp of —— near
the embattled city of —— in his new
role as Ambassador for Save the
War Orphans.**

And I stop, right there on the street, the breath gone from me. I can't ever escape him. He's always there. It's like he's gloating. Like he's still running on the speed he picked up after he hit her. After he threw her body up into the cold night air. After he left her there to die and me beside her, the only one who saw and lived – the one nobody would believe.

I wish there'd been tea at home.

I go home without it.

I get through the door and slide down the wall of the hallway.

I sit there in silence.

Beyond.

The post lands on the mat by my feet and wakes me to the world again. This has to stop. I stand up, give up on tea or meaningful wakefulness, and take myself off to see Leila. Sometimes being near to her is the only thing that'll do and, for the briefest of moments, I can breathe. That's what I really need right now. I need more than anything to breathe and not feel like I'm choking.

At the bus stop there's a five-minute wait and five minutes of standing still right now is too much, so, even though it'll take me an hour, I walk, just to disperse some of this energy. It's the hypocrisy of it that gets me. That he could end a life here and nobody cares, and then get to be some sort of hero for saving some lives somewhere else. It's not even the here and there of it that pisses me off. It's that he point-blank does not deserve to be a seen as a hero. He barely even deserves to be alive. As I stomp along, head to the ground, fists in my hoodie pockets, this is what goes around and around in my head. It hasn't been this bad for a while. Compared to this, I've been feeling pretty normal for months, other than never opening a newspaper for fear of seeing his face and ending up here, this dark place. I even stopped taking my antidepressants, something I should probably have told my NHS therapist about, but she's got enough worries without me adding to them.

Just outside the cemetery I pause to buy flowers, a transaction I manage to complete without uttering a single word. I always slow down as I walk up to her grave, as if I'm scared of startling her, which I know is crazy but I can't stop myself. Her gravestone is made of that pinkish marble and there's a photo of her in a special frame that's a part of it. It's a black-and-white photo, which I think is a pity because you can't see the red of her hair, but her mum chose it and there was nothing I could say. I already felt guilty enough about the fact that I'd been there and done nothing, that I hadn't been able to save her or even bring the guy that hit her to any kind of justice. I wasn't going to argue about what photo of her daughter she chose.

She was beautiful, Leila, there's no getting away from it, but that's not why I loved her. I loved her because she was absolutely the funniest person I knew and when I was with her I laughed more than I have ever done before or since. She was the only antidote I knew to cynicism, to our fucked-up generation, to London itself. For me, she was everything.

In front of her grave there are still the plastic flowers that someone brought on the day of her funeral, faded now and greening round the edges, a little heather bush planted in the earth itself by her mum because her dad had been Scottish, and the daffodils I brought last time, droopy and a little brown, which I pick up now and replace with the new ones. And there's the wreath which turns up every month, a little different each time, seasonal, from an unknown sender. Leila's mum tried to find out who it was once, to thank them, but got nowhere. Everyone thinks they're from some rich ex-boyfriend, but I don't. I knew her from the first day we started secondary school together. There was never anyone else. People say to me that you can't know everything about anyone, even someone you love, so I shut up about it, because otherwise I sound like I'm obsessing, which I am.

We put an old log next to her grave a while ago, her mum and me, so we had somewhere to sit when we wanted to spend some time with her without putting our arses on the grass. The groundskeeper didn't like it, said it looked messy, and kept taking it and putting it next to the bin by the gate, but we kept moving it back so eventually he gave up and today it's here, waiting for me. So I sit and I tell her everything. I have no idea if it's better for her if I speak out loud or in my own head. At least, I say I have no idea, but it's not like I actually believe in God or heaven or an afterlife. I just also don't believe that she can be totally gone, that it could have happened so quickly or have lasted for so long. What would be the point? But then that's the worst bit. There is no point. And that's the punchline to top off the apocalypse chat. We all die, humanity is wiped out, and then absolutely nothing happens and no one or no thing mourns us. Funny.

But right here and now I tell her about the guy in my bed, I tell her about Barry Knight. She is the only one I share it all with. She is the only person with whom I can.

On the way home I go back to the corner shop to successfully purchase tea, and Tilda and Peggy are in there buying milk, the two old ladies that live opposite me. They've been next-door neighbours for over half a century and grew up in the surrounding streets. They like to corner me at least once a week to talk about the war, their lasting trauma, and I appreciate their commitment to it. It stole a husband from Tilda and two brothers from Peggy. Their pain is a smooth round pebble held and nurtured for all these years, its edges softened through use.

'It's gets easier,' says Tilda, often, 'but it never gets easy.'

They don't know about Leila. I moved to this flat after she died. Yet it feels like these words are targeted, like they can see something in me which reflects what they see in the mirror every day and in each other's eyes.

7

COMPOST

ANA

Catherine was not religious. Her will makes no mention of funeral arrangements. Again I find this strange for someone so practical, unless she truly believed she would survive, and maybe she did. She was a fighter, after all. Online, I discover that the world of funerals is made up of relentless choices; the casket, the burial ground, the ceremony or lack thereof. You can be burnt, buried, fired out of a cannon, sunk at sea. There is a theatricality about it that is comforting and disturbing all at the same time. I call Callum to ask him what he thinks, but he's in the middle of service at the restaurant. He tells me to come down and he'll make me something. It's already late and it's a half-hour drive but I decide to go anyway because I don't know what else to do.

In the car – Catherine's car, a relic from the 1990s – I turn on the radio to take my mind off it all, but there's a tape in there already and it starts where it left off, halfway through 'She's Lost Control' by Joy Division. I can't believe this is the last song she listened to, but it must have been her because I'm the only other person that drives the car. I laugh out loud. I didn't even know she liked Joy Division, and yet it's perfectly her, and now of course I'm crying while driving, drumming my hands on the steering wheel. The music's up loud and when I pull up to a traffic light a woman in the car next to mine stares over at me and I wave and make a crazy face, because fuck it.

I'm trying to think when Catherine last drove the car, when exactly she could have listened to this tape. For a moment I think maybe she snuck out one night and paused it exactly in this place, so that when I next drove this is what I would hear. But that's crazy. Though only the same level of crazy as a woman dying of cancer sneaking out and driving around without telling her daughter. I'll probably never know, and this bites at me; the unavailability of the dead.

It's dark when I pull up in the car park. The last time I came here was with Catherine and I remember how I helped her negotiate getting out of the car and over to the entrance without stumbling over the gravel. In those last few months everything became difficult, which in turn made everyday activities surprising achievements. There was always cause to celebrate, right up until the end.

As I walk in, Callum sees me over the kitchen counter. It's an old pub but they took out most of the dividing walls, so now it's big and open with artistically exposed beams, and you can watch him while he cooks. He comes up to me with his arms outstretched like a bear and hugs me tight whispering his sorrys into my ear, and from him I don't mind, from him it feels genuine. It's the first time I've seen him since she died, in fact he's the first person I've really seen at all, and it feels good. He sits me down in a corner by the fire and goes to get us both food. Service has finished and most of the punters have left or are leaving. He comes back with a tray covered in various plates of different sizes and a waiter follows him with two large glasses of wine.

When he sits down I realise he looks exhausted, which he puts down to the thirteen-hour days.

'There's a reason chefs are famously grumpy,' he says, with a smile that only just registers in his creased eyes.

I tell him about Catherine's last days and final hours, I tell him about the house and all her things and how I don't know what to do with them. In between, I eat as if I haven't eaten in days, which on reflection is probably true. I tell him about the online brochures, the glossy pictures of things for dead people. He holds my hand over the table because we are in turn both laughing and crying. He's known Catherine for most of his life thanks to our long history of sleepovers.

'How's Nick?' I ask to change the subject and give us both a breather.

'He's got an exhibition coming up entitled, Where Now What Next. It's about stagnation: the feeling that as a society we're stuck and have lost the ability to dream.'

'Cheerful,' I say and Callum laughs.

'I don't know why you ask about him if this is always going to be your response.'

'I ask about him because we both love him and because he's your husband. I'd be a terrible friend if I ignored his existence completely, even if sometimes it's tempting.'

He stole one of the people I love the most, and I know it's not his fault but, combined with the fact he is also beautiful and successful, it's a lot.

After a moment of silence Callum says, 'I don't think she'd care. A cardboard box, a tree, maybe an oak. She always wanted to have a positive impact on the earth. Let her feed an oak.'

The idea of her feeding an oak is both terrifying and beautiful.

Nick turns up to give Callum a lift home. It's time for me to go too. He offers me his condolences, wraps his long arms around me, his tears wetting my hair. It's good to see him in all his towering height. I promise to give them the details of the funeral, thank Callum for the food, and leave.

The drive home seems to take even longer than the drive there but I arrive at the house determined to start making the arrangements. The dogs jump up and nuzzle me as I come through the door and, not for the first time, I'm glad they are here to welcome me. Without them this would be a far lonelier task.

I turn on the computer, find a version of what Callum suggested and book it. I have not lit the fire, it's too late, and only the table lamp is on in the living room. I'm using Catherine's laptop and the email icon is blinking at me. The dogs are sleeping, one with its head on the body of the other. It's peaceful, and I think of all the nights she spent like this, alone but contented, with enough time to think and to be. And so it shocks me a little when I open up her account and see that she was emailing all over the place right up until the last days, questioning and even threatening, until her last breath. The illusion of calm is gone, and I realise that she was the sort of woman who wouldn't even let dying get in the way of doing the right thing.

The last-but-one email she sent seems to be to the same charity named in the note stuck to the fridge. So I go to the kitchen, stare at her cobweb handwriting in the darkness, and reach out to touch the paper. It's true, it's the same, Save the War Orphans. I wonder why, in the midst of her own pain, she spent time focusing on the pain of others. Perhaps it's easier. You can email about it and rant and try to get something done. You can try to control it, solve it. If it goes well, it is something that can be fixed.

The email is addressed as if to someone she knew, Amanda, another aspect of her life I obviously knew nothing about. Feeling like I know her less and less scares me. It also makes me think of the people who brought me into this world and how little I knew of them, how much I had suppressed their existence. When it finally became possible to know more, I stuck with my imagined histories instead. I lost myself in the increasingly complex nature of cancer care while at the same time holding down a full-time job. Now, having said goodbye to the woman who raised me I wish I had taken the opportunity to say goodbye to the people who inadvertently delivered me to her.

I shake my head to stop these thoughts. It's too late now, the moment has long since passed. Instead, I focus on the content of the email. In it she says that the project they started together has become unrecognisable and she needs to make her thoughts heard before her death. She says they're taking money from a foundation run by a bank that makes investments in the arms trade, that they have stopped their advocacy against the government because of another grant that comes directly from them. She asks at what point do you become a part of the problem that you are trying to solve? She is demanding more financial transparency, questioning some new office building they have and wondering why they need it. She states that in some of the camps where they operate, food aid is being sold by the militia that run the security, that they are inadvertently funding the civil war which has been quietly bubbling away in the country on and off for over a decade. She goes further and lists local NGOs who have stopped operations since they arrived, suggesting that they are destabilising the third-sector economy in the areas where they work. She is saying, when you get to the bottom of it, that they are indirectly supporting the arming of warring groups, maintaining one of the many wars that necessitate their presence in some camps in the first place, while at the same time removing local alternatives. She asks if this is purposeful, an intentional way of keeping the region unstable, of keeping their own jobs?

The reply is an out-of-office response, standard issue. I search the woman's full name in the email search box to see if there's anything else. It comes up again but in an email sent to someone else, someone called Omar. There was no response to her questions, no response at all in fact, just one email, sent into the void. She ends the email by saying, 'Amanda's gone too far this time, you need to go back.'

I close the laptop and consider it. Was she writing an article, or just trying to fix something she still felt responsible for before she died? I put the laptop on the floor and fall asleep in the semi-darkness with one of the dogs resting her head on my lap.

I dream I'm walking along a mountain path in what looks like a dry landscape, but when I look down the slope there are gardens in the valley, overflowing with flowers. There are fruit trees and neat rows of vegetables. I take the path down the hill, following someone I cannot see and when we reach the gardens I bend down to the earth, pick up a lump of soil and rub it between my fingers until I reach its moist centre.

8

YOUR TELEVISED DEATH WILL BE IGNORED

AMANDA

I have felt more at home thousands of miles away in foreign countries than I do right now in this building they call the central office. The carpet is so thick it's like the floor is padded. It steals the sound of your footsteps. Sometimes I imagine that the entire enterprise might actually be run by cats, silently stalking the corridors, occasionally having a little bounce when no one else is looking. The doors are the same. They don't slam, they purr closed, locking out all the air, making it quite hard to breathe as a result.

The other members of the board are already seated when I arrive. I slide between the table and chair and pour myself a coffee. Everything is silent as people look through their paperwork and adjust their glasses, until I accidently put my coffee cup down audibly in this quiet and sacred space. Jesus. The faint clink of china makes everybody look at me. So I angle my shoulders back and stick my tits out like it's the 1980s until they're all satisfied and looking back down at their briefing notes. This is not a place in which you can show fear, especially if you are the CEO.

At our old weekly meetings Jem would have his feet up on the desk, Alex and Omar would be arguing about politics and Ruhi would be reading The Times. Once Jem snatched it from her, balled it up and threw it out the window, lambasting her choice of fascist rag. I sense that this sort of behaviour, in this particular environment, could get you sectioned.

I run my eyes down the list of country updates and stop when I reach the name of the camp I was working on earlier. We're pulling out. Why? This is the camp where Barry Knight should be going. His press office has finally replied to say yes, of course, they'd be honoured, and even though we haven't responded yet, it's already been leaked to the bloody papers. I wanted to wait it out, see how the sex scandal played out in the news. But now, of course, my instinct is to say something immediately. I look up in order to do just that and realise I've been ignoring the opening address. To be honest, I hadn't even noticed that they'd started speaking. Unfortunately, experience has taught me that spontaneity doesn't work with these people. You have to wait until the appropriate part of the meeting, and when the country you're concerned about comes up, you're allowed to say something very concise in an authoritative voice. I will say something like, 'There's clearly been a mistake here, we've now secured a funding stream for this camp and a strong media strategy to sustain it.' And people will nod, and notes will be made. I repeat the sentence several times in my head. It's going to be fine. And if they look confused: shoulders back, tits forward.

John, the chairman of the board, indicates the PowerPoint when they get to my camp and shuffles his papers, tapping them on the table to straighten the edges in time with his words.

'As you can see, in the current round of belt tightening, this is one of the losers. The camp will no doubt receive support from other organisations and we believe the situation is beginning to stabilise.'

I could throttle him. Do these people do any research at all before they make their pronouncements? However, if he hasn't heard about the most recent tensions between the internationally recognised government and its main, heavily armed, opposition, then I'm not going to bring them up right now either.

'No,' I say, slightly louder than intended, shoulders back etc. 'I mean, it's not necessary. We have a new funding strategy and a strong media campaign planned, and there's excess in the Turkish pot leftover from the successful rebuild of the camps in the North to tide us over.'

'When you say media campaign, do you mean Barry Knight?'

'Yes, I mean Barry.'

'Did you see the papers?'

Does he mean the sex scandal or the leak? I'm going to go with the sex scandal. 'I did, but his press office says they're fixing it.'

John pauses, his fingers arched like a little steeple in front of his face. It's supposed to look like he is crunching numbers or deeply contemplating world politics, but having had to endure drinks with him on more than one occasion I know this is supremely unlikely.

'There's also a school project starting there,' I add. 'Classes4All are building two classrooms, we're supporting them with access and contacts. They're all volunteers.'

His head moves to the side, he doesn't like volunteers, but at the end of the day they're free and they build things we can take credit for.

'Okay, with the Turkish money we can do one more quarter, but if Barry doesn't pull it off or the war heats up again, then that's it.'

Shit, he has done some reading after all. I nod and squirm a little in my suit; it seems designed for a slightly different type of animal. I dream of leaving here, getting back to the real office and starting to plan, but John is pouring himself another coffee so I do the same. I wait in perfect silence.

When we're finally released, John catches up with me before I reach the office door. It makes me jump because I didn't hear him coming and he took a hold of my arm without warning.

'Amanda, there's something I think you'll want to know.'

I look at him, trying to work out what on earth this stupid man could know that I would want him to tell me.

'Omar's been in touch, he's not happy.'

'Well, he's not the only one.'

Suddenly it feels like everyone in this stupid fucking airtight office is looking at me and I wish they'd all just leave and stop asking me questions. I make my break for it, stating several times that I do not need a lift, that the Tube will do just fine, thank you. And, of course, when I get to the turnstiles a man in a high-visibility vest tells me the Circle Line is closed, and this is exactly the sort of thing London does to you when you just don't need it, when for a minute or two it would be great if things just went smoothly. It takes me over an hour to get across town and I spend most of that time underground, jammed in with the rest of humanity, standing room only, bumped up against strangers. Though sometimes – or perhaps often, for a devotee of this city – it is preferable to be surrounded by strangers with your own thoughts than confronted by people who actually know you and want you to explain them.

It's already dark when I get home to Greenwich and people who have not been discarded by the person they love are drinking wine together in restaurant windows.

9

RUNNING

OMAR

I pause to get my breath, stretch my calves.

    I bend forward, bring my arms down over my head.

    Reach toward the ground.

    Reach up, lower my arms to my sides.

    Keep my eyes on the stars.

    Head back down.

    Shake out the legs.

    Finally, I take in the street. When you're running on uneven ground it's best to keep your eyes down unless you want a sprained ankle. I'm on an unnamed road and I've lost track of the neighbourhoods I've passed through. I look around and, without meaning to, I find I'm staring directly into someone's home, if you can call it that. A family is gathered around a small fire on low stools. The mother is cooking, the children are looking up at her expectantly, their faces lit by the flames. There are no windows and the broken door is open to the street. The father turns when he senses me watching. I smile and nod. I don't want to cause embarrassment. It's too personal a scene for a stranger to witness. I move on, running through the pain in my muscles, back to the city centre, the traffic and noise. The father's eyes stay with me.

In my small rented room I strip off and wipe myself down with a flannel over a basin of cold water. On a camping stove I boil up some rice and eat it with the sauce left over from the day before. By the evening call to prayer I'm already in bed, the candlelight flickering. Today the electricity did not come on. I think of the children at the orphanage, and hope they have enough candles to get through the night. Most of them struggle to sleep.

I take the notebook from the top of the stack and flick through to the beginning. I started this particular one when we arrived here, the first entry is short.

Amanda is asleep beside me, but for two hours I've lain here in the dark. Tomorrow we go to Gaza. When she asked me earlier how I was feeling I didn't know how to respond. When I was younger I would have said it didn't matter to me, it was all ancient history. Sure, my mother used to go to rallies, my grandad used to tell stories, but I was a Shoreditch kid. It didn't feel like any of this related to me. But now, I feel nervous and I'm having to fight the urge to get straight back on the plane and go anywhere that's not here.

I guess in the end I fell asleep, because that's where it ends. I didn't get on the plane. Today's entry is short. I'm exhausted from work, from my visit with the kids, from the run. I describe briefly how we cleared rubble from the construction site. I place a drawing that Aisha gave me inside – a bomb flying through the air, a house destroyed, a crying face, the colour red. The psychologists say it's good for the kids to express themselves in this way, but it's difficult to see how. Further back in the notebook there's a different picture, of flowers and sunshine, and I take a moment to look at this instead, to remind myself that there is also joy in these kids' lives. For a guy who spent most of his adult life working for Save the War Orphans, I have to say I found kids quite annoying until I got here. I never thought I'd be the one giving art workshops.

I turn on my phone having saved the precious battery for this moment. My hand hovers over the call button, over Amanda's name, but I can't do it. I know that she'll be furious that I emailed the office before calling her. I'm worried about her, about the whole bloody charity, of course I am. Catherine's email was a wake-up call, but I still can't face the questions, and truthfully I don't know if I'm ready to go back.

'Why did you leave?' she'll ask me again.

I have been AWOL.

Like an Israeli refusenik.

I said no.

But at least now I have an answer I can give her that's better than 'this doesn't feel right anymore'.

'What, us, or the charity?' she'd asked.

'Both,' I'd replied, not in one of my most helpful of moods. And just like that, I left, or rather, I refused to leave. I stayed exactly where I was. I stayed in Jerusalem. Amanda caught the first flight out. I did not say goodbye.

I can see how this would look bad.

I didn't mean it to.

But there has to come a time when we stop moving, in order to grow. A strange thing for a runner to think, an addict of constant motion. I needed to take myself apart and I'm just about done with the rebuild.

I probably shouldn't have emailed the Central Office first, but the very fact that there is one underlines my concerns. The reason I left, the reason I stayed away and the reason I'm going back, are all the same. A distance had grown between us and the people we worked with; the kids and their guardians, the wider communities that surrounded and supported them. Our jobs made us better off, but what we provided did little more than alleviate immediate suffering. It changed nothing – at least, it changed nothing but us. We got used to taking planes and eating out and staying in hotels. We got used to unimpeded travel. We were living in the 2%.

Some people might refer to this sort of erratic behaviour as a breakdown. But surely it's crazier to carry on pretending everything's okay, even if you're good at it, even if you're British?

At least now I finally know exactly how little I need.

10

TRUTH IS A SALTY BISCUIT YOU THOUGHT WAS SWEET

SALEEMA

I try not to think about the time before, but I cannot control my dreams. Sometimes, in the middle of the night, I forget to forget. The flapping of the tarp and the murmur of the neighbours becomes the breeze through my old bedroom windows and the low chatter of my parents in the kitchen; their worried, rushed voices. At first, they tried to protect me from the truth. They said the protesters and the shouting on the streets would soon be over. The government would fall, and the world would become a safe place for me to grow up in. But then the bombs started and my school closed and for a while they stopped saying anything about anything at all. I'd ask a question, I'd ask why, and they'd shush me as if the walls were listening. This is when I realised that we were not even safe in our home.

Tonight, my dream is of my old best friend, Yara. I see her running along in front of me. Her hair is long and free. She's laughing but I don't remember why. There are kites in the sky and we're running towards the place where her older brother and his friends are flying them, a bombed-out patch of land that used to be something else. It's at the edge of town and beyond it I can see the orange trees. I see her as she falls to the ground. I think she's stumbled over a rock, but there is shouting and I also drop to the ground. There is the sound of gunfire, the rat-tat-tat doesn't stop. Yara is still lying in the dust and I want to get to her but I don't know how. I'm stuck behind a broken piece of wall. I can only see her properly, lying still on the road, by poking my head around the side of the jagged stones and when I do this the rat-tat-tat starts again. My whole body is shaking but I'm not crying – that comes much later. I stay there until it's dark. I think I drift off to sleep, a short nightmare. When I wake I'm still there, my body is stiff and I can hear Yara's brother talking quietly in the road. I move out from behind the wall and see him cradling his sister's head, his friends standing in a circle, staring, stony-eyed. When I walk towards them it's like I'm moving through thick sand; everything is heavy.

I wake up in the real world, in the shelter, just before I see her face. But as I wake her face comes to me anyway, what was left of it, her long beautiful hair matted with blood. One of her brother's friends came back with adults, and they picked us up and carried us away. Now, in the real world, I'm crying. I wasn't then. The next day I had a terrible fever, my skin was hot to the touch and every pore leaked water, but my eyes remained dry.

It's still dark and my mother is sleeping, so I stick my head out of the shelter for some air, resting it on the ground and looking up at the million upon millions of stars. I stare into them until my mind is only starlight, until I am as far away as they are, hovering above it all, watching all these people and their craziness. It feels as if time has stopped, everything that has happened, is happening, and will happen, is all happening now. It's beautiful and terrifying, and the immensity of it sends me back to sleep until I wake to the first light of day.

Not far from us, there's a big tent full of kids without their parents. By the time I wake again my mother has already left to prepare their breakfast; she does this every morning with a group of women from the camp. Sometimes I think she likes them more than me, and I wonder if it's because they don't remind her of my father and brother. I heat myself a little water for tea on the camping stove. If she was here she'd tell me not to waste the gas, but she is not. When the tea is ready I drink it slowly, sitting on an old blanket outside the shelter. It is already too hot to be in the sun or to be inside. It is too hot to be anywhere.

I watch the world as it wakes and passes. I listen to all the different languages that are spoken here. Sometimes I get a word or two, even if it's a language I don't actually speak. I look out at the children younger than me, toddling around or kicking rocks, and the few girls that are a bit older lost in their thoughts, their headscarves trailing behind them, untucked. I wonder what will happen to us with no school and no place to go. I don't believe in the classrooms they're building. This is not a life. Those classrooms will not be a school. My dream has broken the wall down between now and then, and I think of Yara and all the plans we had together, to finish school and go to university, to travel all around the world and live in different countries. Grown-up dreams for little girls to have, but ours nonetheless. I hold my tea glass tighter. I close my eyes. Inside my head I build the wall back up. Those places no longer exist; my old bedroom where we made our plans, the world in which we could carry them out. Not even the girls remain; in different ways, both of us are gone.

I reach for the book I'm reading, the middle one of a series. I've read all of them a hundred times already. In it children grow and learn and fight off evil and survive, they live to be grown-ups and to have children of their own and though some people do die, it's never so many as to kill the living too. It's fiction, of course, and right now I can't take it.

My father was a journalist. He was a believer in facts,

and every day he would repeat his mantra: 'Help will come.' He ended up spending most of his time talking to foreign journalists abroad because his own newspaper had been closed by the government. As a result, we had hardly any money and each week my mother would come back with less from the market, but we didn't complain because even the walls could hear us and because we were alive and together and this was becoming unique. Half our street had already left and even we had applied to the UNHCR to save us, but no word ever came from them. In the meantime, my father felt that leaving would be a betrayal of all the people we would have to leave behind. My parents had never argued, but now they would spend the evenings chasing each other round in circles. 'You should take Saleema and go,' my father would say, and my mother would reply that we must stay together, and my father would end up saying yes, this was all he wanted, but right now it wasn't safe and so my mother would say that if it wasn't safe we should all go, and he would counter by saying that if he left now, how would anyone in the rest of the world know what was happening, and on and on they would go. It became my new lullaby.

I walk to the edge of the camp. I lean my head up against the stone wall until I can feel it leaving marks on my forehead. I pinch the skin around my stomach. We used to say they were starving us in our country, but the hunger followed us, and I feel as hollow now as I did then. I watch as the sand picks itself up and spins out a dance, then falls again. I watch as the shadows move across its surface, slowly, drawing out the story of the day, its passing, the death of the sun. In this place time does all sorts of things, things you never knew it could do. Some minutes are the longest you've ever lived through and then other days pass in seconds because you're not really here, you've transported yourself to one of your other lives, either the ones you've survived, or the ones you've dreamed of. Both types of time can give you headaches, headaches that can last for days and stop you sleeping. My mother says that this is nonsense and it's not time that does this but the fact that the standpipe is only turned on for a few hours a day and we can't drink enough water. Maybe she has a point. Maybe it is both.

My skin is cracked and itchy and I realise I should move to get out of the sun but I can't make myself. I look up instead to my favourite hiding place among the rocks, up above the camp. It seems too hot and too impossible to get there today. Everything seems too much.

'Saleema!' Someone is shouting my name. It's Noor. I turn slowly and she's hurtling towards me, making me feel like time is doing another thing. She is on fast forward and I am on stop.

'What's wrong with you? I haven't seen you all morning!'

I don't know how to explain my various theories on time or about how a dream I had took me home again, and no matter how hard I try I can't get back to now, but luckily I don't have to because she takes my hand and pulls me out of stop and into fast forward with her, and, even though it is too hot to do this and we are nearly too old for such childish things, suddenly the very feeling of running is everything. My body wakes up as we take a corner too tight and have to jump a tent peg, leaving adults shouting in our wake.

'Where are we going?' I scream after her and she briefly turns to me and then starts laughing as she runs, like it's the funniest thing I've ever said, or she's ever heard.

'Are you crazy? We're not going anywhere! We're just running because we can!'

And then I start laughing too, because of course we're not going anywhere and because the running feels good and then we collapse in the shade of the big tent for the kids with no parents, but round the side, where no one else can see us. I can hear my mother's voice; she's telling one of them off for making a mess, and I can tell from the tone of her voice that she doesn't love them more. For a moment, everything feels lighter.

'Have you heard?' Noor is asking me, 'The big boss charity lady and a famous man are coming soon.'

'I haven't, but what does it matter?'

'I dunno, it's just something, isn't it?' she says, and I feel bad.

'Yeah, it is, you're right. Who's the famous person?'

'I don't know, but when I find out I'll tell you. My dad's been helping with translations in the office so he hears everything.'

I nod, exhausted again. Maybe it's interesting, maybe it's not, I don't know.

'Thirsty?' Noor asks me and holds out her ancient plastic bottle, half full of sun-warmed water.

I take it with a smile and consume a few precious drops.

'You're a good friend,' I tell her and she laughs again.

'I know!'

Next thing, she's up again and grabbing my hand for another few laps of the camp, zigzagging up and down the rows, and we truly are exhausted. My stomach growls so loudly that Noor can hear it.

'Come on,' she says, 'someone in the office gave Dad biscuits, don't tell anyone.'

'I won't,' I say. I never would.

11

GHOSTS – THE LIVING AND THE DEAD

SOL

I realise I'm washing glasses with more ferocity than is required. The radio is playing in the pub and as a Barry Knight song comes on my hand slips and the glass breaks. I pull my hand back to investigate the damage, already bleeding and swearing, and Sharon, the manager, comes over to see what's up. She lifts my hand up to look at it under the bar lights and holding me by the wrist and keeping my hand raised, manoeuvres me into the back office, to where we keep the first aid kit.

'What's up with you tonight?' she asks, as she fetches antiseptic wipes and a blue plaster, her blond curls and gold hoops moving in a blur before me.

It's a long time since I told anyone the truth about my episodes, so I lie and say I'm just tired, which is actually only a bit of a lie because I haven't been sleeping since I saw the article in the paper. The pain of the cut is actually good; it gives me a point of focus, something to cling onto. I've worked at this bar for five months, which is not bad for me. Since I lost Leila I've found it hard to concentrate on things for too long, and I've lost count of the shitty jobs I've had servicing the lives of those who are really living, at least on the surface.

Sharon's not much older than me, but under the hard shell she wears for the day-to-day, night-to-night running of this place, she is open and caring and I respect her for this. I guess that's why I've stuck it out for so long. Now, she finishes sticking the plaster down with one hand and cups my face in the other, lifting it so she can see my eyes. She holds it there, her hand over my ear, pressing my earring into my neck. Whenever I try to lower my gaze, and focus instead on the serpent that twists around her forearm, she shakes me a little until my gaze settles on hers.

'One day, if you want to, you can tell me what all of this is about, and I'll listen,' she says, when I'm calm enough to hear it.

I nod, my eyes sting and I squeeze them shut, but she shakes me again to open them.

'Okay?' she asks.

And I reply, yes, and she releases me.

'Take a minute,' she says and leaves me.

The noise of the bar erupts into the room for a moment when she opens the door, and disappears again as it closes with a soft hiss. I lean back in the office chair and no matter how hard I try, there's nothing I can do and saltwater tears slide down my face. I sit forward to try and gather myself. Every fucking bit of me aches for Leila, and the years that have passed mean nothing when confronted by this, but I push it all down, and a form of resolve configures within me. I will do something to end this. I will work out what this is. I have to.

I get up, walk back into the bar, meet Sharon's eye and give her a nod to say I'm okay. The rest of my shift is whatever, it passes, and while I wash and serve and collect and stack and wash again an idea forms. I'm going to find him, talk to him, confront him, look him in the eye, and I know how I'm going to do it.

As soon as I get home, I go to my laptop, look up the country, look up the camp. It's impossible to imagine him in it, but it may be the only place in the world where shit's so fucked up that I could actually talk to him. Surrounded by all that, even he might find a bit of honesty. And if he could just say the words, if I could just hear them – one moment of truth among all the bullshit – maybe that would be enough.

I click through until I find it, the charity that'll take me out there, and nearly lose it when I see they don't take volunteers. It takes a couple of minutes to realise I'm actually relieved. What have I got to offer anyway?

I take a minute, I breathe. I don't believe in all this 'it's meant or not meant to be' crap, but despite this I think maybe it's true in this case. I'm not meant to go . . . It was a mental idea anyway.

And then I see it. A link at the bottom of the page to a classroom-building project run by another group. I complete the form, send the email, and sit back. I've put myself down for construction work; it's literally the only time I've been thankful for the year I spent on building sites. My hands shake but I shut my eyes and do not cry.

In an attempt to keep myself sane I do a circuit of the flat, then another. Pointless movement. A distraction tactic. In the kitchen I stop and stare out of the window. There's a fox out there, looking right at me. It holds my eye, like it recognises the animal in me. The need to fuck, to fight, to feel safe, to feel wild, to feel free, to claim this freedom as our animal right. And yet what have we both done with this freedom? We have boxed it, in different ways, between tarmac and brick. We have put limits on ourselves to survive our environments. The fox sniffs the air, suddenly aware of some unseen threat, it runs and I continue pacing until I find myself in the bedroom.

The note from the guy from the night before is still on my bedside table. It's next to the picture of Leila that is face down, hiding her, and I can't remember who did it, the guy or me. For now I leave it there. I can't quite face her. Instead I pick up the phone number; turn it over in my hands like there might be a clue to something hidden there. I run my finger over the number and inadvertently look at my phone. I sit down with it, landing on the bed with a sigh I didn't intend. It's a lot to carry, I realise – these things inside me. Leila's death, Barry Knight, the guilt. It's a lot to carry alone, but it seems impossible to explain to anyone else. I didn't even manage to tell the therapist half of it.

Next thing I know I'm holding the phone, quiet and placid, and the note is still in my other hand. I've opened the dial screen, but I don't quite remember doing it. It's as if there's something inside of me struggling to get out and it freaks me out a bit that I've become this divided self, the ghost of who I was, fighting against the ghost of who I am now. I put both things down and leave the room to pace around the sitting room.

I'm waiting for the email back from the charity, half hoping they'll say yes, half hoping it'll be an outright no. Realistically I know that it will just be some sort of confirmation of receipt at this stage, but even that will be proof the ball is rolling, proof that I pushed it to get it started. They want to know that you'll be ready to go within eight weeks, that you can give at least four, that you can complete an online criminal check, that you can make yourself available for an orientation day and training session, and I just said yes to all of it without thinking, and now I'm wondering if that was sensible, seeing as I actually have a job and a bit of a life and bills to pay. But I push all that to the background for now. They'll probably say no anyway. And even if they say yes, how likely is it that'll I'll be there at the same time as Barry? And even if I am, how likely is it that I'll be able to talk to him? Fuck it. I've done it now.

My laptop keeps going into sleep mode, so occasionally, as I pass it in my pacing, I tap the enter key to wake it up and double check they haven't responded, but then I look at the clock and it's passed 3am. Of course it is, I don't even know what time I got back from work. Stupid, they'll never answer now. So, to block everything out until morning, I go to bed and fall asleep quicker than I thought I would.

By 5am I'm awake again, but the dream I was in is still with me, and for a moment I catch a glimpse of Leila, sitting cross-legged on the end of my bed, in the middle of saying something and I can't work out what. I close my eyes to try and visualise it, to lip read my own dream, but I don't get anywhere. I think maybe if I go to sleep again then she'll come back and I can try again to understand, but now of course it's impossible to sleep and whenever I close my eyes all I can see is her face and her silent words in an unintelligible loop.

I try to break it. I can't.

This thing can still get me when I least expect it; my heart seizes up, my lungs stop taking in air, and it's like I'm drowning in my own fluids, which is actually, technically, what happened to her. We're just echoes, us lot, in a pointless, endless cycle of repetition. Learning from nothing, changing fuck all. Round and round we go, and always the same result at the end. Kaboom!

Pick any potential apocalypse you like – and I often do, in the middle of the night – the result's the same. Excess begets extinction. We can't live well, so we die badly too. It's almost fair, apart from the majority of us don't have a choice in it. The majority of humanity didn't choose to fuck up the atmosphere or pollute the seas. Loads of us weren't even born when the decisions that affect us were made, but it doesn't matter, we still get to bear the consequences of flights we didn't travel on, oil we didn't burn, meat we didn't eat, plastic we didn't use, wars we didn't wage, angry words we didn't speak, rules made by people we didn't vote for or can't vote for because they weren't elected in the first place, or we ourselves are considered ineligible to partake in the voting process to begin with.

And we drink coffee shipped in from Kenya because it's

the only way to stay awake, we buy the shoes and the phone and the £5 pints because it's the only thing that feels good when you're burnt-out working a dead-end minimum-wage job to pay the extortionate rents in your lonely little hovel with mould spores infecting your lungs on a street so busy that the pollution fucks with your asthma.

The British Government tells us we're the lucky ones. But from where I'm standing we're not the ones who're winning, which is not to say there aren't some who are. This is why I go to late-night lectures on the plight of humanity – climate change, fracking, Kurdistani militancy, refugee deaths at sea, enclosure of public space, privatisation of the NHS. I'm looking for answers. I want to know what it all actually means, but the search always pulls a blank. So I leave just before they ask you to actually do something about it, because it's all too fucking much.

12

THE FUNERAL

ANA

I guess the point of the funeral is to end the isolation. Some people have extra family members around for moments like this. I, however, have even managed to put off my friends until now. I just needed a little bit of space around it all. I wanted to process her passing myself before I had to hand it on to others, to explain my feelings to them, and to witness their loss on top of my own, and I couldn't have them need me in any way. I didn't want to feel the pressure of having to feel one thing or the other, to cry at the right time, to accept their apologies as if it was their fault she was dead, as if the finger could be pointed in some discernible direction.

My mother was not a person who searched for faith in her last moments; she didn't look for meaning in it all. She looked instead to her passion, and it drove her forward just a little longer. She planted seeds that would grow after her own death, she left footprints, and she has me to walk in them and then carry on where they've left off. I just hope I'm up to the task.

This morning I looked back at her old blog posts just to feel her voice.

Am I an invalid? Or. Maybe it's time for a bike...

Today at the petrol station a young man rushed to my aid, concerned that I was not capable of refuelling my own car. I know he was just trying to be helpful, complete his good deed for the day, but I have survived nearly 70 years on this earth and over 40 of them filling up my own petrol. Stand back. I am not an invalid, just an angry old woman looking to burn some miles.

Writing this, I'm realising the amount of CO_2 I'm responsible for. Maybe it's time for a bike.

It made me laugh, then cry, then laugh again.

Now, there's a huddle of people in the kitchen. They're talking quietly among themselves, unpacking boxes of sandwiches they've brought from home for the wake after the funeral. They stretch out cling film as silently as possible and I want to tell them not to bother, to talk and laugh as normal, but I can't quite pluck up the courage. I have to admit that this loss is not mine alone, and it's possible that they're quiet for their own reasons, that being the only child of an exceptional woman does not mean the world revolves around me.

It's only when Callum and Nick arrive, weighed down with Tupperware, that for a moment I manage to relax. They move among the strangers easily, Callum answering their questions about where things are so I don't have to. Catherine's younger brother, Oliver, is here now too and the rest of his family; wife, daughter and son, none of whom I've met before. His wife kisses me on both cheeks, says how sorry she is that this is how we get to meet, and smooths her hair and skirt down one too many times. It's a long way to come for a family member you haven't seen for years and a stranger. Their teenage kids are both in the back garden, right down the bottom near the woods, throwing sticks for the dogs. It makes me smile to see them. They still don't know shit about life and I envy them.

Oliver left the UK to go backpacking when he was in his twenties and never made it back. Catherine went to visit when he'd settled in America after travelling all the way up from Argentina overland. He came to visit us a couple of times too, before the kids were born, but since then the only communication between them had been long-distance phone calls and emails. But even with all that distance, I'd hear them laughing over the phone at some shared joke in the middle of the night long after I'd gone to bed, trying to match up time zones and family schedules. She was nearly ten years older than him. Their parents had thought they could no longer have children when they had him, unexpected, just like me, and thinking of this now, seeing his children, I feel close to him for the first time. I always wanted to visit them. He sounded like a grand adventurer when I was a child, but a social-work wage doesn't stretch to two long-haul flights, and when I finally went travelling on my own I chose Australia because I had no interest in going to any of those hippy places where people say you might find yourself. I'd long since purposefully decided to leave what was unknown exactly that.

It's time to leave for the funeral, and although Oliver offers to give me a lift in his hire car I insist on driving myself. I need the space and the quiet for a moment. The journey passes in a blur of non-thought, and when I get there I find I can't get out of the vehicle, Catherine's car – I can't seem to make myself move. I'm not crying. I don't even feel that sad, just frozen in place. But then the hearse pulls up and Catherine's body, safely ensconced in wicker, is taken out and taken away again, and suddenly I'm rushing, as if I'm afraid I'll miss her. Together with her brother and two of her friends from work I help to take the weight of her and we walk slowly and carefully to the grave. She is both lighter and heavier than I imagined.

We place the casket on the pieces of rope with which we will lower her in and, after the humanist minister has said her words, we do so, gently, not wanting to knock her against the side of the grave, not wanting to wake her up. I let go of the rope. I step back. I can still feel the markings of the rope on my hand. I can still feel the exact weight of her as we lowered her. I realise people are waiting for me and I take a handful of earth and throw it down on top of her, while wondering at how strange we humans are with our rites and our rituals and our ways of saying goodbye. When I say the words I prepared, none of them sound like a farewell, and I sense she will not leave me until I am ready, and also that I have no idea what this means.

As I drive back to the house for the wake, so carefully prepared by so many caring hands, I realise I am completely and utterly exhausted, drained of everything, empty. I would give anything to be allowed to go to bed with a glass of whisky while these people spend all the time they need with each other. Maybe it's the only-child thing again, but I have often wondered at people's need for each other. I find it nice to be with people. I do not find it necessary. And right now I find it neither of these things.

After a round of pleasantries and hugs with people I barely know, but who knew her from somewhere, I walk out into the garden, glass in hand, and head towards the woods, leaving Callum to deal with the guests. Oliver is down there already, leaning on the wooden fence, looking out into the trees, his tie undone and his suit jacket crumpled. His eyes are red and swollen, and I'm about to apologise and turn away when he stops me.

'Stay,' he says simply, and hands me a long cigarette; the smell tells me it isn't shop bought.

'You know, I probably shouldn't tell you this, but it was your mum that first introduced me to this particular herb. She used to grow it in this very garden, before the social work, of course, before she got so serious.'

I take it from him, along with this further piece of the jigsaw puzzle that was my mother, and find myself laughing. I never knew this about her. There was so much I didn't know.

'She was like a second mother to me too you know. Our parents were pretty old by the time I was ready to explore the world and she already had this place. I'd come here to feel sane and escape them and the city. She kept me on the straight and narrow, more or less. I sometimes wondered if that's why she got into social work in the first place.'

'What was she like,' I have to ask him, 'when she was young?'

'Stubborn, political, always right. Just like she was when she was old,' he says, and turns to me to give me the half-smile of a person trying to think of happier things. 'There was a time after our parents died when I asked her, and you of course, to come and live with us in the States. We were expecting. I thought it would be nice for you to see your cousins grow up and for her to try something different. Of course she said no, told me I was crazy for suggesting she uproot you like that, but I think she was your only root. I think the pair of you could have grown well anywhere together.'

I think about this for a moment. 'You're probably right. She never even told me you asked.'

'Well, that's the social worker at work, making other people's decisions for them. Once you start it's hard to stop.'

I try to imagine what my life would have been like had I grown up in America, but it's too much of a foreign idea. I can't get my head around it and there's little point in trying.

'You'd still be very welcome, you know. There's always a home for you with us.'

I smile, and thank him, and wonder at this family I have, and how until today I'd assumed I meant nothing to them.

'Do you know if she was involved with Save the War Orphans?' I ask, thinking of the email I read.

He takes a moment to consider.

'Yeah, I think she was. I met a few of the people she worked with once, they were having a meeting or something here, but she left long before it became anything like the size it is now. She said they were just kids and their approach was all wrong.'

I smile in response. This sounds exactly like something

she would have said, and knowing this makes me feel like I did understand her a bit after all.

'Shall we?' he asks, and we head slowly back to the house, meeting the kids as they duck out of the back door, up to something.

'It's a shame she didn't have a chance to get to know them better.'

'My biggest regret,' he says as we enter, and I leave him for a moment and go back to the crowd, newly interested in what they may reveal about my mother and the many other selves she had been before she took that role.

There are her college friends here too, Joan and Dave, who I know from dinner parties over the years, and they're laughing and crying at the same time about something or other that they got up to when they were young. They catch me as I pass to tell me how proud she was of me and I wonder if it is true. I wish it to be, but what have I achieved to make her proud? As I go to the fridge to get ice for another guest I see her note again, the one about the article, and this time I pocket it, because maybe this is something I can actually do for her. I can finish her work and her words.

Oliver and his family are leaving. I offered them the house to stay in but instead they booked a hotel in a village nearby. I hold them close and thank them for coming, realising I'm actually glad that they did.

'Remember what I said,' says Oliver as he leaves, and I promise I'll consider it.

Back in the fray I feel lost again now they've left. There's music playing somewhere, Joni Mitchell – one of Catherine's favourites, at least of the ones I knew about, it seems – but a little too sad for now. I stop myself from asking them to turn it off; they're playing it for her. Callum and Nick come to save me from myself.

'How are you holding up?' Callum asks, while Nick pours me a drink. I know I don't have to reply, and this is a relief.

They help me tidy up as everyone starts to leave, and offer

to stay the night, but I tell them that I'll be okay. When the house is finally empty I light the fire, sit down in Catherine's chair and doze off. When I wake I am cold and one of the dogs is licking my arm. It's dark outside and I've ended up with my hand wedged between my thigh and the arm of the chair. I'm getting pins and needles. I try to move it but it's no good. I shake it around in the darkness and still it hurts. I stand up and stamp around even though the pins and needles are not in my feet. I look for distractions.

Catherine's address book is next to the fireplace ready for burning, but each day I start the fire I look at it and leave it there. I don't know why I want to burn it and I also don't know why I can't. I've already copied all the useful numbers down, there is no need for it. It is one thing in this great mess of things that can go. Right now, as I stamp around, it feels like the moment has finally come. But as I pick it up a piece of paper falls to the floor. On it is a number and a name I don't recognise which I must have missed. I feel terrible that this may be the number of someone who cared for her whom I did not tell about her funeral. Without thinking, regardless of the time, I pick up the phone and dial. The number has a country code I don't recognise and rings with that strange tone reserved for telephone calls over large distances. A woman picks up and answers in a language I don't speak. As soon as I hear her voice I realise my mistake and, in a panic, I slam the phone down with sweating palms and then stand and back away from it as if it may start to act independently – and it does, it rings. I hover, unable to move forward or back. When it rings off there is a brief second of peace before it starts again, and this time I edge myself closer, I reach my hand out, pick up the receiver. The pins and needles have finally gone.

'Anahita? Is that you?' says the woman, this time in hesitant English. Nobody calls me by that name and I have no idea how to reply so she does it for me, 'I knew,' she says, 'I knew it was you as soon as the phone rang.'

13

THE PORNOGRAPHY
OF THE MASSES

BARRY

We're sitting in the TV room on and surrounded by beige sofas, like they're planning a takeover, like they've already won. Sam's doing that thing he does when he looks at me as if I'm stupid and I'm reminded once again that he stuck it out in school long enough to go to university, that he got a degree, that he could probably have done more with his life than arse around the world with me, Barry the-fuck-up Knight.

'We have to own the story,' he's saying, and I'm nodding but he's fully aware that I'm not really paying attention, because by now it all seems daft to me and pointless. Sam will do what Sam does. All will be well. But then I think about the way the lawyer looked at me, and I'm not sure. Maybe it's time for the empire to crumble.

'If we do this right, it'll save your career. If we do it wrong, it's over, mate,' he says, trying to drive it home to me, but I've gone to some other place in my head, and I'm not sure that I want to get away with it, and I'm not sure that I can do that again, and if I'm one hundred percent honest, I'm a bit scared of going to that faraway country, with war so close by, with all that pain.

'You are coming, aren't you?' I ask Sam out of context, and he glares at me but he nods and this helps me to concentrate a bit better.

'We need to say that this is the real reason the tour was put on hold, that the media just put two and two together and got six, but that we didn't give an official statement, they printed all that stuff with no input from us and they twisted that poor girl's story and the words of her parents. It was essentially a slur campaign, which we've been trying to ignore because we want to focus on bigger issues, like this refugee camp. Nod if you understand.'

I nod, and I understand well enough to know that to a sane person this would make no bloody sense.

'Good. You'll be giving an interview tonight.'

'What? I can't. Please don't make me go out there. I'll fuck it up, you know it as well I do.'

'No, you won't, you'll be fine, mate. We'll go through it all a few more times beforehand. It'll be a breeze.'

A hot, foul-smelling breeze, a stinking gale.

'Okay,' I say, because what else am I supposed to do?

He's laying it out for me. The girl, Jade, was drunk. She did stay over, but only for her own good, and her parents knew. In fact, they thanked us.

'Thanked us?'

'Yes, mate, thanked us for taking care of their wayward daughter for a night.'

I might be sick, and it's not just the vodka hangover. I often have the feeling of being lost in a tunnel and not knowing how I got there or how to get out, and that's exactly how I feel now. Completely fucking lost.

'We say you'd been planning to visit the camp for some time, but because of the political situation over there we weren't sure it would be safe, and we didn't want to announce anything until we knew you could definitely do it.'

'Then why did we plan the tour for these dates if we'd known about it for such a bloody long time?'

'It was a fuck-up, we apologise to the fans. We'd hoped to be able to finish the whole thing but then the charity told us we needed to act fast, that help was needed now, not in two months' time.'

'And they'll believe us?'

'Does it matter?'

'Well, then what's the point?'

'That's a big question, Barry, one better left for another day.'

This is all making me feel deeply depressed. My body's gone heavy. I'd be perfectly happy to never move off this beige sofa ever again. Eventually they could just lay me out and bury me on it.

Sam hands me the laptop and commands me to read about the camp in question in case I'm asked any questions about it, and all of my worst fears are confirmed. It's a horrible shit hole, where actual people have to live, and this is one of those moments where I'm not sure if it's better to be sober or drunk. There's a website about the charity too, and a picture of this woman's face – Amanda, the founder – smiling like she really believes in what she's doing and I both envy and hate her for it.

At the TV studio I'm cleansed and buffed by the makeup guy, and he coos reassuringly at me about how young they'll make me look, tells me I shouldn't frown so much, that I'll crease my forehead, even though I can see my forehead in the mirror and I'm aware it's already pretty fucking creased. He packs so much shit onto my face that I feel like I could actually melt and am probably combustible and I hope this is true; both are preferable options to talking to this TV host woman who's staring at me in a way that says she's planning all the different ways she can catch me out and boost her own ratings by instigating my downfall and this, if nothing else, convinces me I shall not break, I shall not give her the satisfaction.

'So, Barry,' she purrs, in that way that tells me I was dead-on about her intentions, 'Tell us, in your own words, what happened between you and Jade.'

Luckily I have tucked all my own words deep down inside myself in some unreachable cavern; they'll hear none of them. I give them the words of do-gooder Barry Knight instead. I've heard he's a nice bloke, though I've never met him.

'A terrible misunderstanding,' I begin, and the woman scowls at me and I know that she knows that I know I deserve it, but I carry on going, because I have to, for Sam's sake if not for my own. I tell them the story Sam told me, and that's when I notice that Jade is actually in the audience and – worse than that – her parents are here with her and her dad looks younger than me. I wonder how much we paid them, or if we paid them, and then I bury that thought along with all my other words in the secret place.

The TV woman is pissed off and not hiding it very well, which means I'm winning.

'And have you worked with Save the War Orphans for long?'

'Well…' I begin. Luckily this is another part I rehearsed earlier, and because this is just a performance like all the others, and for the purposes of performances you create a character to hide behind, I can actually carry on. I'm not even sweating. I'm just being another version of myself, a better one, if you discount all the lying. 'I don't really like to talk about it, I try to keep my charity work separate, but yes.'

And the really fucked-up thing is that I can tell the audience is on my side. They are a supportive presence in the background, and this, again, encourages me, but not too much; I can't let myself get carried away.

'Interesting. I guess that makes sense, seeing as your rock star persona can, and often has, led to some rather uncomfortable rumours and accusations. The incident in

London, for example, when it was suggested that you were involved in a hit-and-run?'

How does she know that? It wasn't in the papers. I want to ask her.

'Barry?'

It was a fox. It wasn't a fox. It was a girl.

'Are you okay?'

'Yes, sorry… I find these accusations very upsetting, as I'm sure you can understand.'

'Of course, but you were cleared of any crime in that case, weren't you? Just as you have been now… so there's nothing to worry about.'

Suddenly I feel like the audience is no longer on my side. I can feel them staring at me. The pain is in my chest. The room is getting smaller. I'm just about to stand up and walk off when I see Sam standing to the edge of the stage and he keeps eye contact with me until I calm down enough to continue.

'That's correct, and the problem with being in the public eye is that these things do happen from time to time, but you have to roll with the punches. It's not like I'm stuck in a refugee camp, you know? There are a lot of privileges that come with media attention and a few difficulties as well. All I want to do is use the privilege that I have to do a bit of good in the world.'

And the audience are back with me, and my breathing is normal again, the room the correct size.

'Thank you for your time today, Barry, it's been enlightening,' the TV woman growls at me. I've done it and I could faint with relief.

14

LAUGHING GIANTS

SALEEMA

I wake up to the sound of men shouting. My mother wraps a shawl around herself and leans the top half of her body out of the shelter, reaching one hand out behind her to keep me from joining her. The shouting's getting louder, and now it's not just men but women, too. I ask her what's happening but she shushes me with a wave of her hand as she leans out further. When she turns to finally tell me I realise for myself; the smell of burning, the smoke, is making my eyes sting. Before I know it we are out of the tent and running. I have my book clutched in my hand, nothing else. We run towards the front of the camp, up to the gate where the Portakabins are. The air is crackling. Sparks fly up like tiny demons, behind us things explode, different-sized explosions for different-sized things – cooking stoves and gas bottles, electronic devices and siphoned fuel reserves. Each explosion makes us duck as we run, but we are trained for this; even as you duck you do not stop running.

I hope that Noor is okay, that they got out too. By the time we finally stop we can see the fire spreading along our row, licking at the wall. I hear my mother swallow down her tears. There was a picture of my father in the shelter, she slept with it under her pillow. She has carried it all this way. He's smiling at the camera, confident in his ability to keep on living, his shirt is striped and ironed, his hair is combed off to the left, and behind him you can see our old curtains. I squeeze her hand and she squeezes back to let me know she's okay really. We still have each other. But just as I think this she stands to leave.

'I have to help with the children. Stay here.'

Alone, I watch the light of the fire bouncing off the faces of those around me and the rock walls that surround us. The desert cliffs cast shadows like laughing giants that stretch and break and disappear only to come back again, more menacing, angrier. The roar of the fire is their roar, the screams, their screams. Young men are running in and out of the light carrying water in buckets. Luckily the standpipe is working but the flow is slow and no matter how much water they take to the fire the flames just eat it and carry on regardless. All of our things, gone, again.

People are still running from their shelters. Older people and children are being carried. Everyone looks scared, some people are crying. I search the crowd for Noor but cannot find her, and then I close my eyes in case I find her and discover she's hurt. There are babies screaming and people with burns shouting for medicine, but there is no one here to bring it. This much noise in the night is alien compared to the usual desert silence, and it gets louder and louder as it echoes back and forth. I want to tell them all to be quiet. I want the fire to be a dream.

My mother comes back. The children are safe now with a group of women not so far away from us. She takes my hand, but I can see she's tired and so I pull her gently to the floor with me and we sit surrounded by the others who have also started to settle into this new situation. Our homes are gone anyway. Tonight, where we sit is where we live. A woman next to me is breastfeeding her child and for a moment he seems completely content, oblivious to all of this despite his mother's quiet tears. I envy him.

The flames are finally calming down. I look across at all the people from the camp, stuck here together in the light of the fire, and it's almost beautiful. It feels like we come from every corner of the earth, and here we are, lit by firelight in the desert.

Eventually I fall asleep, my head resting on my mother's knee, and when I wake the fire is out, and the dawn is grey with the smoke. I stand to see how far it reached, and it looks like the two back rows are mostly gone. There are people moving among the debris picking up scraps. I scan the crowd around us again and finally see Noor, still sleeping, wrapped together with her family in some blankets they had the foresight to bring out with them. I breathe in the knowledge that she is alive.

I start walking towards our shelter. My mother calls out for me to stop, and when I don't she runs to catch up with me.

It's a charred pile of melted, smouldering plastic and wood. I find a stick to poke around in the mess. We have one small metal trunk which serves as both storage and table and this seems intact. We touch it gingerly at first to see if it's still hot but it's okay so we pull it free. Under it, by some pure act of magic, my father's photo appears, unharmed. My mother picks it up and holds it to her chest. I poke through the rest of the pile but nothing else is salvageable. I ask my mother what we do now.

'We build another shelter,' she says, and we drag our trunk up to the front gate past the smouldering half-built walls of the classrooms, and wait for the workers to arrive.

Noor sees me just as we're sitting back down and comes over to give me a hug.

'I'm so glad you're okay,' she says over and over again, crying at the same time. And although we never really talk about it, I understand now that she had a friend like Yara once too and that something bad probably happened to her. And realising this makes me hug her back all the harder.

My mum's talking to a group of other women; they're saying an old woman died last night. She was in the far corner and didn't have any family. She probably slept through it all, they say, when they see us watching them. She probably didn't feel a thing, they say. Me and Noor look at each other and hold hands. Probably doesn't mean definitely, probably is a wish. The thought of being surrounded by the fire and not being able to get out makes my skin feel prickly, and the only way to get rid of the feeling is to move. Me and Noor both start off at the same time, running like there's no other option, running like we're actually going somewhere, and today we are, we're going anywhere that's not here. We run straight out through the front gates and in the confusion nobody stops us. We head towards the rocks, we run until our lungs hurt, until the thought of being burned alive has left us. We run further from the camp than we have ever gone before, kicking up sand, only to stop abruptly, teetering on the edge of a precipice.

Below us the ground suddenly opens up into a hard-lined square, an empty box shape in the sand the size of a house. But when we look more closely it's not empty, at least not exactly, we can see what look like small doors on each of the walls. They're rounded at the top but mostly covered in sand. In the corner diagonally opposite to us there are some old steps, difficult to make out but there nonetheless. We walk around the outside of the pit, calm now, absorbed in our discovery. When we get to the steps Noor pauses and turns to look at me. I nod and take her hand as she takes the first step down. As soon as she's confident I let go and follow, trying to hold onto the stones of the wall hidden just under the sand. It's almost too hot to touch at first, but the lower we get the cooler the sand becomes. At the bottom we make our way to the nearest archway. Only a few inches of it is exposed so we start to dig with our hands not minding the heat or the sweat or even the sand as it works its way quickly into our clothes.

We find some rough old wood; not a real door, I guess that broke a long time ago, just a few planks to keep the sand out, although they don't seem to have done a very good job. Noor howls out in pain when she gets a splinter from our scrabbling. She sticks her finger in her mouth, and I ask her to take it out again and show me so I can help her to get it out.

'It doesn't matter,' she says, 'let's look when we're inside,' and this is when I realise how determined she is.

We carry on for maybe another hour until we've made enough of a dent around the entrance to be able to shift the wood, but the planks are heavy and after a few attempts we decide to move the rest of the sand from around the bottom of them. When we've finished it's still a struggle; really we need a lever but there's nothing around. The door is tiny, far too small for any adult I know. It's like it was built for us, a tiny magic place that we can't quite get to.

'Wait a minute,' says Noor, and she grabs one edge of the piece of wood closest to her. 'Hold it steady,' she instructs me and I do, I hold on to the main body of the plank while she wrestles with it. I'm not quite sure what she's doing, but eventually there's a great cracking noise and she falls backwards. I worry she's hurt herself, but she's okay. She's laughing and holding a long narrow piece of wood that she's managed to separate from the plank along a fault line in its grain.

Her laughing makes me laugh. She's holding her hand out for me to help her up. I try but fall in the mess of sand we've created around ourselves, and we're both hysterical. To recover we crawl into the shade by the wall. When the laughing has finally left us Noor stands triumphantly with her stick and levers the now-broken plank away from the entrance, revealing a space so cool and dark that it's like staring into the night sky when there are no stars.

We walk inside about halfway, letting our eyes adjust. The sand is piled up in here, as well. Noor takes my hand and leads me further back. Even with our eyes adjusting to the light from the door, it is still hard to see. When we reach the back wall we place our hands upon it, feel its coolness, its roughness. It looks like it used to be painted white and I can just make out the shape of benches running along both the sidewalls, covered in sand.

'I'm glad you didn't die in the fire,' says Noor to me. I nod in response, but I realise she can't see me.

'I'm glad neither of us did,' I reply, still not looking at her.

'If we'd have known about this place, we could have come here.'

'My mum would kill me if she knew we'd gone so far from the camp. She says it's not safe out here, that if the wrong men find you, they'll sell you for less than a hot dinner.'

Noor looks down at her scuffed sandals and scuffs them some more by kicking at the wall, 'Yeah, mine too.'

'But at least we know it's here.'

We walk back out into the sun, suddenly hungry and tired. It's difficult to scrabble up the broken sand-covered steps and I fall back once, but make it out the second time. When we get to the camp, which takes much longer now we are not running, we are careful not to be seen and sneak in through the hole in the wall.

'Where have you been?' asks my mother, when she sees me. There's a smear of soot across her forehead and I want to wipe it off for her but she's in the sort of mood where an unexpected move might lead to a slap.

'Sorry,' I say, because it's not really a question. 'Is there any food?' This is a question.

She can't bring herself to utter the actual words so she just shakes her head and says, 'The main store burnt down. The charity people say they'll bring something later. But they gave us this for now,' and she holds out a sheet of tarp.

I nod and lower my head so she can't see my tears. My stomach rages and I almost wish we hadn't run so far, hadn't used up so much energy with no purpose, because now it feels like my body is eating itself. But there is no other option, so me and my mum set about putting up our new shelter.

15

LOVE WILL TEAR
YOU APART

AMANDA

The cat, Thomas, is waiting for me when I finally get home
after another pointless day at the office. He's sitting on the
outside mat, his ginger fur standing slightly on end, untold
accusations emanating from him. He does not get up to rub
against my legs as I look for my keys.

'I'm sorry I'm late.'

He refuses to look at me, staring instead directly into the
branches of the tree by the front gate. I turn to see if there's
anything there. Of course, there is nothing. And if cats could
laugh, Thomas would be laughing – 'Made you look.'

'There's no need to be mean. It's not like I do it on
purpose.'

I open the door and Thomas makes a show of going in
before me. He walks slowly and with purpose. His tail raised. I
turn the lights on, go through to the kitchen and dump my bag
on the table. Thomas is finally willing to make eye contact,

but only because he's standing next to his food bowl. Cats are straightforward; it's why I prefer them to people.

'Didn't find any innocent mice to murder today then?' I ask lightly, avoiding the hot topic – the fact that his preferred human, Omar, has been in contact. It's supposed to be a joke, but Thomas, his intense green eyes now focused on the tin of meat in my hand, has no intention of taking it as such.

I scrape the meat onto his plate and then search for my own meal, extracting a ready-made cottage pie from the freezer. I put it in the oven and sit down in the silence of a home lived in by a single woman and a cat.

I try to think of something to say to him, but Thomas has just finished his meat and is now walking towards the sitting room and his favourite spot on the sofa. He is not in the mood to listen.

'You bastard,' I whisper as I pour a glass of red wine from the bottle I opened yesterday. It's much less painful to be annoyed by the cat, who was equally as abandoned as me, than with the abandoner himself.

To pass the thirty-five minutes until the oven timer tells me the food is hot and almost edible, I go upstairs to my bedroom, the bedroom that used to be ours, and open the wardrobe. Omar's clothes are still in it. He didn't bother to come back for them. I kept telling myself that I'd find time to get rid of them and then I gave up lying to myself and just left them there. I touch the fabric of a worn shirt and think of how long it was since a warm, breathing body was inside it, and then I rip it from the hanger and don't stop throwing clothes onto the floor until the timer goes.

To think he contacted head office and didn't even bother to call me. He will not return to find I commemorated him in any way. He will never know.

The food is tasteless. I eat three forkfuls and give up. Eating seems pointless. Drinking seems sensible. I finish the bottle and then go back upstairs with a bin bag. I heap all the shirts and jumpers, trousers and shorts, socks and underwear into three black bags and take them straight outside. I know I should deliver them to a charity shop or to a clothes recycling place, but even the possibility of seeing someone else wearing them is awful.

Next I go to the bedside table on his side. I know it might seem strange that over the last months I have not emptied this, but time passes quickly, especially when you're keeping yourself so busy you can't think. I pick up the half-finished novels and throw them in another black bag. I take the photo of me which he took and which he kept there and put that in the bag with them. The pens he last touched are added to the mix. The notebooks are missing. I don't care. I do not want to understand him. I take this bin bag outside as well. I try to remember when the next rubbish collection is and pray that the bin men come soon. I want it all gone.

Back in the house again, Thomas is staring at me from the sofa as if he no longer recognises me. It scares me a little, so I sit down next to him and turn on my laptop. I open the work emails I haven't looked at yet. There's the one from the Catherine who says she knows me, so – to replace one sort of anger with another – I open it.

Catherine, of course. Catherine who thought we were all wrong from the beginning.

And if there's one thing that's abundantly clear from her email, it's that her general opinion hasn't changed. I want to close the laptop and not think about it, but if I do that I know it'll be the only thing I think about. So to put off the worry I type a quick reply saying we'll look into the claims and close the laptop, and then I'm left with the silence again, which Thomas breaks, in a moment of kindness, by purring.

16

HOME IS THE PLACE
WE LEFT

OMAR

About the mental breakdown. I've been to war zones all over the world, but never my own. When my grandfather left in '48, he was a refugee of the Catastrophe. Our village in Gaza, where he and his father before him had lived, was destroyed. My mother named me after him. When I finally got here and saw what had befallen these people, who could have been me and mine, I could no longer separate my personal feelings from my work.

But at the same time... I didn't want to deal with it.

I couldn't.

The night after Amanda went back to the UK, I travelled back to the Erez crossing and returned to the Gaza strip, still under the guise of the charity. I showed my passport and government permissions to the guy in the hut inside, got waved through the huge metal perimeter fence and made my way into the glass-fronted Israeli border control building. It looks just like a shiny airport terminal, apart from all the security guards with automatic weapons.

Once inside, I showed my papers again and the questions began. It seems that Israeli border personnel often like to begin by asking about my first name. My standard line has become that my mother liked the actor, Omar Sharif. I do not mention Palestine. Luckily my paperwork from Save the War Orphans was still valid, and, although they didn't like the idea of me leaving and coming back again, there wasn't much they could do about it without causing a scene. Not that they mind causing a scene, as such, but harassing international NGO workers tends to lead to bad international press. I threw in a line about some of our local workers being refused travel permits for good measure, because it's true, even if it had nothing to do with my actual reason for coming back.

I got through and began the lonely walk to Gaza.

Down a high-walled narrow corridor.

Through two turnstiles.

Through a secure prison-like metal door, remotely operated by unseen hands.

Past the ancient wheelchairs.

Down a kilometre-long caged passage that took me through the buffer zone.

(You may hear gunfire or see a lonesome shepherd through the mesh, it depends on the day.)

Through another turnstile.

Into a taxi.

Hamas immigration service awaited me at a small table, under a tree.

My passport was checked, my luggage examined.

My ID number was handwritten into the ledger.

When I finally looked up, I saw the broken mess of buildings around me and knew I was home, but I still didn't realise that I wouldn't be going back to London. At that point my plan was limited – take a walk around the city, maybe go to stare at the sea, work out what to do next. When I got to the beach I stopped a while by a cart selling hot tea, still clutching my pink exit card, and listened to the conversations of those around me, even though I couldn't understand much of what they were saying. It was my mother's great pain that she had never been here, and my grandfather's that he had never returned. I saw glimpses of them both in the people passing their evenings together, knowing I looked to them just like any other foreigner – an NGO worker who would stride in and stride out again, while nothing changed for them in the interim, at least not for the better.

So I walked a little further, down to the sea itself, took my shoes and socks off and dug my feet into the sand, let the waves wash over me. I sat there, looking out to the far horizon, until the sun came up again. Even then, I thought I would go back to the hotel, but first I took out an old scrap of paper from my wallet. My mother had written down for me, years ago so that I would never forget, the name of our village. After a protracted negotiation with a taxi driver, I got a lift there and he agreed to wait for me.

The wire fence that surrounded the area was rusty, and there were signs prohibited me from entering. I couldn't decide what to do, to go forward or to go back. I thought of my grandfather and his tales of olive trees older than the cities that surrounded them, but I could see none. At some point, I knelt on the ground, and I wept. When I finally stepped across the fence, I knew that I could not go back to Jerusalem, or follow Amanda back to London, until this pain within me had been resolved. How I thought this would happen, I have no idea. I've finally realised that it can only be survived, and at best, fought against.

Among the roots of the pine tree that grew from our hearth, I placed my grandfather's ring. I had worn it since his death. It was his strength, not my own, that got me standing again. I had never expected to feel such a connection to a place I had never been to before.

On the way back to town the taxi driver kept checking on me in the rear-view mirror. When I met his eyes, I knew he understood.

The charity wouldn't pay me to stay; the jobs at the orphanage we'd opened went to locals, and rightly so. I couldn't make myself work for another NGO. Instead I walked the streets looking for anything to pay the rent. Abdul, a guy from the local market I'd met with Amanda, found me my first odd job, humouring the foreigner who he assumed had lost his mind, something he was probably right about. I dug myself right into the hardest life I could forge. I only took manual labour jobs, only ran down the most torn-up streets and through the most blackened shells of burnt-out buildings destroyed by missile strikes in 2014. Yet all the while, other people, in the neighbouring streets, got up every day, took their kids to school, went to work in their office jobs and spent the occasional weekend in the countryside. But I couldn't let myself acknowledge this. Wherever I looked, I only saw pain. That's why I started volunteering with the kids. They brought me back to myself. They were the reason I'd stayed in the first place.

And now I've come to say goodbye to them, and the workers are telling me what good progress they've made, and the kids are asking if my wife will come with me when I return. They don't listen when I explain we're not married, but I say I hope so, and I realise it's true.

In my room, I pack up my few possessions and before I leave I call my mother. She runs through her usual questions – have I seen Amanda yet, have I worked out what I needed to – and she cries when I say I will be back in London in a few weeks.

'Me and your dad can't wait for you to be home,' she says, but we both know it's not that simple, that coming home is what I have been trying to do all along.

17

THE EDGE OF THE KNOWN MULTIVERSE

SOL

To calm myself down, I stopped looking at my emails for a few days. I know, in the rational part of myself, that constantly checking my inbox and prolonged bouts of staring at its contents will not make them answer any sooner, but this new obsession takes over from my other, older obsessions. Instead of silently firing my anger into the void of Barry Knight, I now spend my time thinking about the person who will open the application. I think about the type of day they will be having when they answer, what sort of mood they will be in. They will have no idea how important their verdict is to me. To them it'll be just another volunteer application, one more human desperate to help. New alleyways of doubt open up to me. I worry that they will turn me down due to a lack of qualifications and inadequate work experience. This makes me think for long hours about my other general failures, which in turn leads me to another place all together; the realisation that I care what these people think. I actually want to go to this place not only because of Barry Knight, but because of something deeper, another kind of need altogether, one that I thought I had long ago put to bed and closed the door on. I want meaning. I want to do something meaningful. And this astounds me. It suggests I'm alive after all. By this point I'm convinced they'll say no, but it's Friday, the end of the week with a long weekend of spilt beer and general abuse ahead of me, and so I check anyway, and the email is there.

I hover the mouse over it, and I'm fascinated by my own behaviour, how this suddenly means so much, but eventually I get up the strength for all possible outcomes and I click. It's open. They've accepted my application. There's been a fire at the camp, the project has fallen behind and they need people ASAP. I've been invited to an orientation and training day, after which I can leave as soon as I'm ready. They'll fast-track all the other paperwork. I read it again, and realise something else, that there is a type of freedom to this. It will take me away from the pub and my flat and Tilda and Peggy, and what I feel is joy, and I can't remember the last time I felt this.

I look at the clock. I'm late, so I grab my keys and run out the door without a jacket, but I don't have time to go back and for once it's not raining, so I run to the bus without getting soaked. On the bus I stand near the front. I'm too full of conflicting emotions to sit down. I draw the normal stares from the affronted middle-aged for my scruffy hair and piercings, but for once it doesn't make me want to turn away and hide, it makes me smile. I smile at them, and that freaks them out even more. At least, most of them. One lady smiles back. I am not scary.

In the pub, Sharon gives me a once over and sees I'm feeling better. We're still not open, so I go around taking all the stools off the tables, wiping down the ones that were missed last night.

'You might want to check the toilets,' Sharon calls to me as she heads into the back to get the float, and when I get in there there's dried vomit all over the floor.

'Thanks!' I holler back to her even though she probably can't hear, but even dried vomit doesn't seem able to get me down tonight. I scrub away with the mop and the disinfectant. It's like I'm high or something. The music comes on and I dance around with the mop until I finish the job.

I catch myself in the mirror as I turn to leave and I have to take a second look because something's changed, and I can't work out what, but it's something. I'm still trying to figure out what's going on with me while I'm stacking the glasses and Sharon shouts that we're open. The couple of guys that come in are wearing business suits. It's the end of the week for them, a whole different life choice. They're talking between themselves like they're still in a meeting and it sounds boring as hell – the economic impact of so and so, the gross profit of blah blah. I might not know what I'm doing with my life, but at least I'm not doing that. In fact, I hope I never even have to learn what 'that' is. After I've poured their pints, they sit down and carry on without even loosening their ties.

The rest of the staff won't be here for another couple of hours, so for now it's just me and Sharon. She comes and leans next to me against the back of the bar. I can tell she wants to ask me about the other day, and I'm not exactly sure how I feel about it. This new mood I'm in could mean anything, could mean it might feel good to tell her, or it could mean the opposite, and then maybe telling her would bring me plummeting right back down. She's smart and she can sense the indecision in me, so for now she backs off and goes to have a cigarette by the front door. I stay where I am, my arms wrapped around myself, trying to keep myself up while I'm up, but I'm slipping already.

I feel like maybe I'm already overloading this experience, and I'm not even talking about Barry Knight. I'm worried that suddenly I'm off on some quest for some kind of real encounter, something not clogged up by all the clap-backs, call-outs and late-night chirpsing. If I am, then that's definitely problematic.

And if that's what's up, then that's shit. That's going to meet a whole group of people who are already in the middle of their own shit and expecting them to somehow heal me.

As if them needing something I can help with, or their pain or something, is going to put me back together.

Now obviously, there are two separate situations here, and maybe that's why it feels so confusing. There's the potential to confront Barry Knight, which is the purpose and the primary moment of release I need, and then there's the bit that's about escaping, which was completely secondary, but suddenly seems to have taken a joint front seat. And who goes off to visit people forced to live in what is essentially a giant desert prison to get a rush of freedom?

Sharon comes back from her cigarette, the smell of it still on her, delicious and forbidden.

'You're thinking too much again, I can tell just from looking at you. I literally left you for two seconds.'

I say nothing and luckily a few more punters are coming in, and for a moment I have the opportunity to get out of my head and do something. Fridays are a bit of a double-edged thing because on the surface everyone's relieved the week is over, but what they really want is to get so drunk that they forget the week ever even happened, so there's an impatience in the air and I can feel it building already, even though there's only five people at the bar. By Saturday everyone's usually relaxed into the weekend a little, they can let go, they have time. But on Fridays they're ferocious. A 'hurry the fuck up' lands on me just as Sharon returns with the first stack of glasses. I've tried to tell her the others should come in an hour earlier, but she says she can't afford it, that it's fine with just the two of us. But people don't feel they can scream at her the same way they feel they can scream at me, and I don't know if it's a gender thing or an age thing – and both can definitely also work the other way round in a different set of circumstances or even in the same set of circumstances in a different bar – but anyway, here, that's how it goes.

The night slides on and I realise I should have taken the opportunity to talk to Sharon earlier about me going away, because I like her and I don't want to leave her in the lurch. It's after twelve when the punters are all finally packed off home or to even sweatier clubs. Sharon lets the others leave before telling me to sit down and pouring me a pint.

'It's good having you here,' she says and I feel even worse about what I'm about to tell her, but by now I have to plough on anyway.

'I know it's a lot to ask, but is it alright if I take a month off?' I ask her. She puts her head on the side and looks at me like she's trying to work me out, so I tell her about the volunteering and about the feeling I've had since I got the response back and I manage to put it into better words for her. I miss out all the stuff about Barry Knight and Leila.

'You running away from something?' she asks, and I pause, because the answer's yes, but it's also no, because I'm running to something.

'I need a bit of time to work some stuff out,' I say, which is lame and she deserves more, but she takes me at my word and nods her ascent.

I tell her I'll let her know the dates as soon as I know them, and I leave to go home, but of course now it's raining again and I wish I'd turned back for just long enough to get my jacket when I left the house. I get to the bus stop, but ten minutes waiting without moving sounds like murder, so I carry on walking, hands in pockets, keeping up a brisk pace, and soon the cold's not so bad and I can't believe I'm planning to do what I'm planning to do, but I am and I will and it feels good.

I'm home and completely drenched so I strip off my clothes as soon as I'm in the door and leave them in a sodden pile. I'm about to take a shower when I see the note again on my bed. I pick it up and read his name: Caspian. I get my phone. I call him.

He picks up within a few rings and it's only when I hear his sleep-drenched voice that it occurs to me that it is nearly 2am. I feel stupid, waking him up in the middle of the night, but when I tell him who it is he sounds pleased to hear from me, almost as if he had been waiting for my call. I apologise over and over for the time.

'Hey, it's okay, I'd only just gone to bed, I was studying for an exam tomorrow.'

And I apologise some more until he shushes me and tells me to meet him for lunch after the exam. I agree and hang up. I lay back in my bed, the phone on my chest, a smile on my lips. I pick up Leila's photo, and she smiles back at me. Every misadventure of the last few years has felt like a failure in her eyes. I've felt her chiding me for getting stuck this way, for being unable to move on. So many times I wondered how it would have been if it had been the other way round, if we were just walking on opposite sides of the pavement and it had been me and not her that had been taken. I've wished for this scenario, or for a multiverse in which somewhere out there this is a possibility. All I know is that she would have coped better, that the world needed her much more than me. I sleep with her photograph clutched to my chest.

The rush of students outside the campus is overwhelming. I never went to university and I feel instantly inadequate. When I was younger, I thought about it. My grades had been good enough, even if most of the kids in my school hadn't gone, but after Leila, nothing seemed possible. I didn't want that kind of big-F future. I ignored her silent pleas.

It's a whole other life, this. People seem to bounce along as if they know the world is made for them, as if they know what to do about it. And okay, sometimes when I come to talks they're in these buildings, but they're always at night, you can always hide in the semi-dark. Now that there's a rare moment of sunshine, everything seems too exposed, most notably me, and, although I know it's highly unlikely, it feels like they're staring at me, asking themselves and each other why I'm here.

Eventually, I see Caspian and realise it's the first time I've seen him in daylight. He's wearing wire glasses and his hair's tied up in a bun. He lollops, if that is a word that can be used for humans. His stride is giant, almost as big as his smile. He's casual in his greeting when he gets to me and asks me to follow him to a café nearby where he says they have good sandwiches and great coffee and several other things in a rush which suggests he's also a bit nervous and this makes me relax a bit.

We get there and it's small and cosy, not too many people. I ask him how his exam was and he shrugs it off with an okay. I don't even know what he studies and when he tells me I don't know if he's joking. Physics. I don't know what to say and he laughs at my reaction, or lack of it.

'It's just trying to figure out how stuff works,' he says.

'What stuff?'

'All stuff.'

I ask him what's good and we order the same thing. To be honest, I don't spend that much time in cafés. The spots around where I live are more caff than café, and serve tea and chips rather than lattes and grilled sandwiches, and that difference, I realise, is everything. I tell him this and he says he likes tea and chips just fine. I want to impress him with something so I tell him about volunteering with the charity, how I'll hopefully be leaving in a few weeks or so. He nods in a way that says he's not surprised I'd be doing something like that, like that's exactly the sort of thing which he'd expect a guy like me to be doing, which is crazy because I'm still surprised as hell.

'It's brave,' he says.

'Is it?'

'I think so.'

'I think the people having to live there are probably much braver.'

'True.'

Our coffees arrive and I realise I haven't done anything like this since Leila, and then it was normally a pint we went for. I think he can see I'm still feeling uncomfortable so he tells me a bit about his life; his part-time job in a bakery which means three days a week he has to get up at around the same time I'm going to bed. The village he grew up in where you could see all the stars. I don't know if I've ever been to a place where this is possible and he explains it's not really possible in many places, even in his village there's light pollution. I ask him if this is why he wanted to study physics and he says maybe, but it's more likely he just wanted to feel like he understood what was going on around him. As a kid he was diagnosed as autistic and he thinks that's one of the reasons he's good at science. He tells me about his mums and how they wouldn't let him watch TV when he was a kid and this I really can't imagine. By the time we've finished our sandwiches I feel like I've known him for a lot longer than the few days it's been.

He apologises for talking too much. 'When I'm nervous I either shut up completely or I can't stop.'

I tend to err on the side of shutting up completely, so for me this has worked out quite well. He gently persists and in the end I give in and talk about myself but I keep it brief; parents, school, social worker, council flat, a few fights as a kid, fewer friends than some but nothing unusual, nothing of interest. The highlights were a couple of holidays in Spain – but mainly for the weather; seemed like the people were the same we'd left behind, or maybe they'd followed us, or maybe we'd followed them, all chasing our own tails – and Leila, but not any of the complicated bits. Just this.

'What would you have studied if you'd gone to university?' he asks me, and it's so long since I thought about it that I can't remember immediately what the word is and then it comes to me.

'Anthropology. I wanted to know why humans do the things they do.'

He has a lecture to get to so we both stand up to leave. It's a little awkward as we hug goodbye, not knowing the level of intimacy to aim for, and then just as he's about to pull away he kisses me, just once, right there, in the middle of the coffee shop. I can't quite believe it. I thought I lived in a world in which the only thing that could still surprise me was how humans as a species can continuously dig themselves deeper into the shit. I was wrong.

18

RECLAMATION

ANA

I am picking through Catherine's life bit by bit and piling it neatly, and not so neatly, in different parts of the house. I feel like I'm undoing a jigsaw puzzle that no one will ever be able to put back together, like I'm unmaking her one piece at a time. The more I dig and uncover the less I understand of the woman I knew, and the more complex she becomes. I wonder at who she was before I came into her life, at her love of Joy Division, at her relationship to one of the biggest children's charities in the country, at her keeping my aunt's number as if she knew one day I'd find it when I needed it.

And as I pack up Catherine's things, I can't get my aunt's voice out of my head – the timbre of it, the closest thing I would ever hear to my birth mother's. After all these years, a lifetime, we actually said very little to each other. I briefly explained that Catherine (I hesitated as I said her name and did not call her my mother) had died. She told me she was my birth mother's sister, and that she had been waiting for me to call for a very long time. I tried to think of something else to say, but between us a giant chasm opened and felt as if it might swallow us both. In the end I thanked her for her call and hung up, even though I had really called her first and the whole thing had been an accident. When I hung up the phone my hands were shaking.

I wish I could talk to Catherine about this, ask her what I should do, hear her voice one last time. I know that sooner or later I will have to re-enter the real world, but I no longer know where I fit into it. I take the note out of my pocket, the one I took from the fridge, and look at it again. I hold it, purely to hold something my mother held, something recent that she was thinking about in her last days.

I stop myself from speaking out loud to her, not because I'm scared someone will hear, but because I'm afraid of the road it will lead me down. I am afraid of the lack of response and the confirmation it would imply. I do not mind being on my own, but I do mind being without her. I wonder what she would have thought of the funeral, if she would have enjoyed it. It's not a sensible thought, but I still want to know if I did it right.

To stop my mind from turning in these circles I switch on the radio and the news trickles out. I keep it low so I don't have to actually deal with it, so it's just the sound of someone quietly talking, a little muffled, as if they were in the next room. But then something catches my attention. The news announcer is talking about the charity Catherine used to be involved in and how Barry Knight, of all people, is going to visit one of the camps they work in. I check Catherine's note. It's the same camp. I'm wondering which one of them was most desperate, Barry or the charity, but it's soon clear that this must be of benefit to both of them. He's obviously trying to clean up his image after the bad press in America and the charity must either have entirely missed the #MeToo movement or they're just broke, which makes me wonder what other compromises they may have made.

Despite everything, my journalist's instinct kicks in and I pick up the phone, call Pete and tell him I'll be at the next pitch meeting, ignoring his protestations and kind words. Everything else can wait. This is something I can do for all my parents, the one who could travel freely and the two who couldn't, who died just because they attempted it. I say their names out loud, Banesh and Zemar. I do not know if I have ever spoken their names before.

19

FREEDOM OF MOVEMENT FOR ALL

BARRY

So it's all set up. We're heading back to London town and I'm packing some pointless shit I probably won't need into a suitcase. The flight's in the morning. We will traverse the hemisphere once again. Sam says the band didn't care about cancelling the tour and I'm not surprised. I mean, would you want to tour with someone accused of taking advantage of a young girl? If they decide to 'own the narrative' like Sam's always going on about, then they'll say they left before they were pushed, that they chose the moral high ground over all the dollar, and to be honest, maybe this is just as well. Why fuck up everybody else's life, being responsible for my own is bad enough.

Sam's clattering about in the kitchen like a demented worker bee, which is ridiculous because the actual cleaning lady will come when we've gone, the Spanish-speaking one Sam likes to practice his language skills on, and I hope nothing else, because I'm pretty sure she has an angry husband somewhere and a million kids already.

'Stop it,' I shout, but I know he won't. He's even worse at this moving bullshit than I am. He panics about packing his toothbrush and then forgets it every time, he deposits a trail of them around all the houses and hotels we pass through like he's leaving clues so we can find our way home, which to be honest, might not be such a bad bloody idea.

I've had enough of all this packing shit and so I go to the TV room and turn on the box. Even though the court case has been dropped, my face is still all over the bloody news or current affairs programme or whatever it is that comes on straightaway, so I turn it off. Now that I'm heading back to England, I suddenly realise it will have made the news there too and that my brother is going to kill me if he sees me, a situation best avoided.

When we were growing up, our flat was on an estate in East London in a block of a million other flats thirty storeys high, in which the lift was most often broken. My mum, Nancy, was a nurse, and hardly ever home. I never knew if it was because of the hours or because of us. My dad was a mechanic, or at least he was when I knew him, after he left who the fuck knows what he was – who the fuck cares? They're both dead now anyway.

Ian, my brother, was the first kid. Nancy was still in school when she got knocked up. A brief family shit storm ensued, my grandad threw her out, and my dad, Phil, picked her up in his red convertible and swept her off to a new life in the flat where I grew up. She clearly believed he was someone he obviously wasn't.

My brother, Ian, is now an insurance broker. We speak once or twice a year on the phone and we see each other even less. He's got a wife and three kids. They live in a semi-detached off Southend. Every year they invite me for Christmas. Sometimes I make it. Often I make my excuses and try to get Sam to go to some bar in whatever city in whatever country we find ourselves in. But now Sam has a girlfriend and I've been dumped, so for the last three years I've spent Christmas in Miami, in the beige house with a bottle of vodka and a Clint Eastwood box set. Far a-fucking-way. The sheer distance is a good enough excuse to give Ian, and they don't really want me there anyway. It's easier for everyone concerned if these last vestiges of familial responsibility are let go of, and this latest news will surely see to that.

I guess some of this would have to go into the book, but I'd like to tart it up a bit. Is there a way to make 'broken home' sexy?

I turn on my phone to distract myself. I don't look at the internet because I've had enough bad news recently, just flick to the messages, or at least try to. I probably haven't turned the damn thing on since I got back from the pig station and now it's starting to pop and ping incessantly and I wish I hadn't bothered to turn it on at all. What all these noises seem to mean is that regardless of whether brother Ian actually saw the interview, word of my predicament's definitely reached England, and there's an untold number of missed calls and messages exploding all over my phone. I catch glimpses of their contents as they momentarily appear at the top of my screen. They say things like, 'you never think about the kids', 'your behaviour', 'sick and tired,' and I can't stop them flashing up and I can't stop the binging noise, no matter how many buttons I press, so I throw the damn thing across the room, but I can still hear it, so I go to find Sam.

He's finally calmed down and is in the kitchen, cooking. I walk over to see what's on the hob and he slaps my hand away.

'One day, you should learn to cook for yourself.'

I hang my head. It's true I have never cooked a real meal in my life, unless you count packet noodles, and most people don't.

'When we get back from the orphans I'll take a course,' I say.

He shakes his head at me. 'I don't think there's a course in this world that's ready for you.'

He takes out two plates and starts to dish up, and I rejoice. I have clearly won him back. We sit down at the island and I make appreciative noises until he tells me to shut up.

'It's delicious,' I say instead.

'You'll take care over there, won't you,' he says, and I ask him what he means, because we're going together. We'll take care of each other.

'Of course, mate, I just mean don't do anything stupid,' and I promise him I won't, Brownie's honour, etc. But the way he said it scares me.

20

THE LANGUAGE
OF HUNGER

SALEEMA

For three days now there have been strangers outside the camp, up near the front gate. I don't know where they've come from. Our parents all tell us not to talk to them, but there are two girls who look the same age as me and Noor, and yesterday one of them waved at us. They have no water out there. They have no food. Noor's dad heard the camp management talking, saying they don't have enough to give them anything, and that after the fire there's no place for them to live either. They said these people need to go back to town and register with the police.

They have no tarps and are sleeping out on a couple of blankets. To hide from the heat during the day they put one blanket up on sticks so the baby can play and doze in the shade. He has one blue teddy bear. I think some people must be giving them water else surely they'd be dead.

'We should go to them,' says Noor, as we sit in the shade

of the big tent for kids with no parents. 'We could find them some food and take it to them. Imagine if it was us out there.'

This is so like her. She once saved a baby lizard and kept it until it was big enough to fend for itself and ran back out into the desert. But I'm not sure. We don't know them and they probably speak a totally different language.

'It doesn't matter,' says Noor, 'food is something everyone understands.'

She means hunger. She means we all know what it is to feel like your body is eating itself, that hunger is a language in and of itself. I look at her, and wonder when we grew up and where we left our childhoods. I know she's right. We both speak this language. So, in the end, I nod – but where to get the food?

'There will be a distribution tonight, we can save our portions and take them to them.'

Again I nod. My own hunger upon my lips remains unspoken as does Noor's.

Sometimes I think I was never a child at all. I listen to my own voice; I don't even sound like a child. I listen to Noor's and she doesn't either. But we were children, we still are, and just because life has led us down paths that have altered our childhoods, it does not make them any less real or give them any less weight. I saw my UNHCR form once. It said that I'm a minor. I asked someone what it meant and was told it means I am too young to have responsibility for myself. What a luxury, to have such a time in your life.

We're finally standing in the distribution line with our pots and can hear the adults talking about the people outside. They say they came from the sea after trying to cross over and being caught. When they left on the boat the father was with them, but by the time they got back he was gone. He was lost. When they landed, people came to take them to a centre that they knew was bad, a place they'd been before and had paid to get out of. They say they ran away all together to be free, that this is why they will not go back to town.

'If I was them, I'd rather starve quickly out there with my

freedom, than starve slowly in that hell hole,' one man says to another.

I look at Noor, and silently we renew our pledge to take them food. She knows I tried to cross the sea before with my mother. She knows we got locked up too. That we were lucky to get out, even if it meant we ended up here in this nowhere place. We cannot let them be forced back to town. We have both heard what can happen in the buildings where they lock you up, the sort of things your parents don't want you to hear about, the sort of words we wouldn't even be allowed to say out loud.

When we have our portions we walk to the wall, a little bit away from the gate, and whistle quietly to get their attention. It looks like the mother is asleep, the baby is crawling around, gurgling to himself. The two kids that look our age walk up to us and it is only when they get close that we realise they look exactly the same as each other apart from one is wearing green and the other blue. We stare, because we have never seen this before. We push the bowls of food under the fence towards them, unsure of what to say. My hand touches the hand of the girl wearing green and I look up into her dark eyes. In them I find that actually we share a lot. We both hold the gaze a minute, taking each other in.

'Thank you,' she whispers, in a language we both speak, but with a different accent.

I don't want to leave them, but Noor pulls me silently away.

'Quickly,' she says under her breath, 'before we are seen,' and with the heat still in the day we go back to sit in the shadow of the tent. One of the children without parents is crying and we peek our heads under to see who it is. It's Jasmine, she's only three. Noor crawls under the canvas and picks her up, cradling her to her body. I crawl under too and try and distract her from crying by making funny faces. The mums who look after them must have gone to get food. We stay with her until she is calm and the food arrives and then, to stop ourselves from taking the food right out of their hands, we leave.

21

FLIGHT PLAN

AMANDA

Outside the house the bags are still there, but wet now from the rain. They take up half the pavement and they're clearly in the way. I pick them up one by one and put them, dripping, in the hallway. Thomas is not impressed and I don't know what to say to him, or how to explain. He gives me his 'you'd better be back on time' look as I leave and I respond with my 'I'll try' shrug.

Finally I'm at work and it's a relief to have something else to concentrate on.

'Did you upload the footage of the boat going down?' I ask Sophie through the open door.

'Yes.'

'And the statement from the European Commission?'

'Of course.'

'Not that'll it make any bloody difference.'

We live in a world where people die at sea every other day, why should anyone pay attention to these particular people? Not when there are cappuccinos to drink and things to do. On the subject of which, Sophie comes to the door with two cups of coffee in her hands.

'Do you want to talk about it?'

'The boat?'

'Omar.'

Not my favourite topic, but I don't say this because I haven't always been like this, and remembering this fact is one of the hardest things about Omar turning up again with his opinions. Sophie has taken my silence as an invitation and has brought the coffee in and placed it on my desk. It's my favourite, cappuccino with hazelnut syrup – I can smell it from here. She must have ordered it from over the road specially for this little chat, and I have to admit it was nice of her, this innocent child.

'Thank you,' I say, to avoid saying anything else.

'How do you feel?'

One of my least favourite questions, but okay, I'll go with it (mainly to prove to myself that I can still have open conversations with humans, not just cats).

'Angry.'

'Oh.'

'Not what you were expecting?'

'Well.'

'He left me. He didn't have the balls to tell me why. And now he's emailing head office complaining about the work we do.'

'I guess, when you put it like that…'

'How else is there to put it?'

'I mean, someone you care about, and were worried about, missed, has got back in contact. That's a good thing, right?'

Is it?

'Maybe.' I've run out of energy for this already. 'Thanks for the coffee.'

'Of course,' and she takes the hint and leaves, but she's brought Omar back into the room and now I can't get rid of him.

It was never an easy relationship and not one that any one of our friends would have predicted, but it worked – we worked – in our own way. He was an idealist, whereas I could never let myself have that much faith in humanity. Too many terrible things have been enacted by one human on another. It's in our nature. There's no way to escape it. He accused me of having a limited imagination. I accused him of naivety. And round and round we would go. In our best phases we made each other better people. He became more practical, I more forgiving. In our worst it was like World War Three without the need for nuclear weapons, the plates in the kitchen were enough.

I stretch out my legs under the desk and slouch down until my head rests on the back of the chair. Fuck.

'Did you respond to the cancer woman yet?' asks Sophie, shouting from her desk next door. It's just as well we don't share this office with anyone else anymore. They've all moved to dimmer-switch land.

'I said we'd look into it.'

'And will we?'

'I suppose we have to.'

'But it's not true is it, any of the things she said? We've got nothing to hide, have we?'

'In this game there's never nothing to hide, and even if you think there is, that we're squeaky clean, you're generally proved wrong by women like this. In our job, things can become complicated without you even realising.'

She's back at the door, frowning.

'What do you mean?'

'I mean, we need money, a lot of it, and only certain institutions can provide it.'

'Okay, like who?'

'Like banks.'

'And what's the problem?'

'The problem is where they invest their money, the problem is the tax breaks they get from giving it to us, the problem is the entire fucking system.'

'You sound like the cancer woman.'

'Well, that's because, believe it or not, we started out as friends.'

'And what about the other things she says? It can't all be true...'

Her face is ashen, this conversation is too much for either of us to bear, but we're here now, better to plough on, destroy her faith in humanity before it's too late and she does something stupid like start a charity of her own.

'It's complicated. Here, if someone is hungry, for example, and it is your job as a charity to find them food, you can just go to the supermarket or the corner shop to buy a bit of rice, and if you want to buy a lot then you go to a wholesaler. It's all relatively simple.'

'Okay.'

'But in a country in the middle of a civil war most often the supermarkets and wholesalers are closed or don't have enough of what you need. Sometimes you can get it in as aid, but sometimes the government or faction ruling whatever bit of the country you're in doesn't like that idea.'

'Why?'

'Jesus, I thought you went to university and studied something. Lots of different reasons. Read about it. Anyway, all I'm saying is that to source enough of what you need, in this case rice, you may discover that only some people are willing to sell it you and at quite a high price. These same people may have links to other interested parties, for example, the local government or militia in charge of that area. And, even if you decide to buy the rice anyway, you might find that, instead of it going to the people you bought it for, it ends up in the local market, making more money again for the people who have power in the area.'

'I see.'

'I doubt you do, but it doesn't matter, at least not for now. We operate in a world with limited choices, that's the lesson, that's what to remember.'

This conversation has been even more exhausting than

our first and I try to remind myself to be nice. Once upon a time, I was innocent too.

'Do you still want me to look after Thomas while you're away?'

'Yes, please, that would be great.'

Poor Thomas. My cat probably knows more about the state of the world than Sophie.

'Your flights are all booked, I've emailed you the details.'

I thank her again and consider the journey ahead. Barry Knight and Omar. There couldn't be two more different souls in the whole galaxy. It's tempting to just go to the airport and take a flight to whatever country is in the opposite direction. Take the cat and never look back. Omar did it, apart from he left the cat behind. Why can't I? But I look around the office and think about the board meeting yesterday, the camp, the kids. I still have a role to play here. No far-off sunsets for me, at least not yet.

I take a moment, leaning back in my creaking office chair. They say that suicide rates are higher in men than women because women are more concerned about their responsibilities to others, and maybe this is true (if you discount my recent thoughts about jumping out of windows to raise awareness). Things were difficult between us, but more than that, Omar had been down for a long time. He said he felt lost, like we'd lost our direction somehow. I thought he'd just get over it, everyone feels like that sometimes – God knows I do – but he didn't, he disappeared further into himself. The truth is, I did wonder.

At least if he's sending angry emails it means he's alive and well. I let this knowledge fill me until tears fall for the joy of it, and I close the door and give myself just one moment to feel this. It lasts for about five seconds and suddenly Sophie is shouting at me again.

'I forgot to tell you, head office said you're giving the volunteer orientation briefing tomorrow before the Classes4All training. They say you add an air of authenticity.'

Fuck them.

I sigh. I no longer have the energy to say no. I prepare myself for more eager faces, more innocent and confused eyes and for the briefest moment I wish I was them. I wish I was the future. I wish I had hope. I cannot remember the last time I truly thought I could change this fucked-up world.

22

WALLS AND
OTHER LUXURIES

OMAR

I'm back in Jerusalem and I realise no hotel will take me in looking as I do, so I go to find a barber shop. It's not so far from the centre, a place a colleague recommended once, and as I sit in the chair I hear chanting. The protesters are using a mix of Hebrew, Arabic and English.

When my beard and hair are finished, and I look like an upstanding citizen once again, I follow the sound. There are hundreds of people in Balfour Street outside the prime minister's residence, asking for an end to the occupation. They are Israeli and Palestinian and whoever else is around, and so I join them. I raise up my voice in the languages I know and finally, after longer than I can remember, I sense that there is real hope.

In the crowd I realise I don't feel like a foreigner anymore, but neither do I feel like a local, and this is okay. I am somewhere in-between.

A group of children are holding a blown-up photograph of a school. I got to ask them about it.

'They came with the bulldozers to my cousin's school in the West Bank,' says one girl.

'They did the same to my home in East Jerusalem,' says another girl, tall with dark eyes, serious beyond her years, and quietly desperate to be heard. 'When you go home, tell the people there what has happened.'

I nod, and I want to say more, but the police are beginning to round people up, and we scatter as shouts bounce off the buildings. By the time I've caught my breath, leaning against an ancient wall that could tell more tales of bloodshed than I would care to hear – the pain of all the peoples piled into this small strip of land – I'm glad I didn't get the chance to reply. Because what could I have told her but the truth.

'They know,' I would have said. 'They all know.'

And what would that have left her?

Sometimes, even hope is a luxury.

I walk slowly to the same hotel I stayed in with Amanda, having called ahead to check they have a room. Entering it I take on the mantle of my previous life. In the lift up to my room I can't even look myself in the eye.

Inside, despite myself, I run my hand along the surfaces. The off-white carpet still feels luxurious under my naked feet, the towels, the dressing gown, each one a minor miracle. There have been times when I thought I would never let myself experience this kind of life again.

The sound of running water while the shower warms up.

Steam on mirrors.

Views across a city from above.

Brand new socks, white just to see how clean they are.

Fans that chase the heat away.

Air conditioning.

Aftershave.

It makes me dizzy.

I take a shit on the gleaming white porcelain throne,

cleaner than so many places I have slept. Regal in its pristine perfection, its water flowing freely. More water for one shit than some people in Gaza have in a day. I get into the shower and feel each loving blade of water as it pierces me, embracing me as if it were a waterfall created by eons of geology for just one man, for only me, to enjoy.

My own personal waterfall every day, twice if I feel like it, more.

It's too much.

I drop my towel and lie naked on the floor, the wall at my back, to feel the comfort of a cold, hard surface.

An hour or so later, I'm awake again and anxious about my decision to return. I try to call Amanda and there's no answer. I am incredibly relieved.

The only friend I ever confided in, Abdul, always told me I was crazy, 'You left everything I dream of every day. You have freedom. Take it back, make some babies.' He'd winked at me, and then shook his head as if he still couldn't believe what I'd told him. That I'd left everything I knew behind, just to find out what my life would have been like if my grandfather hadn't escaped in '48. In Abdul's eyes there was no defendable explanation for doing what I'd done, for giving up security and comfort. At worst, I was playing a stupid rich man game. At best, I was just stupid. But I had to, I wanted to say to him, I just couldn't find the words.

I pick myself up off the floor and, without dressing, I go to the wardrobe mirror. I stare at the stranger I have become. My hair cut short, my beard trimmed almost to nonexistence, and my skin paler where it is freshly exposed. I turn to see myself in 360 degrees; my body is still the wiry frame of a worker, of a man who does not have quite enough to eat every day. I have aged more than I would have thought possible, but in some way I am also brand new.

After a deep breath, I pick up the phone to call Amanda again. With the phone pressed to my ear I go to the window and stand there as signals reach across continents and bounce off satellites. She still doesn't pick up, but I don't leave a message. It's been too long for a trivial, 'I'll try you again later.' I press my forehead against the window and stare out into the night. From here on the fifth floor I can see the wall in the far distance, a glowing watchtower. It's supposed to keep me safe from the people I was living next door to only yesterday, from the descendants of my own grandfather's village. I place my hand upon the glass and block it from my view. Nothing changes.

23

ORIENTATION

SOL

The orientation session is in a part of London I wouldn't normally come to and a building I wouldn't normally be let into. I'm wearing my black jeans without holes in. I'm wearing a real shirt, also black and only very slightly patterned. It feels like a job interview even though it's not and, according to the email, will mainly consist of slide shows. A woman at the front desk points me in the direction of the right room. I get there and there's a sign outside with the names of both charities. I cringe a little at the implied white saviour complex, remind myself I'm there for a good reason and head inside. In the room itself, there's tea and coffee neatly placed on a long table on a crisp tablecloth. I make a coffee just to have something to do. This is partly the ex-smoker in me; I need to keep my hands busy.

An assortment of other people are already here, also looking uncomfortable, milling around, choosing seats. The room is large and has a high ceiling. The rows of chairs look fragile and inadequate. They wobble on the carpeted floor whenever someone sits on one of them and all face towards a podium, a blank wall and a projector. I sit right at the back, nursing my coffee, wondering if they'll give us lunch too. A woman appears and walks towards the podium and even she looks uncomfortable, and I wonder how it's possible that humans can be so bad at this sort of thing yet force themselves to do it over and over again.

She taps the mic and begins even though when she tapped it, it made no audible sound.

'Welcome, and thanks to you all for coming. We've relied on co-operating with small charities like Classes4All and volunteers like you for many years in order to be able to carry out our work, and now more than ever we need and appreciate your participation.'

She coughs a little and reaches for her water. If I had to guess, I'd say she tried to get out of this and at the last minute was told she couldn't. She's reading from a little pile of cards that she clearly didn't write.

'Although all of you here have different levels of experience in the field, by the end of this introduction and the Classes4All training I hope you will feel an equal level of preparedness.'

She turns on the projector and then immediately after she looks over my head to the corner of the room behind me where the door is. A younger woman is standing there waving at her and mouthing something I can't get.

'Oh yes,' she says to us, but clearly in response to the other woman, 'my name is Amanda, and given that some of you will be taking part in our emergency response to the fire we'll likely get to know each other a bit better when we're there. I'm the CEO of Save the War Orphans and have been here since the very start.'

Now she starts going through the slides and explaining them, beginning with a sort of disclaimer about going to a country in the middle of a civil war.

'It always looks worse from the outside; people still have to get on with their normal lives, but obviously there is still a risk,' she says before moving to pictures of the camp, of their office, of some children holding onto the dresses of some women. She continues for a while, more photos and more explanations and then stops abruptly.

'The truth is I didn't create this erm... display. It was supposed to be Nigel, our training guy, but his wife's sick so here I am, and what I'd really like to tell you is this. Where you're going the situation is supremely difficult. Our government don't really care because it's in their interest for people to stay there and their government doesn't have the resources to cope with refugees after various internationally backed civil conflicts.'

There is a bout of furious coughing behind me and when I turn to look it's coming from a man standing next to the young woman who was already there. It's pretty clear he's doing it purpose.

'Sorry, I'm being told off. I'm rambling. What I mean is, they are struggling even to care for their own population. And what we do is not perfect, as you will see with your own eyes very soon. There is so much that could be better, but by being there and seeing it and working to make it better at least you are doing something, even if it is not saving the world.'

The room is quiet when she finishes and she looks up to the man and the young woman at the back who, when I turn around, are now talking quietly between themselves.

'I hope that was educational enough,' she says as she steps down leaving the cards behind her, 'I believe you have a twenty minute break before I hand over to Susan from Classes4All.'

By the time she's finished speaking, she's already out of range of the mic.

With that she's gone, and we all look around the room unsure of what to do. I contemplate trying to start a conversation with someone, but I don't know where to begin. So I get up, and, after placing my cup on the side, I investigate the sandwich selection, pick up a couple and decide to eat them outside in the less pressured air. The two women are still in the corridor outside talking to the man who turned up halfway through and I pause for slightly too long trying to hear what they're saying. Amanda, the woman who spoke, looks up and sees me, and I smile at her because what she did seemed kind of brave and, although I have no idea why a woman in her position would feel compelled to do such a thing, she smiles back with a look of relief and gives me a small wave as she turns away. In the giant corridor she looks even more out of place than she did on the podium, but she walks like she could take on the entire world.

I perch on the steps for the ten or so minutes I have to eat and watch the pigeons watching me waiting for the crumbs.

When I get back inside the training bit of the day is just about to start and I sit down quickly at the back. They take us through cultural awareness and child safety and health and safety and other types of safety and then team work. At the end they remind us that although they can take care of our visas etc. they can't afford to cover our flights or accommodation. They'll email us recommendations and a copy of the training manual and various other things. We all nod. Fair enough.

Caspian is waiting to meet me outside and when I get down the steps he holds out his hand for me to take and, even though I'm still a bit tentative about all of this, I take it. In the last couple of weeks we've settled into a sort of friendship with benefits. He knows I'm not ready for a real relationship. I even explained to him about Leila and how he reminds me of her, and he's okay with it. I didn't use the phrase ghost-fucking. I haven't gone as far as telling him about Barry Knight, but he thinks me going away for a bit will be a good thing and I guess I agree, but I feel uncomfortable that he doesn't know the whole story.

We wind our way through the streets and stop when we get to the Thames to stare down into the water, the filthy mass of it. I'm lost in my thoughts about leaving and the orientation thing and Barry Knight and the woman that gave the talk and it takes me a while to realise that Caspian is looking at me.

'Whatever it is, you can tell me,' he says. I feel like people are constantly giving me the opportunity to do what I need to do, but I just can't find the right words.

'Imagine you're in love,' I say, 'and the person you're in love with dies and you're the only person in the world that knows why that person died, but nobody will believe you.'

'Okay.'

I take a deep breath.

'Leila was killed by Barry Knight in a hit-and-run,' I say it and I wait for him to laugh or leave, but he does neither.

'And Barry Knight is going to the same refugee camp as you. I saw it in the papers.'

'Yes.'

'You're going to confront him.'

'If I get the chance, I am.'

'Well, that sounds like the right thing to do.'

'You don't think I'm crazy?'

'No more than I did before.'

I laugh with the relief of it, and it almost chokes me, breathing freely at last, too much oxygen all at once.

'Thank you. I'm sorry to lay this on you,' I say as he leans his elbows on the stone wall looking out over the river, but as I say it he turns away from London and back to me.

'You don't need to thank me and you don't need to say sorry. I'm glad you told me.'

'Why?'

'Because it brings us closer,' he says and gives me one of those smiles that means the person speaking is nervous of how what they've said will be received.

He stands and we turn to walk off the bridge, and this time I take his hand before he offers it. We make our way back to mine and as soon as we're there I start trying to book the flights online. I put in the date. I choose the cheapest flight and then I realise it's virtually impossible to get from my side of town to that airport at that time. I try again, but know I've made it too expensive. Truth is, I've never booked a flight before and I keep ballsing it up. Caspian is trying not to get involved, but in the end he can't stand it anymore and he gently takes the laptop from me and magically sorts it all out, partly by actually reading the email they sent properly.

'There's only one hostel in the town near the camp, so I've booked you into that,' he says and I kiss him to thank him and there's no need to go out for the rest of the night, so we don't. By the end of it I'm almost regretting booking the flights.

24

TERMINUS

ANA

The woman from the charity, Amanda, has sent me, or rather Catherine, one of those standard responses that says nothing, apologises for nothing and promises very little. It is not an outright denial. The tone is not outraged. It's predictable but infuriating. This is a woman who is not telling the whole story.

I begin my research; this is not my speciality. I start with Catherine's blog.

CHARITY? I'M OK.

> People say, as you get older, you get more opinionated, but what they're actually suggesting is that you're making trouble for no reason. Well, I've had enough. Having watched something I helped to start grow into a corporate monstrosity, it's time to ask Save the War Orphans what their priorities are, because it sure as hell doesn't seem to be children fleeing conflict.

It goes on to make the same accusations I found in the email she sent. I need more. Next, with a whisky in my hand – something I will probably soon cut down on – I read about the routes. I read about people forced over borders, overboard, the deflating of boats full of people. I read about Italy and Spain, survivors of rape and torture from camps in Libya run by militia no one controls, not even, it seems, the militias themselves. I read about Greece, and islands isolated in their pain, pregnant women giving birth in the mud, death at sea and on land, and nobody very sure of numbers. I read about a woman who used to be a dentist before war forced her to leave her home in Syria. I find out she lives in a tent now, in the grounds of an abandoned psychiatric hospital, surrounded by a heavily guarded fence for good measure.

I read about the Balkans in general. I read about camps deserted by the governments and organisations responsible for them, people beaten by the police in deep snow. People locked in cages, while others, locals, struggling already with their own lives and the histories of their own wars, help them, give them their own food, their own clothes, the shoes from their own feet. I read about the push and pull of humans shoved from one state to another, in boats, on foot, in police vans. I read about people running from unknown men in balaclavas in the middle of the night. I look at heavily beaten faces, broken noses, and the deep blue of cracked-rib bruises.

I see the bodies of young men splayed on the ground shot by guns no one will take credit for.

I read that some people refer to this as 'the game'.

At around 2am I re-evaluate some ideas I had about Europe.

I read about visa restrictions, low employment rates and growing economies, everything at odds, little making sense. I read about hostility to migrants, to humans fleeing war. I read about human acts of solidarity that cross politics, religion and race.

And I stop, and I breathe, and I carry on.

I read about children dying of the cold in the Alps, limited food, police chases. A little girl shot in the head, dead in her parents' arms in the back of a van.

By 4am I understand why, when I asked Catherine what she was working on, she would often say, 'It's better you don't know.' She was protecting me from readily available, internet-searchable truth, because she was my mother and because she knew I would associate this information with my birth parents. Which, of course, I do. And I'm crying. I'm crying for them. For the family we could have been and the risks that they took which led to me being born here, a course of action which led to their deaths. I wonder now, in the heart of the night, if I was the reason they returned. It's not the first time that this thought has occurred to me, but it is the first time I've confronted it head on, and it wrecks me, tears me from the inside out – to have lost so much and to have caused such loss. I have to wrap my arms around my legs just to hold myself together.

I look deep into the burnt-out fire, no more than ash now, and I sense Catherine there with me, even though at least half of me does not believe this is possible. I feel her hand on my shoulder, her support and her strength, and I promise her that I will find a way to finish this. I sense her nod and as she does I feel a larger presence near her, warm and loving, and I wonder if it's them and then I wake up and realise I have been asleep, dreaming of ghosts.

Tomorrow, or more accurately later today, I will go back to my flat for the first time since all this happened. I will stay the night and go to work the next day just like normal. I will tell them I want to write this article. I will put off collecting my things, or deciding how it feels to be there. I will not contemplate whether I can do the commute that Catherine managed every day when she was a social worker or whether I can stand bringing the dogs into London. I will put no pressure on myself to decide, or at least I will try not to, and until then I will force myself to get a few hours of badly needed sleep.

My flat is oddly silent in that way that tells you no one has been in the space for a while. It has settled in on itself, becoming its own thing which no longer needs or invites my presence. I pick up the pile of post by the door and leaf through it. There's nothing of interest, so I put it straight on the table of the small hall and lean my bike up against the wall from where it has fallen, knocking it with my hip as I then try to move past it.

My living room seems desolate. My kitchen diner, a wasteland. Everything is neatly packed away and ordered, not like the sprawling rooms stacked with books and paperwork at Catherine's. For a moment, I don't recognise my own life and feel constricted by the thought of inhabiting it once again, but then I remember, this is not the time to decide. I take a shower to try and normalise, put some music on and throw on some London clothes. I place my laptop on the kitchen table that is also my desk, turn it on and try and force my mind back to work, perfect my pitch, hone my angle, but I can't concentrate. I stand. I pace. I make coffee. I pace some more.

I call Callum and ask him if he and Nick can look after the dogs while I'm away. He says of course, but he's worried about me scooting halfway round the world for work so soon after losing Catherine.

'The thing is,' I say, 'I accidently called my aunt.'

'You don't have an aunt.'

'Catherine didn't have a sister, but I do have an aunt. In fact, I think I have more than one. The woman I spoke to was my birth mother's sister.'

This stuns him into silence for a moment.

'I didn't even know you had a contact for them. I thought you'd put it all behind you. I mean, I think it's great, I do, but it's a lot, even you must realise that...'

'It is, it's a lot,' and I don't know how to explain more, because even I don't know what I think or feel about this other than it's one of the reasons why I have to write this article. In the end, we say our goodbyes and I promise to see them before I go.

I give up on work. I try reading, I give up on that. I go to bed early, I cannot sleep and so I give up on that too as soon as the light reaches my window.

I take my bike from the hall and head out, triple-locking the door as I do so. It's still very early and the almost carless streets are silent. Even when I turn onto the avenue and pass an electric people carrier there is only a gentle hum, as if an insect is very slowly flying past my ear. For a moment I think I can spot a small hand held up to the glass, but the windows are blacked out so I can't be sure. I wave back just in case.

At this time of day the city feels deserted. It makes cycling easier though, and as I join the main road for one junction I find other two-wheeled commuters enjoying the freedom of the dual carriageway. They, like me, wear tight-fitting helmets, sunglasses and masks over their mouths and noses. The air is untrustworthy in these streets, and breathing too much can kill you. To recover I take a break near Islington. I head to the canal and watch the ducks squabble amongst themselves. When, as a child, Catherine used to bring me into London, we'd often come here to feed them. Once, in winter, I'd stepped onto its frozen surface while she wasn't looking. At first, I'd felt adventurous, but on the third step I took the ice began to crack. I screamed and Catherine came running, her face white but determined. At the water's edge she reached for me and I managed to take her hands. She pulled me to her with a physical strength I did not know she possessed. It was the only time I ever saw my mother cry. Now, I wipe my own tears, pull myself together and continue on my way.

A few shoppers are already emerging along Camden High Street as I arrive. I'm amazed by their dedication. Probably tourists only in town for a few short days, stocking up on second-hand vintage to fly around the world with. I remove my helmet even before I lock my bike to the lamp post opposite my office door. My hair feels like it's glued to my skull and sweat is running into my eyes. Before going in, I grab a couple of coffees from the café next door. The woman who works there smiles at me and asks how I am, and the familiarity is calming. I realise I've missed this routine.

When I enter the Terminus office, most people still haven't arrived but a hush falls upon the three people present.

'It's okay,' I say to try and normalise the whole thing. 'It was my mum that died, not me.'

I go straight to Pete's office and hand him his coffee, one sugar, no funny stuff.

'You're back,' he states, as if this is a surprise and we didn't recently have a phone conversation about my return.

'And what's worse, I've got a plan.'

I swan out before he has a chance to challenge me.

At our morning meeting we trawl through the usual news pieces and I wait my turn to throw out my pitch. Pete keeps giving me sideways glances, wondering what I'm going to hit him with, and when the time comes he gives me the nod because he knows there's no point in trying to stop me.

'I want to do a piece on Save the War Orphans, focusing on the camp Barry Knight is about to visit.'

'You want to do a celebrity piece?' asks Pete, somewhat incredulous.

'Of course not, but the fact he's going there suggests things aren't going well. I've done some research and it looks like funds are being misappropriated, if not by the charity itself, then by the militia that runs their security.'

'Okay, could be interesting. How's the war going out there? I don't want you getting into anything we can't get you out of.'

'As far as I can tell the fighting is contained to only a few areas, the camp's not at risk. At least, not yet.'

'And you're feeling okay to do this? Ready?'

'Of course, I wouldn't suggest it if I wasn't.'

'Okay, well, there we are, folks. Ed will work out your travel itinerary,' he says to me directly, and I nod and stand and wander out of the room feeling like I'm finally moving forward again.

I sit down at my desk and begin the slow and painstaking process of reading old yearly and financial reports, cross-checking information where I can. At lunch, I go back to the café next door for a sandwich and eat it while I continue to work. Before I know it Ed is handing me a bunch of paperwork, saying he'll email me the rest. The work day is over. I cycle home, crash my bike into the hallway and head out of the city and back to Catherine's as quickly as possible, calling Callum on the way and inviting him and Nick over for takeaway.

They arrive not long after me, having already picked up the food, the aroma of which fills the kitchen and makes me realise how hungry a full day of work makes me. I tell them about the article pitch being accepted as we open the containers at the kitchen table. Nick congratulates me, while Callum keeps up his questions about whether it's all too soon.

'What's the worst that can happen?' I ask. 'Food poisoning? Mental breakdown? I'll be fine, and I'll see you when I'm back,' I say, but it's not enough to convince him, and afterwards, when they're leaving, he gives me an extra hug and makes me promise to take care. I'm about to tell him to stop mothering me, but I don't; he's the only mother I've got left.

25

OTHER WORLDS AND DIFFERENT FUTURES

SALEEMA

Celeste and Nadine meet us by the entrance to the camp; we've agreed to show them the underground house we found. Maybe, they can take their family there. Maybe, they will be better off down there than out here in the sun, being stared at by all the people on the other side of the wall.

You can see they think we're crazy when it's been at least fifteen minutes and we're still walking. First we go around the side of the cliff and out of view of the camp, then out into a stretch of open desert, the horizon flat and shimmering. For a moment I worry that we are actually crazy, and that we imagined it, or that we didn't imagine it but that we won't be able to find it again, but then, just like before, the big square hole only becomes visible when we're nearly falling inside it. The weirdest thing about this place is that someone put it here on purpose; they actually chose to live out here, and even if the desert can be beautiful, I don't get it.

Standing at the edge, I turn to look at them to see what

they think. They don't speak much. They are stick-thin, just like us, but taller so they look like young trees when you see them from afar. They have faces that look too old for their ages. Celeste turns towards Nadine and then nods, so we carry on around to the steps.

'What is this place?' asks Nadine.

'Don't know,' replies Noor, 'a house I guess.'

They're twins, Celeste and Nadine, and I think this might be another reason why they don't speak much; they're in constant communication with each other, it's just that nobody else can hear it. We show them how to lever the plank off and expose the room behind.

'There's more rooms,' I tell them, and point to the other half-hidden archways.

'Don't you think someone owns it? Won't they come and tell us off?' asks Nadine.

I shrug. I don't know, we didn't see anyone else out here last time, and I tell them so. Noor agrees; only mad people or people with no choice would come out here.

'Which are we?' asks Celeste, and it's the first time I've seen her laugh.

Together we work at opening another room. It would be better if we could lift the sand out of the box entirely but instead we just pile it up on one side, so while exposing one door we're making it harder to get into another.

'Maybe next time we should bring a bucket,' I say to no one in particular, but I'm pretty sure they all agree, or would if they had the energy after all this digging and lifting in the midday sun, or if any of us actually had a bucket.

We carry on until the boards are exposed and together we prise them off. There is less windblown sand in this room. It must look more or less like it did when the people that lived here left. There's still a rug on the floor, a few dusty pots along a shelf built into the wall. It looks like a real home, and I realise someone must have loved it once.

Noor is holding up a photograph she's found.

'It's the family that used to live here!' she pronounces, pleased with herself and her discovery.

We all rush forward to peer at the grainy black-and-white image. A man and a woman stand next to each other in their loose desert clothes, three children of different heights arranged in front of them. They have the formal gaze of people unused to photographers and cameras and who understand the weight of history.

'I guess all these people are dead,' says Noor.

'I don't want to live in the house of dead people,' says Celeste. 'It has to be bad luck and we have had enough of that already.'

Nadine nods and adds that there is no water and maybe the camp guards are right, they should just go to the town and see if they can find shelter there.

We sit down in the cool of this abandoned room with the ghosts of the dead all around us and try to reach into the future.

'My dad said he heard people saying that the town is not safe anymore. I don't know if you should go, your little brother is too small, you need a safe place,' says Noor and lifts her hand towards the uneven roof above us to make it clear that she means the place we are in, this particular safe space.

The twins look at each other, their words silent.

'We'll talk to our mother,' Celeste says, and lies back on the cool sand.

With nothing better to do, we all follow suit, exhausted from the fire and the clean up after it, from the lack of food and water and the hunger that eats at us.

It's darker outside when we wake and suddenly we are rushing to get back before our parents panic, not wanting to cause any more worry than already exists. The twins help each other climb out and Noor offers a hand to me when I slip in the sand on the last step. For a moment we stand at the top, breathing in the silence of the coming night. It's still hot, but with the sun setting, the sky no longer burns down on us.

As a unit, as if me and Noor have been taken into the secret conference of the twins, we all start walking back at the same time, trudging heavily through the sand, strangely reluctant to return now that the time is upon us. I wish I could have stayed a little longer in the cool of the underground house with the world blocked out far above, far enough away.

When we reach the camp we leave the twins just out of view of the gate and go our separate ways so we can enter through the hole in the wall without being seen. When I join my mother she cuffs the side of my head.

'Where have you been?'

'Nowhere,' I tell her. She would not be interested in the underground house. She would no doubt think it was a foolish thing to spend time doing, but what else is there for me to do?

I used to go to school. I studied my language and literature, maths and geography, history, worlds lost to me now. The only world left is this camp and dust and desert. The only world left lives in books; imagined battles are easier to win.

26

WAR ZONES AND OTHER ZONES

AMANDA

There's something up, I know it as soon as I step off the plane. There's security everywhere and men walking around briskly, talking on mobile phones in that way they do when they don't want anyone to notice them yet they still think they're the most important people in the universe. Men. This is not how I hoped this was going to go. All I need is another bloody conflict to explain to the board. It was supposed to remain contained. There's nothing as expensive as working in an active war zone. Barry Knight had better not chicken out.

As soon as I have reception, I call Sophie in the office.

'Looks like things are heating up over here. If the board asks, say I'm fine and there's nothing to worry about. Say that, whatever the news is reporting, I'm on the ground and I'm saying it's not as bad as it seems. And if Barry's manager calls, tell him the same. And if Susan from Classes4All calls, tell her I'll talk to her later. Got that?'

Of course she has, I only just said it, and perhaps I could

have used a better tone of voice to do so. I ask her about the cat, discover he's fine and hang up. Little bastard's safer where he is anyway. Maybe Sophie can adopt him after my untimely death. A few seconds later I get a message from her, there's something she forgot to tell me. I don't have time for another call now, or at least I don't have the patience, so I ask her to text me about whatever it is, which turns out to be the right decision because the news is that Omar's on his way here. He called the office, asked where I was, and said he would come out and meet me, just like that, after nearly a year. Apparently, he couldn't get through to me, and it's true that I don't answer to numbers I don't know – it's just common sense – but it's also true that he could have tried harder. I have to stop myself from throwing the phone out of the window. I haven't smoked for years, but I desperately want a cigarette. I ask the driver. We both light up and I cough my lungs up but keep on going, inhaling the poisonous fumes like it's my only route to salvation.

At the hotel things aren't looking any better, even the plants outside are cowering. The manager, who I've known for years now, takes me aside as I enter. It's worse than I thought, the war is in danger of reaching us, but he reassures me that we're safe for now. That even though the hostel nearby that was supposed to take the volunteers has been closed they can all be accommodated here. That he has contacts. That he'll keep me informed. I ask him to keep all this between me and him, I don't want to freak out the team unnecessarily, and I also don't want Barry to leg it. If I had a number for the army heading our way I'd call them and ask for more time. I get in the lift and make some more calls, at this point the only answer is mass evacuation of the camp and although I know this is so unlikely to happen that it exists in the realm of things-only-crazy-people-would-say, I have to try anyway. I call the people I know in the big high-ceilinged offices they sit in. I can hear them nodding on the phone. I get the feeling the nod means no.

In my room, the one I stay in every time I come, I unpack

without thinking. I've gone on to automatic; there's too many things competing for my attention, so in the end I try to keep them all out. For all I know, Omar may already be in this building, and Barry will soon be on his way. There's an army somewhere out there in the darkness that's aimed right at us, and in among all of this are the people in the camp, people I told I'd try to help, that I'd do my best, and it looks like I've already completely and utterly failed.

My last resort is journalists, and there's already a few milling around downstairs by the time I make it to the bar. But this lot are foreign correspondents, ready to pounce and out for real blood. Refugees are not their current news story, war is.

I need a softer target and check my email for potential contacts. One name pops out, sounds almost familiar, and although this could be either a good or bad thing I just go with it because a choice has to be made and quickly regardless of what the PR department may or may not have to say about it. She wants to do a piece on the charity for Terminus, and I send off a quick email to confirm the interview before I start working my way towards gentle oblivion.

In the morning we drive out to the camp first thing. The place is still a mess; the last batch of Classes4All volunteers are only halfway through the clean-up after the fire, making things decent for our illustrious guest. The actual classrooms will have to wait, and so will my phone call to Susan. I try to see the place through a stranger's eyes – the charred tents, the barbed-wire-topped wall that's supposed to be here for the safety of the people inside, not the other way round – but I sense that might be a hard sell. I try to envisage a different way of doing it, a way to shine the whole thing up, and the very attempt is exhausting, so I stop and get down to business.

To work out the route we will take through the camp with Barry I take a walk around myself. As I do so, a few people recognise me and run up to ask about their asylum cases, which I explain, again, is not in my remit, so they ask about the toilets and I apologise and apologise again. They ask what can be done to prevent another fire – some of them haven't had shelters since the last one. There are problems with the food they say, not enough of it, and when they get it you can barely eat it. Someone brings an example to show me and asks if I'd feed my children this food. I don't bother to explain that I don't have kids. I already know I wouldn't feed it to my cat. I take out my phone and make notes. They ask about blankets, and though these are technically not in our remit, I take more notes. In a couple of hours I'm exhausted and we make our way back down the road to town.

Halfway back and there's the sound of a far-off explosion, I exchange looks with the driver, Ibrahim, a man I have known and worked with for five years, and he just shakes his head. We both know what's coming. It's been a long time since either of us have heard this sound in this country and neither of us is ready to speak of it, it's too much.

Instead, as I get out of the car at the hotel, he explains that he'll swap the Land Cruiser for a regular Jeep in the morning, no signage, nothing to make us stand out.

I nod, wish his family well, and go inside.

27

TRANSIT

BARRY

The pavement is shimmering in the shivering darkness as the street light falls through the birch trees and scatters like leaves on the tarmac. Poetry. Am I shivering, or is the darkness? Either way it's fucking freezing compared to Miami. But it's also beautiful, in its own way, this rain-soaked town. I can barely even remember the last time I was here, but then sometimes, as I know only too well, it's better to forget.

And as much as I love it here – this London, this home – something out there, creeping about in the darkness, fills me with a kind of dread. I've been out of control in many corners of the world, but at home, I really let things go. And although drinking shouldn't be the answer to the question no fucker asked until that woman on the TV show brought it up the other day, I can think of no other.

To pre-empt all this I started drinking heavily on the plane and have continued to do so on the way from the airport to this street where I now stand swaying a little, bottle in one hand, bag in the other. Balanced. Sam, the bastard, has gone home to see his girlfriend and left me all alone. Bastard. Balanced bastard. Bastard balance. I'm tipping ever so slightly in a direction I don't intend, but luckily there is a lovely hedge waiting for me, springing me back up, light as a drunk guy wearing leather.

I place my burdens on my doorstep and look for my key but it's nowhere, gone, disappeared, and it's taking so long I'm going to have to break my search for a piss. I face out from the doorstep and aim into a nearby bush. Not very discreet, I admit, but an emergency's an emergency – what can I do? A late-night dog-walker wearing a pink raincoat and green beret snarls at me and makes a big show of averting her eyes. I try to avert mine too in an equally exaggerated manner, which makes me wobble a little and get some piss on the front of my trousers. It's her outfit that's done it. Some people shouldn't be allowed to dress themselves. Her poor bastard of a dog has a matching pink and green collar. It would be a kindness to the world to put them both down.

Business completed, I return my energies to accessing my abode. The keys are magically in the inner pocket of my leather coat; of course they are, of course I should have found them there before. I get myself inside, bounce down the corridor covered in photos of award ceremonies and memorable gigs and clatter into the kitchen.

Now, to celebrate my return, and because I am a true gentleman – rough round the edges, admittedly, but underneath it all just misunderstood – I will drink from a glass. I throw my coat onto the floor to release my arms. Freedom! I need my full stretch to reach the ridiculously high cupboard where the glasses are kept. Don't know who put them there, and I don't know why anyone would have. Considering this kitchen cost more than most other things I ever bought put together (if you don't include the houses or the cars, especially the American ones...), it's one of the most impractical spaces I've ever stood in. But it is very pretty.

Glass in hand, I make my way next door and thud onto the sofa. I pour myself an alcoholic beverage from the cut-glass carafe on the table, though I can no longer remember what I put in there, and lay back into the cushions to take in the room. This is my oldest and best house. A great vintage, 1823, and a commemoration of the good old days; I bought it after our first record went platinum, back when we had the real band, back when there were friends to sleep on sofas and other people to drink with. All the other shitholes are modern, angular, and ugly, but highly recommended. I gave up caring long ago. This house here is my house. All the rest are just extended versions of airport lounges.

My eyes are beginning to close, and I should really try to remember what Sam said about the war orphans. Like, when I'm supposed to going. I'm pretty sure I had an answer to this earlier. Tomorrow? The day after? And what day is it now anyway? Saturday? Monday? What does it matter? Sam will come and he'll fix it and it will all be okay. He just has to not let his mind get addled by that girlfriend of his, who doesn't even like me, and never invites me for dinner. Not even a Sunday roast – not a single potato has come my way.

28. LEILA

SOL

I'm packing to go and I can't remember the last time I actually left this island. The charity gave me a list of things I'll need and it's only now that I'm realising I don't have half of them. I must be able to buy things there, right? Like a mosquito net and repellent. Like a torch. There's also recommended reading. I've done a bit better on this, mainly because Caspian insisted on reading some of it out to me, but I feel like I've forgotten it all already. This must be something I can do on the plane. I also wish I'd spent a little more time trying to talk to the other volunteers during the training; then at least I'd be able to get a taxi with someone, or know somebody when I arrive. But it's too late for regrets now. At least I'll recognise the woman from the talk, though I guess she'll be busy doing whatever it is she does.

I'm trying to push all thoughts of what I'll say to Barry Knight to the back of my mind, but obviously it's playing on me a little. When I'm in the middle of doing something like brushing my teeth, I realise I'm writing a speech in my head about who Leila was and how he had no right to take her from us and how he has to face up to what he did. When this happens I discover this amazing well of anger within me and it scares me, so I try to push it all down again, because if I don't then who knows what the fuck I'll do when I'm actually confronted with him. And of course I know there's still a possibility I won't manage to talk to him at all, quite a large one in fact, but the only thing worse than confronting him is not, so I shove that thought away too.

Tonight I've got my last shift in the pub and the flight's early. I hope I don't miss it; Caspian said he'd come by after his bakery shift finishes and make sure I'm up. I find it crazy that he's helping me with this, that it'll be him that sends me off on this mission which started with Leila. But I know she wouldn't mind; she'd be happy for me that I had some back-up. That's what we were for each other. We always knew that no matter what happened we had each other's backs, until that is, we didn't – until I fucked it all up and let her go. One minute she was right there next to me, the next minute she wasn't. It was over before I even understood what was happening. And there it is, the anger again, this time at myself.

I head out to the bar, leaving a heap of stuff on my bed and a half-packed rucksack on the floor next to it. I leave enough time to walk because I need the head space, a bit of time to calm my nerves. The streets are cold but it's refreshing to be out and about in the evening as it's getting dark. When I get to the bar Sharon's there, and she hugs me as I get in to say she's sorry it's my last shift for a while. She won't say the actual words and I don't expect her to.

The cleaning and everything doesn't take that long; it's a relief to have something practical to do that I don't have to think about, the gift of dedicating myself to an easily achievable task. By the time the others get here the bar's already half-full, and knowing that I've served them all myself gives me a strange satisfaction as I look out over the crowd, at their happy faces. I played a part in them feeling that way. Not that they'd ever thank me. It's not like the films; people don't lean over the bar and tell you their problems, ask for your advice, thank you for it after.

There's a DJ in tonight. The booth's right next to the bar and the speaker is pointing just slightly in the wrong direction, which is making it pretty impossible for me to hear anything. The music's mostly a mash-up from the late nineties and early two-thousands, not my thing, but the punters are loving it and a few of them are dancing. This DJ's been in before and she'll start with the easy stuff and move into something with more bass later on. That's my time. For now, I take a moment and go outside onto the street. Once upon a time I would have smoked a cigarette but I haven't smoked since Leila died, one of the only good ideas I had. Either way, I still have the smoker's habit of standing for five minutes in the cold, though actually you can't feel it after being in the bar. I'm only wearing a T-shirt and I'm fine.

There's a couple of women laughing and smoking together, a guy on his own leaning against the wall. Over the road the homeless guy that waits by the cash point is fumbling through the coins in his paper cup while his dog eats the food he just gave him. I pop into the shop next door and get one of those microwaveable sausage rolls and a cup of something like tea from the vending machine and take it to him. He looks at me like I'm crazy, smiles and thanks me and it's a wonder that a guy like this, living a life like this, can find it in himself to say thank you for something he should have anyway when all the people in the bar are swearing because they can't get something they don't even need fast enough.

I used to wonder what his story was and then Sharon told me he used to be a builder but took a fall one day and knocked his head. Since then he'd been a different person. His family couldn't cope with him and so he moved onto the street with his dog. She says he doesn't mind it, says it's a type of freedom, and I wonder what sort of freedom that could be. Not one that I'd be interested in anyway.

I wave at him as I head back in and he's tucking into his sausage roll. Sharon catches me as I do.

'You will come back, won't you?' she asks and I say of course I will, and then she adds that someone's been sick down the front of the DJ booth and laughs. I swear at her in the way you can get away with mates and go to get the mop and bucket from behind the bar.

When I reach the DJ booth everyone's dancing in the sick without realising and pretty soon one of them is going to slip in it. I ask one of the others to hand me the wet floor sign from behind the bar and the sanitizer. I put the sign out and get to work, but by this point the crowd has grown and they're all off their faces, they've got no idea what I'm up to and just think I'm getting in the way. One guy in particular, one of these people that dances mainly with their elbows, is desperately trying to make my job impossible. As I bend down to pick up the bucket he gets me right in the face and I go down from the shock of it. It takes everyone a moment to realise what's happening but when they do Sharon comes up and grabs me. I'm in a hell ton of pain and I think I can feel blood. When we get to the office, and Sharon can actually see what's going on, she's got a look on her face that causes me some level of concern.

'I think we're going to have to get you to the hospital this time,' she says. 'It looks broken.'

I have no idea what she's talking about, so I go and take a look in the old style bar mirror that hangs in the office by the desk and see what she means, my nose is off to the left and seeing it makes the pain worse instantly. She takes me to her car out the back and drives me to the nearest A and E. By now it's nearly closing time so the punters should be leaving soon. Obviously there's a giant line of people waiting in the hospital on a Saturday night, but there's nothing to do but sit down and take my place, while Sharon goes back to lock up and grab my stuff.

It's not that many hours till Caspian's supposed to come

over and in reality it's not actually that many hours till I'm supposed to get my flight. The thought of missing it is a massive disappointment but also a kind of relief. I don't have to go and try and be that guy. I don't have to talk to Barry Knight, I can just let it all fucking be. But can I? Now I've come this far?

When the pain's calmed down enough for me to really take in where I am, it starts to freak me out pretty quickly. I haven't been in a hospital since Leila died, and suddenly I'm right back there again. One minute it's as if it was a million years ago, and the next, it feels like it was only the other day that I was walking down another street, holding hands with her, laughing. Leila by my side, like always. What had it been about, that laughter? I no longer know. I looked into her eyes, thought about pulling her close. We were drunk, wobbling along the road, like a tandem bike with a busted tyre.

We had been to the local. A good, solid London pub, cut-glass and hardwood and smoking inside after hours. We were only seventeen, but nobody cared around there. We were old enough. Walking home, laughing, holding hands. Then, all at the same time, a roaring. A ripping away. A thud with a crack in it. A face staring back at me through an open, blacked out window. Recognition. A cry from the road. Leila looking up at me. All angles. Stroking her face, fumbling in my pocket for my phone. Not breathing. Tears. A far away voice. Questions. The word ambulance. Kissing her forehead. Only realising later that it was the last time. Lights.

They loaded me in to the back of the ambulance with Leila. I tried to hold her hand but it already felt cold. I held it to my lips and then pressed her knuckles deep into my eyes precisely because they were cold and soothing. I kept my eyes closed for the rest of the journey. The interior of the ambulance was too bright. There were too many tubes, shiny surfaces and metal instruments. A modern torture chamber on wheels.

I couldn't stop thinking about all of the people who must have died in there. I tried to make myself think about something else, something more positive, but then I would think of Leila, some good time we'd had, and then I'd think of her lying there, her face pale and her skin cold to the touch, and then I'd go back to thinking about all the people whose lives had ended on the thin little gurney she lay on. It took a very long time to get to the hospital. At least it felt that way.

When we arrived, doctors rushed out to escort Leila inside. Questions were shouted, but not at me. I was off the hook. I was no longer needed. I crumpled myself into a chair in the waiting room. I tried to make myself as small as possible. The dig into my ribs of the plastic ridges between the two chairs I occupied was the only thing that felt real about the whole entire night.

Both our mums arrived an hour or so after we did; somebody must have called them. My mum took my face in her hands and held it there. She looked at me as if she was trying to look into me. It was too much. I turned away and haven't really turned back since.

'I'm sorry, son,' she said to me, like they always say, like it's their fault, but it wasn't her fault, it was mine. I'd been there and I hadn't saved her. That was all on me.

The police arrived and the police did nothing. They didn't care what I'd seen; the face in the car window, recognisable from every tabloid front page, had been photographed elsewhere, at the same time, promise. It was just another hit-and-run in an area that had plenty of problems already and I was just a kid.

And that's why I have to get out of this hospital and get on that plane. That's why I have to go and I don't have any choice.

Sharon's back with my stuff and I'm still waiting, I realise I passed out for a bit and a couple of hours have gone by. There are three missed calls on my phone from Caspian but as I'm about to call him back the doctor finally calls my name, so I leave my things with Sharon and go on in. My nose is still bleeding a bit and he takes the bloody tissues from me and deposits them in a bin for medical waste.

'Get into a fight, did you?' he asks, in a tone that suggests he's just trying to make conversation.

I explain to him what happened and he laughs.

'A hazard of the job, I guess.'

'I bet you have to deal with much worse in here.'

'Well, sometimes, usually weekends, so we have that in common.'

He holds my head in his hands and asks me to tip it back for a second so he can get a good look at what he's dealing with. In the end he tells me it all looks simple enough and asks me if I'm happy for him to proceed. I ask him what time it is. It's only three hours until I have to leave for my flight, but he says it won't take long. I nod and he gives me pain medication. It kicks in quick and I feel much better until he starts moving my nose around, and although it doesn't hurt it feels like bones being ground together and it goes right through me. He notices me flinch and tells me it'll be over soon. I close my eyes and realise that at least I haven't thought about the last night with Leila since he started messing with my nose. Pain, in its own way, is helpful.

I go back out to Sharon all bandaged up and she drives me home.

'Still leaving?' she asks and I nod. 'Well, I'll see you when you're back, just try not to have any more accidents while you're gone.'

I get out of the car and tap the roof as she starts to drive off, to say bye and that I'll miss her, which I reckon she already knows. It's getting light already and as I turn round from the road to my front steps I see Caspian sitting there, leaning up against the railing, asleep. I can't believe he's waited for me, and I go to sit down next to him. As he opens his eyes he gives a start when he sees my face. For a moment I'd forgotten what'd just happened, but when I see his reaction I remember and laugh.

'Difficult night at work,' I say as I stand and take his hand to lead him up the steps to the door.

We get into the house and while I'm explaining what happened he sees the pile of unpacked things on my bed and now it's his turn to laugh.

'You have a shower, I'll deal with this, and be careful of your face.'

I do as he says. This is not the night or morning I'd imagined for us, but I'm glad he's here. By the time I get out of the shower he's packed my bag.

'Do you think they'll let me on the plane?' I ask him, because there are dark circles around my eyes now and a giant bandage over half of my face.

'Well, if they don't maybe I wouldn't be so sad,' he says, and holds me for a moment. 'We'd better go.'

He carries my bag for me to the Underground and waits for me as I get onto the train. There's still nothing settled between us and I wish I'd said something more to him about this, but it's too late now and maybe there's an edge of panic in my eyes when I turn to him to say goodbye because he says, 'We'll talk about it when you're back,' and I give him a quick relief-filled kiss and run to get on the train before the doors close. The last thing I see before we enter the tunnel is him running along the side of the train, waving, his red hair untied, reminding me of Leila.

It feels almost like she sent him to me and I thank Leila all the way to the airport for letting me get this lucky twice. When I get there, airport security eye me like I'm trouble, like I'm a tall, tattooed male with hair they don't understand, but instead of cowering I pull myself up straighter and they let me through. All the way through the shopping section, or whatever you call it, people have a good stare at my bandage and my black eyes, but because I know it's this they're staring at it doesn't bother me. I haven't been in an airport for years and I'm still worried I'm going to miss the flight even though I'm in the airport already, so I work out what gate I'm going to and then head straight in that direction. I purposefully don't stop to look at the newspapers. I don't want to see Barry Knight's face right now.

When I get to the gate there's a stack of people sitting on all the chairs, so I go off and get myself a coffee to keep myself awake until the plane and then I find a corner on the floor and sit there with a book open in front of me that I don't have the brain power to read right now, partly because it's an introduction to physics that Caspian leant me and told me was really interesting, a suggestion that is yet to be proved, and partly because the pain meds are wearing off. I dig around in my bag for my prescription and take a few more.

On the plane I'm sitting next to a guy who says he's from the city we're flying to. He's chatty and normally I struggle a bit with small talk, but this is a whole new world to me and I give the chitchat a go. He asks me why I'm going to his country and I explain about the refugee camp.

'It's good,' he says, 'that you're going, it's difficult for people like me, who live here all the time. We have our own concerns to take care of, jobs and family. If we get involved with projects like this, especially if we give our time for free like you, it can become very difficult for us.'

'How come?' I ask him. It's not something I've thought about really.

'Well, you get to go home afterwards. We have to live here all the time,' he says and laughs. 'If you exhaust yourself, you're young, you can heal. I have a family to look after, I don't have that luxury.'

It's a good point. There's plenty of stuff going on at home I could get involved in, but it's different, in your own country, he's right. It has an impact on your day-to-day; by going to another place I'm entering a space I can leave at any time, there's a freedom to it, a freedom I wouldn't have if I was working right next door.

'Were you travelling for work?' I ask him, because he's wearing a suit and it looks like this could be the case.

He smiles at me before he says, 'I fix broken hearts.' And then he pauses to see if I'll take him seriously, clearly enjoying the confusion on my face. 'I'm a consultant cardiologist,' he clarifies with a chuckle.'

I don't really know what to say to this; it's definitely not a sentence you can follow with, 'Well, I work in a pub,' but of course he asks and then I have to tell him.

'You're young, you have a lot of time. I also worked in a restaurant before I finished my medical degree. If you could do anything in life, what would it be?'

Telling him I have absolutely no idea seems impossible, and anthropology isn't actually a job, it's a degree that you then have to find a job with, and I never got that far in my thinking about it.

'What would you suggest?' I ask him, which really makes him laugh.

'Life is short, do something that will make you happy.'

'And does your job make you happy?'

'It makes me feel useful, and this makes me content. My family makes me happy. For me, this balance works.'

It's a long plane journey and for a while we both doze off. When I wake up we're landing and there's this big rush to get off the plane, as if everybody's late for something already, which is surely impossible. I walk down the steps in the crush and beyond it I can see the sea, deep and blue and beckoning. I wonder what would happen if I left this lot behind and just headed straight over and jumped in? Probably not good things.

Instead, me and the guy I was sitting next to walk to the passport bit together, chatting about nothing in particular and working out if we're heading in the same direction from the airport, which we're not. When we're finally outside he shakes my hand and wishes me good luck. I wave him off and can't believe I've already made a friend here, and that a guy like that would actually take the time of day for a guy like me. Knowing that he has makes me feel pretty good inside.

It's Spain-hot when I step out from the shade, so I duck

back under cover again. Somewhere on my phone I have the address of the hostel that Caspian booked me into, but it takes a bit of searching through my email to find it, and when I do I don't know how to pronounce the address. A taxi driver comes over to me, looks me up and down and asks what I'm doing here. I tell him about the charity and explain I'm not sure where I'm going.

'Do not worry,' he says, 'you people always stay in the same two places and one of them is closed. I'll take you.'

And that's it, the windows are down, the hot air is making my face sweat under the bandages, a country I have never seen before speeds past my window, and I only have a very slight anxiety about whether the hostel I'm supposed to go to is the one that is closed.

I doze off and wake up sticky and confused. We're pulling up to some sort of fancy hotel and I'm trying to explain to the guy that this must be the wrong place, there's no way I'd be allowed to stay here, but he shakes his head and looks at me like I'm stupid.

'This is the only place – unless you want to sleep on the street, which I wouldn't recommend.'

So I climb out of the taxi all nap-woozy, head in through the spinning doors and try not to collide with anything expensive.

29

THE RIGHT TO RETURN

OMAR

I call Amanda again from the airport, but this time it goes straight to answer phone, so I give up. I'm standing in the departure hall, screens and people all around me. It's been nearly a year since I last stood in such a place, a bright, open space like this. I'm surrounded by all these people, packed, ready, moving. Yet, I feel strangely distant from them. Not so long ago I was used to flying from one catastrophe to the next, so much so that the thought of flying for fun revolted me. Yet here these people are, drinking their espressos, laughing, totally unaware of what is happening only a few miles away, a distance you could almost walk if the wall wasn't in the way.

There is no way for me to communicate this to them, but for a moment I think about it, going up to someone, tapping them on the shoulder and saying, 'Hey, there's a refugee camp down the road where children don't have enough food; it's called Gaza.' Of course I don't; they'd look at me like I was an arsehole, and I would feel like one. And this means there's absolutely nothing I can say to any of them, so I don't. We're from different worlds, a language hasn't yet been invented that could bridge that gap.

No language exists that can explain to them that their privilege comes directly from the subjugation of others, from the continued abuse and pain of large swathes of society. I'm starting to feel like a crazy person. I have to leave, but the only way out is on a plane, so I go through the motions and climb aboard.

As we lift off from the runway I take one last look at the divided country below me. I think of all the people that came together last night, all their languages joined in one voice, and I allow myself to hope that one way or another, they'll find a way forward. I rub the space where my grandfather's ring used to be, the white band of skin that marked the place it was for so long has now faded, but I can still feel the weight of it.

I close my eyes, and silently say goodbye.

When we land it's dark. I've already called Ibrahim, a guy I've worked with for years, to pick me up, and he meets me in arrivals. When I see him he shakes my hand warmly, but I can tell he's worried.

'How is the situation here?' I ask, after enquiring about his family and his health.

'I don't know where you've come from this time, but you should probably have stayed there.'

I try to press him further but he doesn't want to speak about it.

'If we're all going to die together that at least let's talk about something interesting.'

I laugh, despite the worrying implication of his words.

'Okay, well, how is Amanda?'

'Ah, not the best place to start. I've seen her look better,' he replies, and so for the rest of the journey we talk football, because whatever happens here, football carries on.

At the hotel I check into my room. Amanda's not in reception or at the bar so I go upstairs to unpack. I take my few possessions out of my rucksack; place my notebooks next to my bed. I'm nervous about seeing her and not quite ready for the confrontation, so I sit on the bed and try to get myself together.

I guess you could say that on the day I left I did try to tell her why, but it got twisted in the telling. It sounded like I was blaming her, specifically, for where we were. But that's not what I meant at all, because she was then, and most likely still is now, trying to do the best she can. Making only the compromises she sees as most necessary, and telling herself every day that what she does is for the greater good, that she is constantly choosing the lesser evil. For a long time I comforted her in that, supported her for as long as I could, while we moved further and further away from the place where we started. On the day I left I did so because I realised I was even more lost than she was.

I never returned to our London flat. Did not pick up my things. Did not write. And I should have done. It's just that the longer I left it the more impossible it became. The more space there was for words the less I could find them. But now I have to. It's time, and I slowly go downstairs. I spot her sitting at the bar, and I know she is waiting for me in this quiet moment while everybody else is in their rooms preparing for the evening and recovering from the day. I walk up to her one step at a time, giving her the opportunity to leave if she wants to. Even though she hasn't turned yet, I can sense she knows I'm there and that she's been preparing something.

'So you thought you could just walk out and then just saunter back into my life when you felt like it?' she says as she turns to me, her skin tinged red from the sun, her anger boiling.

'No, I walked out because I couldn't cope anymore, because I was done with it all.'

And we are instantly in familiar territory. It's as if these last few months were nothing, like the argument we were having on that day never ended. I do not sit down but stay standing, ready to retreat.

'Because you were burnt out, and you didn't think you could go back to London and see a therapist like everybody else?'

'I wasn't thinking straight, I wasn't in a place where that suggestion would have made sense. I'm still not. How can a therapist help when the problems we face are institutional, governmental, ingrained?'

'You're being ridiculous. Of course a therapist will not

solve the world's problems; their job is to help you deal with them better.'

'But don't you get it? The sickness is not in my head, it's in the world. It's everything.'

'Omar, the human race has lived with oppression and destitution for millennia, it's what we do.'

'No, it hasn't, and no, it doesn't have to be this way.'

'You're going to give me the handful of examples from tribal society of true equality?'

I hang my head, there's no way forward.

'Or you want to talk about the great institution of democracy which came from a society reliant on mass slave labour, where only men of social standing were citizens?'

'I just needed some time out.'

'It's been nearly a year, and not a single word from you, that is not a "time out". I'd started to think you were dead for Christ's sake.'

'I needed to strip myself down to the bare minimum. To see what was underneath. I needed to go home.'

'You, Omar, just you, that's what's underneath. Can't you see that the answer is not to deprive yourself of everything, it's to give each other more. And you already had a home, with me, and the bloody cat.'

'The answer is both, the question is how to do it. How to live lightly and to live together. How to unbuild what was built on pain, and rebuild something built on love, or if not love, respect.'

'Well surely you found your answer, enlighten me.'

'Maybe, but I don't think this is the time to talk about it.'

'You make me crazy.'

'I make myself crazy too.'

And this feels like round one of an ongoing battle. I back away, and as I do so her eyes say, 'Yes, leave again why don't you,' and for the moment, that's exactly what I do, because I am the one at fault and she has every right to her anger.

Back in my room I lie in bed and listen to the familiar sound of a war getting closer.

30

DIGGING IN

SALEEMA

The twins and their family have gone, Noor tells me while I'm drinking my morning tea.

'Do you think it's because of the explosions last night?' she asks, and for a moment I pretend not to hear her, because I was hoping the explosions were a part of my dream. But as she says it a helicopter flies overhead, so low that we can feel the very edge of the wind it makes, and both of us automatically duck.

When we're sitting up straight again, I shake my head to say I don't know and I don't want to talk about it, but she keeps on.

'Maybe they've gone to the underground house?'

'Maybe,' I say to show I am listening and can hear, but that I still don't want to talk about it.

'We should take the gun from the man you saw.'

'No,' I reply, because I know what happens to people who carry guns: they get shot.

'It's the only way to keep ourselves safe.'

'Guns don't keep you safe, they get you killed. They got my brother killed.'

And I haven't spoken of him in so long that after I've said that, I don't know how to continue. We buried him in the park where I used to play with Yara.

'I'm sorry,' she replies, and allows us both a moment of silence.

'This life is crazy,' I say after a while, because I feel like nothing makes sense and I don't know how else to explain it, 'Sometimes, when I wake up, I keep my eyes closed and pray that when I open them I'll be at home, late for school. I pray my mother will scream at me to get out of bed, get dressed and go to class.'

Noor looks at the ground and scrapes the floor with a small stick she picked up somewhere, drawing circles. 'I do the same,' she admits, 'which is stupid, because I hated school.'

'I loved it,' I say and breathe in all the available air into my lungs before I let it out again, because it's true I loved it, and because I think I will never go to school again. 'When the famous man comes, I'm going to ask him about it. I'm going to ask him to give us a real school not these half-built classrooms that are burned already.'

'Do you think he will?'

'I have no idea, but he must have a lot of money, and he must know the charity people. Maybe it's possible.'

'It's a good idea to ask.'

I nod and say nothing, because I don't really think it will work, but I want to believe that it could.

Noor takes my hand in hers and holds it, rubbing her thumb over my dry skin.

'We don't know what will happen in the future,' she says, to make me feel better, 'anything is possible. Let's go to see if the twins went to the underground house.'

I don't really want to, but I stand up anyway. Anything is better than sitting doing nothing all day.

'We should take food, in case they're there,' I say, and Noor pulls out a packet of biscuits to show me. She's thought of everything; this was already her plan. So we head out of the camp and back to the house.

'I wonder who lived there before,' says Noor as we walk.

'Local people, I suppose, a family. But I wouldn't live here if I had a choice.'

'Me neither,' she says and we trudge on in silence.

When we get there we can hear them talking before we can see them, and when Celeste notices that we've turned up she waves.

'There's a well!' she shouts, joy and sweat all over her face.

They've been busy digging all morning by the look of it, and it's true, I can see the opening of the well. We greet her mother. Nadine is still digging out another of the rooms, the baby must be sleeping somewhere.

'We forgot to bring a bucket,' Noor says as we walk over.

'We don't have a bucket,' I reply, and for some reason we both find this funny and start laughing, the twins laugh with us and this gets us in the mood to dig, which we do once again with our bare hands.

When we've cleared out the next room we enter and sit in the cool dimness, Noor pulls out the biscuits and we pass the packet around.

'What will you do about food?' she asks Nadine, who looks at her sister.

'We hoped maybe you could bring us some,' Celeste says. 'Tomorrow me and my sister will walk to town and try to beg some.'

Their mother walks in suddenly and interrupts.

'This family does not beg,' she says simply. 'We will ask the people who live here for help. That is not begging, that is humanity.'

'Yes, Mother,' says Celeste, as her mother walks out again.

'And anyway, it's not safe to go to town, not anymore,' she says from the doorway, and I wonder if it was ever safe to go to town and what could possibly have made it worse.

We all look down at the floor, at our feet, at our filthy hands. We all know that the twins shouldn't go, but we also know that we are not people that can make decisions over how we get our food, or over what lengths we will go to.

'We should leave,' I say to Noor. We stand and brush ourselves down.

They thank us and, before we know it, we are on our way back to the camp, both of us wrapped up in our thoughts. We don't have any more food to give them, and this makes us both sad. Noor asks if I want to hear a story her grandmother used to tell her and, because it's a long walk and she's still trying to cheer me up, I say yes.

'Okay,' she says, clearing her throat a little before she begins. 'I probably won't tell it as well as she did,' and she coughs one more time, nervous.

'The first map that was ever was made by a mother for her daughter. The mother had become too old and frail to look after her. It was time the daughter learnt how to look after herself. The place they lived was very dry and rocky. There was one stream but it sometimes dried up in summer. When this happened it was necessary to go to a spring some distance away. The mother drew a map to the place in the dusty earth. It showed her daughter the route to the spring. It showed the curve of the valley she must walk down. It showed some of the bigger rocks as markers,' here she pauses to look at me and check I'm listening; I nod for her to continue.

'It showed the tree next to the spring so she knew she'd reached the right spot. It showed the mountain lion that lived just past the place with the tree. The next day the wind swept the map away. The only people to ever see the map were the woman and her daughter, but it worked. When her mother was sick that summer, the daughter found her way to the spring and brought home fresh, clear water that was cool and delicious to drink.' Here she pauses again while we both consider our own thirst.

'The following year the mother died and the daughter decided to have her own child. The pregnancy and birth went well. The child grew fast and its mother was healthy. Yet, when her child was only five years old and safe at home, the mother was bitten by a snake and died. She never had the chance to pass on the map. As a result, several years after her death, when a drought came, her only child was eaten by the mountain lion.'

'That is not a cheerful story. Why did your grandmother tell it to you?'

'I don't know, I just like it because it is about a grandmother and a mother and daughter, like my family.'

'But they all die, what does it mean?'

'That you should have a really good memory?'

'But the middle woman dies and doesn't even tell her daughter about the map, she couldn't remember it even if she wanted to.'

'That you shouldn't trust lions?'

'Well, that's just obvious. Are there lions where you're from?'

'No, my grandmother said there used to be, but it was a very long time ago.'

'What happened to them?'

'People came, I guess.'

'Or maybe the people were there first and the lion came because he was hungry. Maybe the people killed him because he was eating people.'

'Maybe,' she says, unconvinced. I don't think she cares what it means.

'And what about your grandmother?'

'I don't know,' she says, and I wish I hadn't asked. To take her mind off it, I grab her hand and we run the last bit back to camp. We go together to queue for lunch, ravenous and hot. Our mothers tut tut when they see us, calling us wild children, which makes us smile as soon as they can no longer see our faces. Better wild than bored.

After lunch I take my book to the high place but do not read. There is a slight breeze in the air up here and I concentrate on that, let it cool my skin, clear out my head. I do not want to think about the explosions or about Celeste and Nadine going begging, so of course this is all that occupies my mind. In the end I open my book just to chase all these thoughts away. And suddenly I am in a cold and faraway land where anything truly is possible. Where simple words can make bad things go away and good things happen.

31

HISTORIES

ANA

On the plane I try to organise my notes into two separate folders, one on the camp and one on the charity. I use the two empty chairs next to me as a sort of filing cabinet. Because it's for work, I've ended up in the special curtained-off bit where they're constantly bringing you free things and I'm alternating wine and coffee so I don't get too drunk or too tired to read through the notes. As a result of this combination I have quite high energy and my tap-tap-tapping prompts the woman behind me to touch my shoulder and explain that she is trying to sleep. I apologise, and as I don't know if I can be trusted to type quietly, I close the lid of the laptop. There'll be plenty of time at the hotel.

But now I don't know what to do with myself. My hands fidget on the small table, so I order some nuts to give them something to do, but then I eat them too fast. I turn on the miniature screen and plug in the earphones to see if a film will calm me down, but I only last five minutes. I realise that the type of energy I have right now is actually the product of exhaustion, the deep kind you can't shake off with a coffee, the kind that requires actual rest and emotional calm. I'm starting to think that maybe this was a bad idea. Maybe it's too early to be putting myself under this kind of pressure? But then I think of Catherine and how she spent her last days emailing and fighting, and I stop drinking coffee and instead have one last wine to calm me down and help me sleep because this is clearly what I need.

The wine was a bad idea, because although I do manage to sleep I wake up with a searing headache and have to down several bottles of water. This in turn makes me need to go to the loo, which means pushing past other people's legs from the window seat to the aisle and, even though there's quite a lot of room to move around in this part of the plane, I still manage to wake up at least one person.

The nearest toilet's engaged so I walk unsteadily to the toilet at the other end. When I finally get inside I'm sick into the strange plastic hole. For a moment I feel desperate, and I wish I could call Callum and hear him laugh at my stupidity for following through with this plan. I don't even know why I'm being sick, I don't know if it's the wine, or the nerves, or the flying. I don't know if it's the tiredness. I don't know if it's the sadness. I stay in there for long enough to prompt knocking from a member of the cabin crew. I apologise and flush and clean my face and mouth, and exit, leaving the smell of vomit in my wake. I'm glad I'm sitting all the way at the other end of the plane.

For the rest of the journey I doze, slipping in and out of consciousness. When I finally get to the hotel, I'm surprised I've made it and, after checking in, head straight up to my room and turn on the air-con until I'm a normal temperature again. Really, I just want to sleep, but my stomach won't let me rest, and it's late already, so as soon as I'm feeling a little refreshed, I go downstairs to forage.

I get down to the bar and there's not much on offer at this time of night, but I order what they have, a club sandwich. I'm looking around at the limited number of other guests, the journos and charity people, when I'm sure I see a face I recognise, though he's wearing a bandage across half of it. Sol, a kid Catherine worked with. He even lived with us for a short time once – a few days maybe, no more – when there was trouble at home. I can't remember what exactly happened now, but he was quiet then and it seems he hasn't changed much. He's sitting on his own, holding a book he's not reading while staring out the window. I feel bad now that I didn't tell him about the funeral. I didn't have a number to contact him on, but maybe he wouldn't care, not after all this time.

I'm unsure what to do now. Should I go up to him, ask him what happened to his face? Maybe he would have no idea who I was. Maybe I should wait to see if he comes up to me, but sitting here thinking about it is annoying me, so I get up and walk over. It's a couple of seconds before he realises I'm standing at the table and of course he doesn't recognise me so I explain, and he can't believe it.

'I still think about Catherine you know, she really helped me out back then.'

And this is awful, and I tell him gently that she's dead, and while I'm in the middle of it my sandwich arrives and then my drink, and I don't know how to cope with the reality of meal times combined with the reality of death.

'What was it?' he asks, and I tell him about the cancer and the chemo and about how in the end none of it worked, even though we tried everything, and how it's difficult to do this shit on your own, and how I'm not sure I should have come on this trip for work. In essence, I tell him more than I meant to.

'I remember when you stayed with us,' I say to him, for no particular reason, other than to confirm that I haven't made this fact up.

'Me too, she was great, Catherine. She was different to everybody else. She didn't care what people thought as long as she knew she was doing the right thing.'

'It's seems you knew her pretty well.'

'She worked with my family for a while.'

I'd like to ask more, but I also don't want to let on that I've forgotten anything important, anything he might have told me before, or that Catherine did.

'I haven't seen you up there for years though,' I say instead.

'I didn't want to bother her. She'd retired.'

'She wouldn't have minded. I'm sure she would have liked to see you.'

This seems to be enough conversation for him and he looks out of the window again. I guess he's taking in the information that someone he knew and liked has died.

'I'm sorry for your loss,' he says after a while, and he briefly makes eye contact with me before looking once again out into the darkness.

His presence is useful though, it's taken my mind off everything else. I use his silence and eat my sandwich in peace, while trying to remember more about that summer when he came to stay for a few days, what the reason for his stay was and what we did while he was there. I can picture Catherine talking on the phone in a quiet but commanding voice. She was good at that. She was a social worker, she had to be firm. But all I have is the image not the words.

'Didn't you run away when you were staying with us?'

It's the first time I've seen him smile.

'Yes, but I didn't get very far. You found me.'

And I remember. Catherine calling his parents, asking if he was there, checking with the police, telling them that it didn't matter that he'd only just gone missing, that they had to look for him anyway, and I was worried for the strange quiet boy who'd been staying with us so I went out to find him myself. I went to all the places I had shown him in the garden and in the woods, and I couldn't see him anywhere. I went to the top of the lane and called his name but he did not answer. I walked as far as the bus stop but knew instinctively that this was too obvious a route for someone on the run. So I went back to the woods and through them, out to the wheat field on the far side, and it was true that if you walked through that field you got to another road and from there you could no doubt catch a ride, so I walked along the boundary until I found a place where I could crawl through the fence, and there he was, sitting on the side of the road with his sports bag.

'I told you that you weren't trapped there and that if you really wanted a lift it was probably just easier to ask Catherine.'

'And I did. And she told me I must be crazy if I thought she was some sort of taxi service, and that she'd think about it and I could ask again the next day.'

'But you didn't.'

'Correct. I did not.'

'I miss her,' I say, glad I have someone to say it to, and it feels like in some strange way it is her who has brought us back together.

When we're done I go up to my room to finish the work I need to get through before tomorrow. The human rights report alone will take me hours, and it's all I can do to keep my eyes open.

32

THE TRUTH IS DEAD, LONG LIVE THE TRUTH

AMANDA

The journalist I emailed arrived last night and even though my body and mind are screaming for a moment alone, to work out how I feel about anything at all, I suggest we have a coffee together and get this interview over and done with. She's young, beautiful and straightforward. I wish I could shrink a little further into my desert-hardened skin, my dried-out hair, my chapped cheeks. Instead I sit forward on the plush bar chair and begin.

We roll through the niceties, but I need to make one thing clear from the beginning.

'You need to use the article to call for the evacuation of the camp.'

'So it's that bad already? Does your boy Barry know?'

'No, he's not here yet. The problem is, the situation is fluid, maybe the whole thing will pass us by and I don't want to spook him. You've seen your journalist buddies over there, you know what I'm talking about.'

'I was hoping they were here for the bar. I thought this place was supposed to be dry.'

'I guess they're paying all the right people. But let's get to the point. Will you do it?'

'Of course.'

'Okay, well then, let's get to it, do your worst.'

'Firstly, I think I should tell you, I'm Catherine's daughter.'

And this takes me aback. Catherine. The woman who wanted to take me down before she died.

'Is she…?'

'She passed away recently.'

It's funny, I didn't think this would affect me, or rather I hadn't even thought about it at all, which is a terrible thing to admit. I'd just piled away her illness with all the other bad news that arrives every day. I didn't even say I was sorry that she was sick when I emailed her. It's only now I realise that this was not okay. I only saw the charity. I only saw another long list of complaints. Just more problems to deal with.

'I'm sorry,' I say, and mean it, which is clearly something Ana didn't expect.

'Me too,' she replies, such a simple thing, but the honesty behind her words reminds me of her mother, makes me think of the younger, less complicated self I once was, and it's all I can do to stop myself from crying.

'I'm ready,' I say, even though we both know I'm not, and of course Ana offers to do the interview at another time and apologises for giving me the news in this way. But I don't deserve any of it and in the end she agrees to continue.

'How long have you been involved in this camp?' she begins after some preamble about the background of the charity, how it all started.

'Three years, more or less, but we've worked in the country much longer.'

'A difficult place to work. How do you manage to keep the beneficiaries safe?'

And there I was thinking she was going to give me an easy ride.

'Well, I'm not sure that's ever something we've promised, and it's not as if we're solely responsible for the camp.'

'So who employs the armed militia that work as security?'

'That's a very particular way of describing them; they are an armed force, but they work for the government now. It's the ministry that employs them.'

'And you're okay with this set-up?'

'Like you said, it keeps people safe.'

'Did I say that? I've read testimony that suggests the opposite. That states this group have held people to ransom, have beaten people, robbed them. There are allegations of sexual assault.'

'I don't know what to say. There are always problems in camps like this, even if there aren't guys with guns.'

'Torture? People being sold into slavery? Indentured labour?'

My skin is prickling and I worry that colour is rising to my cheeks. I need to look calm. She, on the other hand, seems to be enjoying herself just fine.

'We don't run the camp. We just provide some basic items and, in emergencies, food.'

'But you do work with the camp management. What about the accusation that funds and goods that you supply are misappropriated and sold on?'

'Unless I cook the rice myself and watch the people eat it, there's just no way that here, during a civil war for Christ's sake, I can know exactly where everything we donate ends up. It's not possible.'

'Your hands are tied.'

'That's not what I said, but yes, in some ways they are.'

'Would you say that you're happy with the level of advocacy your charity is involved in?'

'I mean, I think we could always do more.'

'So, that's a no?'

I'm not in the mood for this.

'Look, the truth is, we do our best. Those people wouldn't be there if they had any other options. It's EU policy. It's UK policy. They don't want them to leave and if they do leave they want them sent straight back. It's not me that doesn't care, it's the bloody government.'

'So there's nothing you can do about the conditions?'

'I'm not saying that, of course there are things we can do, but it's the policy that needs to change, not us.'

'Some people would say it's both.'

'Well, let them; freedom of speech still exists.'

'I can see how you and my mother could have been friends.'

And I take a breath, the interrogation is over.

She smiles awkwardly and stands to leave, and something about the way she does it makes me wonder if I chose the right one after all. It's a risk, this media route. But then I remember that she's Catherine's daughter and I relax, because, strange though it may sound, this makes me trust her more than anything else could.

I arrange a time for her to come to the camp with us, shake her hand confidently and only allow my own hands to tremble when I'm safely in the lift. I know I have to get past my anger with Omar, I know I have to be a grown-up, to calm the fuck down, but on top of that there's everything else as well, it's all tumbling down around me. In my head, the war's already here, it's always been here, and the truth is spilling out all over the place.

For example, it's not quite true that Jem died of lung cancer. It's what I tell myself, and it's true he had it, but what actually killed him was a bullet to the head while transporting school materials. I was with him in the truck. I was sitting next to him. When his head exploded, I was what it exploded on to. And in our line of work, maybe this was even preferable, a quick death, not some drawn-out kidnapping with an unknown outcome.

Omar being away has made it much easier to forget everything. There has been nobody around to remind me of it, nobody else who truly knew. And now he's back and I have absolutely no idea what it means.

33

THE CAMP

SOL

The carcass of a UNHCR tent, its metal ribs blackened, its white canvas skin scourged, hovers above the heat haze; a monolith to a dead civilization. Up close, the air still smells faintly of burnt plastic. I'm right at the back of the camp, cleaning up after the fire. My white overalls are covered in soot, and I mean covered. But if you look towards the front gate there's an unlikely explosion of humanity – children running to and fro, shouting as they climb up one side of a tent just to slide down the other, women chatting as they queue for food and water, fathers playing with their sons and daughters, young men joking and shouting together, staring past the present and over the barbed-wire-topped walls of the camp, trying to catch a glimpse of their future selves, beyond these patchwork shelters and low dark rooms. From afar it doesn't look that bad, but the reality is another matter. Even just cleaning up after the fire makes you realise how precarious all this is, how easily it could be wiped off the map and hushed up. I think of how I'll explain it to Caspian tonight on the phone and wonder what his physics mind will make of it.

I take a break in the shade of one of the bigger tents to think, but it's difficult to form a thought in this place. The stench of the toilet block is overwhelming. The cramped shelters give off their own peculiar odour as well. Unwashed humanity crammed together, sweat, vomit, purification. Hope's dark underbelly. And I thought I had problems.

The girl I'm working with, Sarah, offers me a cigarette and a glug of her water bottle. I thank her and take both. I'm parched and reeling from all this. Everyone I've met so far smokes and I have the sense that it'll ground me. I haven't smoked for years and the first drag makes me cough, but I go with it, hoping Leila wouldn't think I was too much of a loser for picking it up again. The head rush is an old familiar friend, and when it's passed, I do indeed feel more present, and the smell of tobacco is a welcome break from the reek of the toilets.

A woman sits in the dirt opposite us stirring a pot over a small fire while a child plays with the dust and rocks next to her, building small fortresses and then destroying them again. There is not a single person in this place that does not need a get-out card. I wish I had some to give. I look away from the woman towards the horizon; it is only just visible through the row of low rooms along the wall and the expanse of desert beyond, as if the outside world has ceased to exist. For these people I guess this is the only world that matters, this small patch of dust, these home-made shelters and factory-made tents, that wall, the endless flat land leading to town, the red cliffs on every other side. What do they dream of at night? Is this a place in which dreams are even possible?

At orientation they showed us pictures of when this camp was new. They showed brand-new toilet blocks. Shower cubicles by the mile. Fresh, clean running water. Bright white tents. Nice neat rooms. Not the fire damage, not the fire itself – the kids have seen to that already though, holding up their parents' phones to me when I arrived. Look. See. Understand. Their only request, shouted in the myriad languages they speak.

A loudspeaker announcement blasts through the camp in English first and then in at least five other languages. It brings me back to my senses and to the task at hand, which right now, in the heat of the day, seems overwhelming. Luckily it's lunch time and I make my way to the distribution tent with Sarah. In the short time it takes us to walk there, several hundred people have already arrived. They've queued in a single straight line that nearly reaches the fence at the other end. Technically we don't have to queue because we're working, but what sort of bastards would we be to push in front of everyone? I check with Sarah and she agrees, we just can't.

At the back of the queue a young girl wearing taped-up flip-flops grabs my arm as if to check I'm real. I thought she was going to ask me for something – money or food – but she just stares into my eyes for a moment, trying to work something out, and then drops my arm again and stares straight forward once more, towards the distant distribution tent. I rub my arm where she touched me trying to confirm what just happened, but there's no answer to be found, just the slight pain left over from the strong grip of a kid wishing there was something more to do, wondering what it might be, and finding nothing.

After a while, during which absolutely nothing happens unless you count sweating, she tugs the back of my overalls.

'Sorry,' she says to me in English. 'I thought you might be the famous man, but then I realised you definitely weren't.'

Of all things, to be mistaken for Barry bloody Knight. Yet here, surrounded by all this, with this serious-looking girl staring up at me, the weight of my anger suddenly feels less. And the situation, though terrible, is smaller than I thought it to be. I know now that when he arrives I will finally be ready to talk to him.

'It's okay,' I say. 'My name's Sol.'

'I am Saleema,' she replies and holds out her hand to shake.

34

SILENCE

OMAR

I already feel lost here.

Surrounded.

Suffocated.

Trapped.

Strange, given I just left a place often referred to as the largest open-air prison in the world. But it's not just the hotel; it's the feeling on the streets. I read the papers on my way back from the market. I saw the men's eyes. These people know war and thought they'd said goodbye to it. Nobody wants what's about to happen and yet nobody can stop it. This seems to be the nature of all wars.

I don't know how long I can stand to stay here, but having seen Amanda I also know I can't leave without her. So I have spent another day waiting, even though I know she'll never come to find me. It has to be me. Finally, I gather the courage and walk the flight of stairs from my room to hers, not knowing if she'll be there or not. When I reach her door I stand there for a moment to get myself in order and rehearse my speech, but as I'm doing this I hear a sound from within.

I hear her crying, and without thinking I knock and after a pause she opens the door. As soon as she sees me she slaps me hard across the face, but her tears are still falling. She steps backwards and I step in after her. She collapses on the bed and sits there on the edge of it, looking at her own hands, refusing to meet my eyes.

'I'd started to think you were dead, you bastard,' she says, but quietly and I go to her and kneel on the floor in front of her. I'm about to speak but she silences me and draws me to her. She pulls me onto the bed with her.

'I don't know how to fix this,' she says as the tears continue, and we stay that way, wrapped in each other as we have been so many times before, in silence, but in a strange kind of peace, her breath eventually settling, and it's only when it does that I realise mine has too.

35

THE LIST

SALEEMA

This morning there's more people outside the camp. I heard the adults say that they escaped from another centre that was attacked. They look sick, and even though I know I should try to help them, I don't want to get sick too.

Noor comes running up to me and I think she's going to try and convince me to take them water, but it turns out she's saying something else entirely.

'Did you hear about the man in the hut next to the government office?'

'No,' I say, and from the way Noor is speaking I don't know if I want to. I want to cover my ears.

'He's dead, he killed himself.'

'How do you know?' I ask, maybe she is wrong.

'Everyone is outside the hut, the men that live in there with him found him.'

I look at her and I don't know what to say. Why would an adult kill themselves? But then, living here, why live? We all hear things in the night, nightmares from our old lives, but also real things from now; people calling out, sometimes there is screaming. My mother always tells me not to think about it, not to look, not to ask. It feels like pretending, but at the same time I don't know what else to do. If there are such terrible things happening that grown-ups can't cope, then what chance do we have?

Noor's just standing there like she doesn't know what to do either and I hold my arms open. She steps forward and we hug each other. We keep each other safe from our own thoughts.

'Yesterday I thought I saw the famous man,' I tell her, 'but it turned out it was just one of the new charity people. He looked strange, tall and pale with drawings all over his skin and earrings even though he was a man.'

She pulls back from our embrace.

'Really?' she asks, wiping her eyes. I didn't even realise she was crying.

'Really. I think we should make a list of questions for when the real famous man comes. We need to find a safe way to leave this place.'

Noor nods. She doesn't look convinced, but she sits down with me outside the shelter anyway while I search the floor for my pencil stub. The only paper I have is the book I'm reading, so we just use the inside back page.

'Do you think we should go to see if the twins went begging?' asks Noor.

But it doesn't seem like a good idea, not with all the new people outside and how they're sick.

'I think they will have stayed at home.'

'But then what will they eat?'

'I don't know.'

I put the pencil and the book down. There doesn't seem any point anymore.

'Why do you think they came here?'

'Who?' I ask her back.

'The new people outside.'

'I suppose it wasn't safe anymore where they lived.'

'But why come here, when it isn't safe either? It doesn't make sense.'

'I think it must be very hard to find a safe place to live. I don't know why. I'll add it to the questions.'

'Okay, let's write them down,' says Noor and we begin, and soon the page is full.

36

AIRPORT EXTENSIONS

BARRY

I lie awake on the sofa, still clutching my glass, though the contents have long since spilled. The phone is ringing. The room is bright thanks to the un-pulled curtains. My head hurts, which may just be the natural state of my head. I try shouting for Sam, but remember his absence and stop – after a few more tries, just in case he turned up in the night and because it's a part of my morning routine.

I give in and answer the phone myself.

'Barry, mate?'

It's Sam.

'Yes, mate.'

'You shouldn't be there.'

'What, why?'

'You're supposed to be at the airport.'

'Airport?'

'On your way to make the war orphan video, the plane leaves in like an hour and a half.'

'They're going to have to book me another one, nobody told me.'

'I told you.'

'I have no recollection of that conversation,' I say, which is true.

'Damn it, Barry, you're impossible.'

'I'm an artist.'

'Oh fuck off, I'll ring them and see what they can do. And in the meantime put yourself in the shower and try not to drink.'

I look down at myself. He may have a point. There are several things amiss.

The phone's gone dead.

How is it that I fucking hate airports and yet it feels like I spend the majority of my time in them? They're too bright, too full of people, and they're always reminding you that you're not at home, hinting at the fact that you don't really know where it is anyway and suggesting that even if you did there'd be no one waiting there for you when you returned, which may be why you left in the first place, because you are inherently unlovable. To rub it in, the endless attendants and border guards and police officers and even their dogs all whisper, 'At least we've got each other,' as you pass them, horrible little fascists.

The war orphan people have managed to change my flight to a more reasonable time. I've washed. I've changed my clothes. I look almost like a fully presentable example of the human species. I'm looking forward to a bloody Mary and a nap even though Sam said several very strict things about drinking on the plane. The thing is, Sam's not here because of his awful girlfriend, so fuck him and fuck her too. I'm going to have a double, several of them. I make my way to the place where people like me can sit without having to look at the great unwashed.

From my seat in the first-class lounge I'm watching the planes landing and taking off, zooming down the runways.

Everything is bland apart from this, even the heavily spiced drink with the celery stick poking out of it that I'm clutching in one hand. I've always fancied the idea of becoming a pilot, or at least of learning to fly. You get to go so fast, so much faster than you can when you're stuck in a little four-wheeler on the streets of London, heaped in traffic, struggling to breathe. Though, as we know, I've had my moments. None of them will go in the book.

It's been a while since I've been on one of these charity gigs. These days they're normally all London- or New York-based; talk in front of the camera about something that's supposed to be awful, wear a very clean T-shirt that says something on it, have a latte, go home. They don't usually expect you to travel to the actual place anymore. The insurance, for a start, is a nightmare. There are so many dangers, so many things to be insured against. So many knowns and even more unknowns, both of which may largely be made up or entirely true, it's impossible to grab at these things anymore. Nothing stays still. Nothing is fixed. Nothing is actually knowable anyway, and – even if you wanted to know it, which luckily, I don't – you would never be able to trust it. I can't even begin to imagine the insurance conversation. How do they work that out? But ultimately they must have, and now I'm thinking about it I'd like to ask someone. Sam would know. I'd like to know, exactly how much my life is worth – in pounds, I can't do dollars or euros.

A woman comes over to usher me towards the plane. It's time, and I get to do the sort of boarding that no one else even knows about. My passport is but an inconvenience, it's my face that's the ticket, even if it's not as fresh as it once was. When I was a kid we didn't go on a plane once, not even to Tenerife like everybody else. This sort of stuff still shocks me a little, when I'm sober enough to notice it.

The plane feels claustrophobic and airless as soon as I climb inside it, and, to make matters worse, a troop of medical practitioners pile in as soon as everyone is seated and start talking sternly to an old guy who lost consciousness for a moment in a not-just-having-a-nap way. I can hear everything they're saying and it's awful. The old guy is supposed to be visiting his daughter, they're estranged but she invited him to her wedding. He's pleading with them to let him go and talking about the grandchildren he has never met, but they just keep saying 'no' in an infuriatingly calm way. Tests, they repeat, as if tests are in themselves the answer.

What they don't get, but what I fully understand, is that this guy would rather die than spend one more day alone.

I try not to make eye contact with any of them, as if I too could become affected by this strange fainting disease, or whatever it is. Finally they convince him to leave, and although I feel for him, my main emotion is relief, as if I've escaped the same fate. The doors close with that strange sucking sound and now there's no way out. I take a sleeping pill to knock myself out for a bit, it's the safest way.

When I wake, I have no idea how many hours more I have to be on the plane or how many hours I have survived so far. If it wasn't such a stupid question I'd ask someone, but people expect you to know these things as if everyone has a bloody watch or a phone programmed to the second with all the details of their lives saved and organised. I should have brought some stronger sedatives with me and I wonder if they have any on the plane, but again, how to ask? I wish bloody Sam was here. Why hasn't he come? He knows I hate travelling by plane on my own. He knows it freaks me the fuck out.

Breathe.

More things that will not go in the book, and who knows maybe the book will be written after all. Barry saves the war orphans etc.

I went through a brief yoga phase a few years back, when I first begun having panic attacks after a very pretty girl turned down my offer of a good time. It had never happened to me before. I nearly choked on the information, didn't know what to do with it. For a second afterwards everything around me went silent, as if I'd fallen off the edge of something very tall and now all I could hear was the whistling of the wind in my ears as I fell. Gradually the world came back, but some bit of me remained in the abyss. The yoga, I had hoped, would help to bring it back.

I went to Thailand for a retreat, a very expensive one, and one of the things they taught me was how to breathe. I had never breathed correctly in my life they informed me, never once in all my years of singing even had I allowed in balance, the simple inner balance, that can be achieved by proper breathing. This blew my, admittedly rather fragile, mind. How was it possible that people didn't know how to breathe right? Surely it was simple? Surely it was all anyone ever did, the one thing we all had in common, the breathing in and out to remain alive thing? And yet, we are, as a species, consistently doing it wrong. Crazy. For a brief moment I did wonder if this had more far reaching consequences – if there were other things held fundamentally correct and acceptable that were not so – but only for the briefest of moments, because a long time ago I taught myself not to give a shit.

I manage to normalise my breathing now by quietly reminding myself of the statistics for deaths on planes (not a method they taught on the retreat). My slight fear of flying is the real reason that I've never actually taken lessons. It's not that I can't afford it, of course I can, but whenever I think of the potential to crash into a mountainside, the careening, out of control descent, the lack of options for escape, my breath leaves me as quickly as if I had been sucking on a vacuum cleaner. And ultimately, famous people do die in planes, especially when they're flying them themselves – fact.

A few doubles later it's all gone away: the anxiety, the fear, the image of the old guy's face as he was led away. Fuck you, Sam, I can do just fine without you.

In the sorry excuse of an arrivals hall a fat man with dark glasses, who speaks so quickly and quietly that I can hardly hear what he's saying, ushers me out to a waiting car. We wind our way towards the hotel, which I can only assume, due to the length of the drive, is actually in another country.

I try to avoid looking out of the window. It's dry as dust out there. An endless expanse of absolutely fuck-all. And I don't ask any questions. I've already realised I'd rather not know.

Eventually we get to a hotel in a long row of all the other hotels I've been in recently, a row which concertinas in on itself; they are, in fact, all the same hotel, a time travelling, non-space into which I have been cast.

It's only when I step through the door and get a sense of the room that I realise this one's different; that there is something undeniably fucked-up going on.

37

BARRY KNIGHT
WILL SAVE US

AMANDA

Barry's here, and when I finally catch a glimpse of him through the constant camera flashes I'm shocked by how fragile he looks in person, a crumpled half-man, something that was and is no longer. I almost feel sorry for him.

As I stand, having had a couple of drinks to prepare for his arrival, I suddenly realise that the alcohol's kicked in. I'm feeling a little light-headed, so I make my way to the bathroom to quickly splash some water on my face and try to wake up. I haven't been sleeping too well. I find I can't stop crying whenever I'm alone, and even though me and Omar have regained something of what we were there's still so much I don't know, and no longer know if I want to. He's back, and right now, in the middle of all this, maybe that's enough. But it doesn't help with the sleeping and neither do the mosquitoes, or all the other thoughts – the camp, the carnage of life lived in the extreme, the kid I saw yesterday talking to one of the volunteers, trailing around with her Harry Potter book, dressed in someone else's clothes, her jumper down to her knees, her taped-up flip-flops, her perfectly combed hair. I slap myself gently across the cheek and then a little harder. There it is. The brief shock of pain brings me to myself again. I brush back my hair with my hands, smooth down my shirt.

After the glare of the toilets the bar seems dark and it takes me a moment to refocus, to find Barry in the dim light. He's made it a few metres further forward. There's a journalist questioning him intently and I dread to think what's coming out of his mouth in response to this woman's questions. I half-run towards them and it looks like I'm coming to rescue him, which of course I'm not. I'm coming to rescue us, the project, the kid with the wizard book, and I don't pause to wonder what Omar would think of this thought, my white saviour complex, my liberalism, etc..

I extend my hand through the crush for him to shake.

'Amanda, Save the War Orphans,' I say to introduce myself and then begin to try and order the press. There'll be an official press conference tomorrow, I tell them, plenty of time to question the poor bastard then. And it's happened again, feeling sorry for him, this man who could own the world if he was only clever enough – he certainly has enough money. The photographers and the journalists are ushered out and, although I can guess the answer, I ask Barry if he'd like to go up to his room or have a refreshment to settle in first. It's the latter, of course. If there's anything we all know about this man it's that he loves a drink and whatever else he can find to go with it.

We make our way over the padded red-patterned carpet, the sort favoured by bars the world over – it hides the stains. Barry orders a double gin and tonic and, against my better judgement, I do the same. There's something about the tension here and in me that makes it seem okay, even correct, and I've noticed one too many foreign correspondents ambling around with their straight whisky as if they know the world's about to end but nobody's said it out loud yet. They're waiting for something and they'll be ready to pounce when it happens.

We sit down and I try out the pleasantries, ask how his journey was, but he just stares at me and looks back down at his drink.

'Where the fuck have you brought me?' he asks, and I find it difficult to know how to respond so instead I drink a little more of my gin a little faster than necessary. 'There's one thing you learn doing gigs year in and year out, especially at the beginning, in the dodgy bars and clubs; you learn to sense when something's about to kick off, when shit's about to go down. The air changes, you can taste it, smell it... and this place reeks.'

I look down at my hands, notice the dry skin, the way they look more like my mother's hands every day. My phones flashes silently to life; it's Susan. I turn it over. I still haven't called her. I think it was their team leader who knocked on my door this morning when I was still searching for the elusive moment of rest I crave.

'It's not a bloody holiday, Barry. You wouldn't even have come if it wasn't for the mess in the papers. Yes, this country's in the shit – what did you expect?' All my inside words have come out. It's the gin.

'Well, at least we can be honest with each other,' he says, not angry, not looking for praise, and this to me, seems strange. 'I can think of about billion places I would rather be, and they all have better gin in them.'

'I can think of a couple I'd rather be in myself, and you're not in any of them.'

'Well, let's drink to that, to being someplace else, with other people, as soon as fucking possible.'

I raise my glass. I almost laugh. I don't.

'I guess we both need each other, just for very different reasons, and luckily for a short length of time,' I say instead.

'Are our reasons that different? When was the last time you introduced yourself without your charity's name attached?

You are this operation, you're the last one left just like me. We're both maintaining a brand.'

I take some time to consider this, astounded by him knowing even this about me, this simple internet searchable fact – it means he actually read something before he arrived.

'Don't look at me like that. I read. We're not so different, you and me, both too good at sticking around even when all our reasons for doing the thing in the first place have already walked out the door, even when we hate it, even when we hate ourselves.'

More gin is arriving, and I'm no longer sure if this is the first time this has happened, or even how it happened this time. Do people like Barry just have to think of the thing they want and it arrives? Even though he's getting on, he has a certain charm about him. I must be drunk.

'Probably time to call it a night,' I say as I stand, swaying a little.

'Oh, come on, drink up, don't let it go to waste,' he cajoles me, as he must have done so many women before me.

'I'm sure you won't be short of company,' I say as I leave him, small and hunched at the little bar table in the giant, worryingly empty bar. The journos must have gone out on the hunt.

I take the lift up to my room, get off on the wrong floor, and walk the final flight of stairs holding onto the banister for comfort. It takes a long time, with each step I drag myself up a little further. When I get there Omar is propped up on the bed reading, one of the most familiar sights I know, so for now I let it be.

38

WARRIOR GIRL

SOL

My phone is sitting in silence in front of me on the bar table. I pick it up and call Caspian. He answers in only a few rings like he's been waiting. Hearing his voice feels like pure relief after today. I tell him about the camp and the girl I met, and it's only then, after I've got over the fact she thought I might be Barry Knight, that I understand what really got me about her.

'She was like a little warrior, her grip was so strong and her eyes were so clear,' I say to him, but he doesn't get it straight away – not literal enough – so I try again.

'Even surrounded by all that shit, she hasn't lost who she is. She's a fighter. She still has hope.'

He gets it this time, and he asks her name and I tell him.

'I miss you,' he says, and the directness of it takes me back. But truth is I miss him too and I tell him.

When I hang up the phone there's a hole where his voice was. I rub my chest hard to try and ease all the feelings that rest there. There's still a rawness in me after being in the camp today; it's fierce, it's animal. It makes me think of the fox in my garden, of what he was trying to tell me with his eyes. Life is precarious in ways you do not understand, he said to me, unless you come to realise this you will remain forever a child. And now I'm loading a wild animal with all my emotional crap, poor bugger. It's just as well I'm on the other side of the planet, otherwise I'd probably invite him in for a cuppa and force him to listen to my first-world problems.

I wish I could be as strong as that girl.

For the first time in a long time I think about calling my mum and hearing what she thinks about all this. I pick up the phone again, but as I do there's a commotion by the doorway and before I even see him I know it's Barry Knight. My heart's up in my ears, my whole body is beating with it boom boom boom. I find I'm stuck. I can't fucking move. I sit there and watch as the woman from the charity walks over to him, leads him away like a lost lamb. They sit, and they talk, and at some point they even laugh, and for the whole time I swear I'm not even breathing.

I am not ready, not at all.

I only come to when I realise he's walking towards me. The woman has gone. My beer is flat. He's getting closer and closer and I swear to fuck he's smiling at me and holding out a gin and tonic. Ice and a slice clinking and floating together, melting from the heat of him.

'Hello,' he says, and I'm still just staring. 'Don't suppose you want to keep a guy company? I've just been dumped.'

Fucking say something.

'The woman from the charity?' I manage, my throat so dry that I've taken the drink from his hand and downed half of it without even realising, no communication between my conscious brain and my hands whatsoever.

'Yeah, the charity woman,' he says as he sits down opposite me.

I find myself rubbing my face, massaging my eyes, but when I open them again he's still there.

'Difficult day?' he asks, and I can't stop myself replying. It's like I'm a character in a video game being played remotely by some other dumb fuck I've never even met, who has no fucking idea why I wouldn't want this to be happening.

'Yeah, actually, I went to the camp for the first time. I totally wasn't prepared for how bad it was.'

'I've not been yet. To be honest, I'm hoping to still be drunk when I have to deal with it tomorrow.'

'They won't let you in.'

'What? I'm the star of the fucking show!'

Dick.

'I mean, they won't let you in if you're drunk. For a start it's illegal here, and anyway there's kids living there and some extra security alert. If you looked off your face I don't think they'd let you in. So, if you don't want to piss off the woman from the charity, you'd better get some shut-eye.'

'Shit, I wish Sam was here.'

'Who's Sam?'

'He's my, well... I was going to say my manager, but if I'm honest, he's my best mate. He was supposed to come, but he didn't. I don't know... we've been having some difficulties.'

I have to remember who this man is, what he did. I can't get drawn in.

'I hope you work them out,' is all I give him as my half-hearted response, because this guy is clearly lonely and even though he deserves it, it's hard to watch. 'Well,' I say, standing, 'thanks for the drink.'

'Fancy another for the road?'

'We've only got to walk up the stairs, mate, though I guess you're a little higher up than I am.'

'Penthouse! Want to see it?'

'No, you're alright, thanks though.'

I thanked him, the man that killed Leila.

This is next level crazy.

'Night, then,' he's calling after me as I scramble for the stairs.

By the time I get to my small first-floor room I can barely breathe. I've read the news. I'm not stupid. Only an active war zone could bring the two of us into the same space like this. I was supposed to be at the hostel down the road, but it's closed. Some bullshit about the end of season, but I've seen the guards hanging out smoking cigarettes around the perimeter of this place. The guns they're carrying say enough. I half-expected the charity to load us straight back onto the next plane out, but I guess they really need the cash Barry Knight'll bring in. They can't open their eyes to the problem until the last moment. I just hope we all live long enough to see it.

I open the window and let the air wash over me, and, hot and sticky and mosquito-laden though it is, it makes it a little easier to breathe. There are lights on the far horizon, all the way out there in the darkness, bright one minute, faded to nothing the next. I wonder what it feels like to watch them from the cage of the camp.

I used to stare out of my bedroom window at my parents' house in London watching all the cars pile up on the ring road, pushing each other forward one short rev at a time. At night I could still see the lights, moving a little faster now, flashing through my curtains, speeding across my ceiling, disappearing into the night, into nothingness. I used to think, I may never come across these people again, this is our one-and-only interaction in this city full to the brim with humans. I wanted to cling to each moment, this couple of seconds of contact through light.

A few years later, I told Leila about how I'd felt, as I traced the pattern of a car's headlights across her body with my hand. This time the light came through a different window, the one in her bedroom in her parents' first-floor flat. She was the only person I knew in the world who would not laugh if I told her, and I was right. Instead, she nodded, pulled me closer and whispered in my ear. The most important thing in life is to recognise the moments when yours touches someone else's and to try to understand the reason for each one, to not be fooled by the good or bad of it, to let it settle until it's clear.

Sometimes, I think she'd done all her learning already. When she left, she was already complete.

I always wondered what she saw in me, even when we were deep in our love, inseparable and safe with one another. I would look at her at moments like that one, all wisdom and beauty, and think, why me? What makes me special enough to share this time with you? I never asked her. I was scared of the answer, but also scared that by asking I would highlight my inadequacies. That she'd suddenly wake up to reality and realise I was nothing, less than worthy, and that she'd leave at that very moment and I'd be alone and empty.

Now, in this hotel room, that, though small, is nicer than any other place I've ever stayed, it's still her I miss the most, more than Caspian with all his realness and the actual weight of his physical presence. I guess I've got used to the ghost of her. I've lived with her loss for almost as long as I lived with her presence, and maybe, what I'm really worried about, is that Caspian could chase her away. I'm scared of losing her even though she's long gone.

39

SHIT GETS REAL

BARRY

Well, fuck me, seems it's hard to have a good time round here. Even most of the journos have fucked off somewhere and the ones that are left are peering into their screens, waiting for something to happen, their faces blueish and their bodies tense despite the whisky. Probably good drinkers, happy to while away the wee small hours, but generally not my type, and it's not just the dust-covered neck scarves; I've had a few too many difficulties with their kind. Shame though, it'd be nice to have a partner in this taking-the-edge-off exercise I'm involved in. A solo project, it seems. Bloody Sam.

Just to move my body, I walk myself to the bar and the barman greets me with another gin. I guess he's from here, so I ask him what's going on with the journos, why they showed up in the first place, where the rest of them have buggered off to. They're obviously not here for me, not this lot anyway. But he's following the hotel line – nothing to see here, all's well that seems well, journalists often stop off here on their way to other, more exciting places, it's common, usual, nothing to worry about – and everything about his overtly calm voice puts me on edge. I wonder how much gin they have and if the minibar in my room is well stocked enough.

I wander off to another chair to better observe the remaining press, see if I can gain any intel without having to actually talk to them. They murmur among themselves, too low to catch much except phrases that could come from any article about almost any country that's ever gone through a civil war: political tension, firing line, border skirmishes. Jesus, I could write this shit in my sleep. I look back towards the barman. He's been polishing a glass for a good five minutes, all on his own behind that giant, well shined bar. The wood is gleaming, the taps are golden. For all he's tried to take his mind off it, whatever is worrying him is dead centre in his thoughts. He hasn't even noticed me staring. What is he thinking? As soon as he knocks off work is he going to gather up his family and get the fuck out? Should I? I don't even have a family to gather. I don't even have Sam. Maybe I'm ready. If this is going to be it for me, maybe I'm okay with that.

To get my next gin (and maybe my last, because the kid was probably right about the camp), I have to go back to the bar again. The guy is still busy planning his escape route or whatever. It's like I've woken him up when I turn up in front of him and, caught off guard, he accidently asks me a question.

'Do you have a family?' he says, and I don't know exactly how to reply. I have a brother… but he means kids, a wife, the fabled cat.

'No,' I say back, and I've lost him again, but the gin's in front of me so I can't really complain.

This time I walk to one of the windows that look out onto the street. It's silent out there, but far in the distance, only just visible from here, there's a red glow along the horizon and it's well past sunset. To get a better look I go outside, round the roundy door, gin in hand. I only get as far as the first step before someone 'Sirs' me from the darkness. It's obviously not the night for an evening stroll in this town. He waves me back in with what I realise is an automatic weapon. For once I keep my bloody mouth shut and step backwards into the safety of the foyer, though it suddenly doesn't feel that safe after all.

Probably best to call it a night before I wind myself up any more. I down the gin, leave the glass on a table as I walk past and head to the lift. Strange, that in so many other situations my body sends me into a panic, yet here, potentially closer to death than I have ever been in real life, at least consciously, I feel worryingly fucking calm. In the mirror in the lift I even catch myself smiling. Maybe I have more of a death wish than even I ever realised.

A penthouse suite is pointless on your own. I wander around it, finally. My bags have already been brought up and are stacked neatly just inside the door, next to the giant wardrobe I probably won't even open. There's a bedroom, a sitting room with a little breakfast table in front of the night-filled window, and a bathroom with one of those baths half-set into the floor that has a little step up to it that goes all the way around, so no matter what angle you enter from, or how many of you there are, you can all slide in with ease. This reminds me of another story, and a different hotel room, but I tuck the thoughts away. They'll just make me lonelier in the now.

I open the taps because I might as well and it'll sober me up a bit. I chuck in all the things in little bottles until it's frothing like a motherfucker. I might have gone a little over the top. I throw all my clothes into a heap on the floor and catch a glimpse of my pale little body in the steaming mirror as I slide in. It feels good, there's no denying it. I dunk my head under to clear it and come up covered in suds. If I was to go now, disappear into this night or into this country's earth in the coming days, who would notice? Who would care? Sam, maybe, but his girlfriend would soon talk him down, put a positive sheen on it of some sort. He'd forget quick enough. And the band, if you can even call it that, they've probably already moved on to their next gig, propping up some other has-been. My brother? Well, he's got his kids to worry about; real life, actual family. I could tiptoe out of this bloody window now, naked and covered in bubbles and maybe the world could even be described as a better place as a result. One less fuck-up to look after, one less problem child. I don't even pay very much tax – not even the state would miss me. Arseholes.

Shut up.

The guy who had the bricks before and did all that laughing is peering at me through a hole in the enormous wall he built. He's telling me that even though he doesn't like me there is a way out and this is it: do the charity gig, write the book, or, more likely, get someone else to write it for you. Stop bloody moaning, enough of the self-pity. He's saying, you're doing my head in, and I'm not even real, which means you're doing your own head in. Stop it.

He has a point.

I get up, do the towelling, do the getting-into-bed thing. I lie there on my back, light off, and look up at the ceiling, stare into the darkness, willing my eyes to close. But whether it's the jet lag, or getting the gin level wrong, or this fucking place, I can't get my brain to stop. It won't let me sleep, because under all of this, without Sam around to bury it with his words and the stuff he keeps in his wallet, lies only the truth. The truth about who Barry Knight really is. And it's not pretty.

The minibar is calling out to me, and I vaguely wonder if it's covered by the charity, but then I put my foot down. Tomorrow, and even if only tomorrow, I will actually try to do the right thing. I will go and meet these people and their kids in this shithole they live in and I will try and get the world to care. Even if this is all I do, maybe it is something good and maybe it'll let a little light into this dark space inside me that never gets filled, that only gets bigger. With this thought, I notice that the sun is rising, stretching across the far off hills, and I finally close my eyes and in the half-hour of sleep I get I dream of a holiday we had in Cornwall when I was a kid, caravanning with my folks and my brother before my dad fucked off, and I wake up strangely happy because this is one of the few times I actually was, and I'd completely forgotten about it – the winding lanes, the flat tyre, the way my mum looked at my dad when he took a wrong turning and blamed her because she had the map, even though she'd told him to go the other way, waking up in the morning to the beach, to the sun, sand in my toes, dancing in the dunes to the radio with my brother, laughing.

40

FAMOUS WORLD TRAVELLER

SALEEMA

It's today that the famous man, Barry Knight, will come, and they've told us not to bother him, not to follow him, not to ask questions, and, if we can, to stay inside. Of course, they have, because they know that this man can answer our questions. Noor says it would be crazy to listen to them, the man is famous and he is coming to visit us. So we've decided to go and see him anyway. Despite everything that's been going on I feel quite excited to meet him.

The only people who have been asked to stay outside are the people who have musical instruments and they will play for him. Apparently they might even be in a video. Some people are also allowed to dance. People who live with more than one family in their tent have to go to the canteen, which is a big tent that they put up after the fire and called the canteen. I'm not quite sure why it is called that. It has no tea or food. It is where the sick people who just got here sleep. My mum says they did it so that the famous man doesn't see them sleeping outside on the floor. But today it is full of benches and tables I have never seen before. They take up a lot of room. I don't understand where they have hidden them up until now or where the sick people have gone. My mother says there is no point in asking, that they will only lie.

Last night one of the boys who lives near to our shelter looked up this Barry Knight on the internet and played his songs; he must have paid a security guard to charge his phone from an office generator. For a few moments people were laughing and dancing outside the boy's room but then the old man that lives next door to them shouted and asked why they were cheering for a man from a country who cared nothing for them, who would rather spit on them then take them in, and the dancing stopped – which was a shame because some of them are actually quite good dancers.

When I went to bed I told my mum I wanted to speak to him and ask him some questions. She told me I wasn't allowed and rolled over. I don't understand why people already hate him when he hasn't even arrived yet and he is coming as a guest. In our old life we always welcomed visitors; we gave them the best of everything. Right now we don't have the best or even the worst of anything to give, but that doesn't mean we cannot invite the man in and give him tea. If my dad was here, I think this is what he would do. He would want to talk too, to find out what this man thinks and what is really happening in the world out there. Maybe he knows all the things that the people that work here won't tell us. Maybe he knows what the red lights in the sky at night are, the lights that remind me of home, bring back my nightmares and make even my mother fall silent.

After my mother went to sleep, I checked the list of questions on the back page of my Harry Potter book with the pencil I stole from the UNHCR woman. I know it is bad to write in books. I know it is wrong to steal. I just really don't want to forget our questions, and getting them right is important. We included things we've heard our parents asking. Noor thought they would find it helpful if we could get the answers for them, especially seeing as none of them want to ask him themselves.

Our questions are:

Why don't the people that work here usually clean everything, why did they clean when you came?

Why did they make some of the people hide?

Where did all the benches and the tables come from?

Why are your government and their friends and the UNHCR not coming to help us like my dad said they would?

Why do they pay the government in this country to keep us in this big outside cage?

When can we leave?

When we leave, how long will it take us to get someplace better, someplace safe?

How long will it be until I can go back to school and if we can't leave to go to school can we have one here?

Is there a war coming?

If there is, will we be okay?

Why do some of the men that work here have guns?

Can you take us with you when you leave?

Do you come from a very small country and is that why they don't want us to come?

Is it very difficult to find a safe place to live even there?

What is happening at night to make people scream?

We have a lot of questions. I'm not sure how many it is rude to ask.

I check them one more time and then Noor turns up, but she can't read, so I read them out loud to her. Her mum wants us to add an extra one so I do.

Can we have electricity?

I fell asleep holding my book and wake up as it gets light. I use a little of my breakfast water for washing my face. My mum is plaiting my hair for me. Noor arrives with a business-like expression on her face.

'I'm ready,' she says seriously.

My mum ties up my hair and stands to view us both.

'I still don't want you to go, but I can see that you're determined.'

'We are,' I say and open my book to show her the list.

She takes a moment to read it.

'Sometimes,' she says as she cups my face in one hand, 'you are just like your father.' And the way she says it makes me unsure if this is a good or a bad thing.

We wait to hear if we have permission.

'Stay safe,' she says eventually, and briefly leans down to kiss me.

I take my book and my pencil, in case I forget anything or need to take notes. I carry my father with me in my heart, and hope that being the daughter of a journalist will come in useful. I'm wearing my only good dress, which is quite clean and quite new, and Noor is also looking pretty smart.

'I wish the twins were here,' she says, 'I bet they have some questions too.'

'We can tell them the answers afterwards and we can ask him for some food for them.'

'Good idea,' she replies, her eyes focused on the gate and the road to town beyond it.

We hold hands while we wait, more nervous than we thought we'd be.

41

WARNING SIGNS

ANA

Sol's at the breakfast buffet when I get there. I ask him if he's coming to the camp today, but his team has the day off because Amanda didn't want them getting in the way on the first day of filming.

'We'll be there tomorrow though,' he says quietly. 'They want us in the background wearing flak jackets with the logo on, looking useful.'

'I'd have thought you'd be happier about it.'

'Well, it's not really what I came out here to do, pose wearing a special jacket, especially not while all those people are struggling, living like that. It seems wrong.'

I agree with him, and once we've sat down with our breakfasts I pull out my notepad and take some notes.

'So,' he says, 'what are you, Barry Knight's fan club? You writing an article about him?'

There's a bitterness in his voice I can't place.

'No, I'm writing about the charity and the camp,' I say, and I'm about to say more but I stop myself. He's working for them after all.

Either way, he doesn't seem that interested in this line of conversation, so I ask him about the bandage he's been wearing, which this morning he's finally taken off and this shifts his mood as he tells me about the bar where he works and his non-boyfriend.

'We're going to talk about it when I'm back,' he says with a small laugh, like he can't believe it.

I'd like to sit here longer, to find out more about his life during all the missing years, but I have to get ready before leaving for the camp with Barry and Amanda. As soon as I finish, I get up to go and apologise.

'Don't go,' he says, serious again. 'I know you said you're not writing about him, but there's something I need to tell you about Barry Knight.'

He has his hand on my arm, so I sit back down again and what he tells me is shocking but plausible. I don't know exactly how to respond, it's a lot to take in, so I stick to journalist mode.

'Okay, but to publish this we'd need facts, witnesses, corroborating evidence.'

'Like what?'

'Start with the basic stuff. What car was he driving? Was anyone with him? Did anyone else see it happen?'

He looks so sad when I tell him this that I can't stop myself trying to help.

'I'll call my office and see if there's anything they can dig up in London. Is this why you came here?'

He nods, but doesn't lift his eyes from the table, so I reach out to take his hand.

'Can you talk to him? See if he confesses? I thought I could do it but when I saw him the yesterday I just froze.'

'I'll try,' I say, because what else can I do. 'I'm sorry, I've got to go.'

I stand again and this time I actually leave and head back upstairs to get ready. I don't want to believe that they'd cover up this sort of thing, a hit-and-run, but then people with money can buy pretty much anything.

My instinct is to ring Catherine and ask her what she thinks, which says a lot about instinct, so instead I try to imagine what she would say to me in this moment. She would say, take them all down, do what's right.

And I know she would want me to talk to Barry about Sol and about the girl in the US too. That she wouldn't trust the authorities to tell the truth. That she would want me to do my best to get the people in the camp to safety. That she would forgive Amanda, who was once her friend, but that she would not let her off the hook or make excuses for the behaviour of the charity.

I take a deep breath.

How can someone so strong just go ahead and die? How could she leave me when I was still so busy learning from her? I can feel the grief threatening to overtake me, immobilise me in the moment when I desperately need to move.

I take another breath to steady myself. One breath at a time I will get through this. I will go on breathing in and out until my body, like Catherine's, fails me. Because, like her, I must be strong.

For now, to ground myself, I deal with the here and now. The practicalities of life. I message Callum about the dogs. I tell him I'm coping just fine out here, and then I call Pete to fill him in about my conversation with Sol and ask him to look further into the accusations against Barry. I summarise my interview with Amanda, tell him that I'll be calling for the evacuation of the camp, ask him for the front page.

'You should get out of there while you still can,' he cautions me, and I promise him that as long as he does what I've asked I'll return the favour and be back as soon as I can.

He gives in, and wishes me luck. I hang up and finish getting my stuff together. I've made a pretty extensive checklist of things that I want to understand from my visit to the camp today. For now, I'll focus primarily on documenting material conditions and setting up interviews for tomorrow. If I do a good job of it, I should be ready to leave in a couple of days.

I'm in danger of being late, but I hesitate by the door, suddenly nervous. It doesn't make sense. I've seen people living in all sorts of terrible conditions all over the world, but this is affecting me more than usual. The logical part of my brain, which knows what it takes to get through a day of work in an environment like this, has built up a pretty big wall between the situation in this camp and how my birth parents died, but the other part of my brain is drawing all sorts of comparisons and parallels between their experiences and the experiences of people here. Catherine's voice is also present, confirming my worst fears by saying it's true, it's connected; the same systems and prejudices resulting in different outcomes.

I shake my head to clear my mind. I don't want to make this about me and my family, we're already irreparably broken. I have to focus on the people in the camp for my own sanity, but also because for them there is still a thin sliver of hope.

42

ALL AS IT IS MEANT TO BE

OMAR

Amanda's getting ready to leave, pulling her clothes on, disguising herself for the outside world.

'You could come?' she offers, already knowing my answer.

'You could stay,' I reply, already knowing hers.

She leaves me in the room and goes to find breakfast and Barry, and deal with journalists and documentary film-makers. I lie where I am and think, none of it's real, it's all just show, even though I know this isn't quite true. The money is needed. The fame brings the money. The people eat. This is the equation they're working from. It's an old and proven one, but for me the maths are wrong, there's a flaw in the working out that nobody's willing to admit to. Least of all Barry Knight, and right now, not even Amanda. I have to give it time.

To pass the hours I go out and walk towards the market, nodding greetings to the few people I meet. The market is cave-like and covered, supported by ancient pillars, and a great relief from the heat. In the clothes I now wear I am very noticeably a stranger here and attract some stares. I've slipped back into this life so easily that it scares me and soon I'll be heading home to London. I haven't seen my parents in over a year, but I've thought about them a lot.

My mother, the doctor. My dad, a lecturer in the local college. A good job, but not as cool as saving lives, to my child mind. I don't have any brothers or sisters. My parents always say I was more than enough for one working family to deal with, as they tried to maintain order while I streaked in and out of the house, content with my back garden projects, my childhood interest in bird-spotting, generally ruined by our family cat.

My mum would come home tired from work. I guessed it was because she got back late and had difficult cases. I'd try to ask her what happened at work but she never let me delve. 'Doctor-patient confidentiality,' she'd say, 'and anyway, you're too young.' I was ten, nearly eleven, and pretty sure I could handle anything. But then, on my eleventh birthday, I fell off a low tree branch in the back garden while I was trying to show off to the children who had come to my party. It was pretty clear my arm was broken. Dad drove me to the A & E where Mum was working, and we sat and waited while I tried not to cry. Mum was busy when we got there so we couldn't see her immediately, and when she appeared she was walking down the corridor towards us with a man and a woman.

'Please,' the woman was saying, 'we want to see the real doctor in charge of the case, we want a second opinion.'

'Exactly, Miss... what was your name again?'

'Dr Thurgood.'

'Really? Well, Miss Thurgood, we're sure you understand, we just want the best for our daughter.'

I saw my mother sigh, and I knew now why she was so tired when she got home each day. I didn't ask her about work so much after that, but I did still tell all my friends that she was a doctor and not only that she was a doctor, but that she was the best.

Now, as an adult I understand that we live in an inherently racist society, but as a child I did not. I thought they were just being mean, mean people, saying mean things. But racism is a fact we all have to confront in different ways. Its history is so long, its dimensions are so deep and so wide, that we cannot even see the edges. It is endemic. It underpins our most basic infrastructure; it could almost be considered an infrastructure in its own right. My parents are both British. I am British. But my parents are British in different ways. My father is Viking British. My mother is Palestinian British. My father moves through the world unchallenged. My mother does not.

The maths is wrong. This is the flaw in the equation. It's not an accident that the people stuck over here – reliant on the good grace of Barry Knight, of Save the War Orphans and world governments – have black and brown skin and often come from formally colonised countries; it's exactly as it is designed to be.

This is why me and Amanda used to argue so much. I haven't thought about it for a while, but this is definitely the reason. Different world views, with the bridges built between them continually in need of construction work and maintenance. It's not that she denies that racism exists, it's that she thinks she can plaster over it. And the situation's got worse, not better, during my time away. Now, the camps have spread to Europe. Now, army barracks and concentration camps from the Second World War are seen as an effective way to house refugees within the EU. Now, human rights are optional and lawyers who fight for them are 'activists,' as if such rights exist outside of democratic values instead of being the foundations of them.

But what do I expect from Amanda? And what do I hope to achieve from whatever it is I expect? How does this all end? How can any of us move forward without first examining our past, understanding our present and looking towards making our future a better place?

I look at the scene around me – the people going on with their daily lives, the fruit stalls, the dried goods piled up in sacks, the olives, the earthenware pots perfectly crafted – and I know that even here, probably not so far away, human beings could be added to this list of saleable wares. And no matter how many questions I ask, I still cannot work out how we got here.

43

WELCOME TO THE SHOW

BARRY

The headache's not as bad as it could be, but it's not great, so I chug down a couple more of the big pink pills in the back of this godawful Jeep that, despite its upmarket suspension, seems attuned to every single rut, bump, hole and crater in this hellish road that I can only assume leads to somewhere even worse. I'm trying to catch a little extra shut-eye by resting my head against the window, but every time I get close some fucking obstacle throws us in the air and cracks my head against the glass. A small voice is trying to remind me of the drunken promises I made myself last night – do the right thing, etc. – but right now I could happily clamber aboard the next plane out of here and drug myself stupid until solid London streets were once again under my boots.

We're slowly getting there, I guess. In the distance, through the heat haze, I can see a long uneven line of a darker shade and as we get closer it takes on shapes – walls, boxy little containers, tents, very few humans. I don't blame them.

It's weirdly flat here on the valley floor, like it's been carved out especially as some sort of container. The camp and the road that leads to it seem to be the only signs that humanity even exists. The valley walls are red rock and far apart, when I squint my eyes I can see the occasional little dot of green, but squinting makes my head hurt more, so I stop.

I feel like asking the charity woman why these people are here, in the middle of nowhere, but I'm still sore at her for walking out on me at the bar last night, so I'll sit on it a while longer. The only other option for conversation is some journalist they've got sitting next to me. I'll just keep shtum for now. In the front seat, the charity woman hasn't taken her gaze from the desert the whole way and hasn't said a word since she good-morninged me at the hotel. Even the driver, who says he's worked with her for years, only got a nod. Her dark glasses are hiding her eyes but I'm guessing they're not a pretty sight and wonder what's got her so wound up. Not likely to be the camp, she must be used to it. She's spent most of her adult life in places like this, dancing around at the edge of war zones. It's kind of sexy, when you think of it like that. But I won't mention that to her either, probably not the time.

The drugs finally start to kick in as we pull up to the gate; the first gate – there are two. Some police or security guards are lounging around the way they do and sort of lazily wave at us to go through. From what the guy last night said I thought they'd be more on it, but it turns out he was right, as soon as we're through the first gate some more security types or charity types or both – it's hard to tell when you're sweating into your own eyes – walk towards us and start looking at the paperwork of the people of the vehicle in front. But when they get to us they see the charity woman and back down.

We get through the second gate, sending up a big cloud of dust as we turn the corner, and there's two girls just standing there like they're waiting for us, but as soon as I see them one of the security-charity-whoever starts trying to move them on. I catch one of them wave at me, but just as I raise my own hand she's turned around and pointed in the direction of the tents. I get out of the car and am led to a Portakabin. Out of the corner of my eye I can see a sign painted in big black letters saying HELP US pinned to a tent. I wonder if it's meant for me and what I'm supposed to do about it.

The Portakabin has a fan on, running off a generator that purrs out the back like a big cat. If I was on my own I'd rip off all my clothes right here and stand in front of it, but I'm guessing these guys wouldn't be up for that. The charity woman seems to be waking up, talking to the people in the Portakabin, a woman and a man. The camera crew are trundling across the yard behind us. I can see them through the slats of the window blind, and when they open the door they bring in a wave of hot air that nearly topples me. They're talking among themselves too. It'll be a two-day shoot; they're discussing angles, light, other films they've done together. I have no idea how to interact with either of these groups so I stand in front of the fan, which is conveniently positioned next to the coffee machine, and make myself a drink. Another thing I'd do if I was on my own is empty my hipflask into the cup, but the voice in my head thinks I can do better and won't let me. So I stand there sipping the hot beverage, trying to ignore the shaking of my hands, trying not to make eye contact with the journo, who also looks totally out of place and is clearly trying to make eye contact with me. To be honest, she's not bad-looking, and in another situation I would, but this is not a place for taking risks, and nor is it the time in my life. I'm literally going to kill Sam for leaving me in this position.

It takes me a minute to realise that the charity woman is actually addressing me. She says we'll start with a little tour, like we're in some sort of bloody theme park or on safari. I almost make a joke about looking forward to seeing the hippos, but I stop myself, and congratulate myself a little for doing so. When we go back outside the HELP US banner has gone. I prepare the smile I practiced earlier. I'm hoping it says, 'I'm sorry about your shitty situation,' while at the same time not really encouraging conversation. That, at least, is the dream.

Outside, the heat is brutal; the sun weighs down on my head like it has actual density, like it's trying to push me into the dry earth, where I would gladly go, if only a shady chasm would open up under my feet. I bring out my dark glasses – not the most friendly look, the goody-goody voice says to me from inside my own skull – but without them I can't bloody see. It's too damn bright, in a way that just doesn't happen in England. This whole place is pulsating light. It's like being on stage under the lamps, but the crowd's different; in fact, there isn't one, there's hardly anyone at all.

'Where are all the people?' I ask, but no one answers. I try again to find out how many people live here, but everyone is suddenly distracted by the view and their clipboards and their fluttering little badges with their names on and the organisations they represent. I give up.

Whenever there is a brief gust of wind, any momentary relief you might feel is immediately compromised by the dust that blows into your eyes. I was right, this place is even worse than the shitty road that led here. I wonder if they built the road just for the camp, but there seems no point in asking – they won't bloody reply anyway. I'll have to get one of them drunk later to get any fucking answers out of them. I might even have to talk to the journalist who seems to be just trailing along behind us scribbling in her little pad, not so interested in me after all.

I'm pretty sure that the kids I saw at the gate are following us too. I've seen them a couple of times now, slipping between the big whitish tents. At the far end of the compound there's a big multi-coloured area that looks like a festival campground, but when you look closer it's all bits of old fabric and tarp sewn and wrapped together. I guess people live there. I guess that must be pretty fucking shit. No air-con or fans in one of those shitty little shelters, no room to move, even if you were on your own, which I'm guessing they're not. I wonder how many people you can fit in there.

The kids are at the edge of my vision again, just for a second. It's the dress of the one who waved at me that catches my eye each time; it's long and blue and slightly too big for her. I'm surprised she doesn't trip on it as she runs.

We've come to an abrupt halt outside one of the big white tents and the charity woman is telling me to come forward and meet the family. A young guy with sad eyes is lying on a low bed just inside the tent. I ask what's wrong with him and after some discussion the interpreter tells me he has a shrapnel wound which needs to be operated on. When I ask how it happened the family go quiet, like they understand the question before it's even translated. At home, the interpreter says avoiding the question, it happened just before they left.

'Why hasn't a doctor seen to him?' I ask the charity woman, and she tells me there's a waiting list, but that if we raise enough money the charity might be able to get more local doctors, and that hits me hard. Suddenly it's like she's made it my responsibility, and I take a few steps back. She looks at me like I'm an idiot or a child or both, an idiot child. I nod and suddenly they're moving me on again, and the journalist is still taking photos and furiously scribbling and it's beginning to set me on edge. What the fuck is she writing in there?

There's music coming from somewhere and as we go round the side of the last tent in the row I see a group of five guys playing a collection of instruments I'd find pretty hard to name, apart from the guitar. There's no one else about and it's clear they've been asked to put on some sort of show for me. A sick feeling starts rising somewhere in my gut. I don't want to offend them, the music's fucking good, but the idea that they've been asked to do this in the middle of all this, just for me, makes me feel, I don't know, I don't have the words. I may never have felt this, whatever it is, ever before.

I take a few deeps breaths – hard when every breath is hotter than the further reaches of hell, but I do it – and I raise my head and take a proper look around for what feels like the first time. I see the red cliffs rising up all around us. I see how small and fragile the walls and the barbed wire look in comparison to them. I see how dirty and torn the once-white tents are, and that we've walked down a row of the newest ones. I see some faces half-hidden behind canvas and tarp, staring out at me. Finally, it's back, the pain in my chest and the tightening of my lungs, and it's almost a relief because it means I'm feeling something, but I push through it. Without looking at the charity woman I go to shake the hands of the guys who've been playing and then head back unsteadily towards the entrance. The charity woman is chasing me, saying loads of words and getting a bit shrill. I can't even turn to look at her until we get back to the Jeeps.

'What the fuck, Barry?' she's screaming at me.

It takes me a minute to respond. I lean my head on the Jeep, but the metal's hot as hell and I have to stop myself from shrieking. I'm breathing like I've run a long way, but it's just the heat and this feeling I'm having and the panic attack I'm teetering on the edge of.

'I know you think I'm a dick, some useless fucking rock diva, but this...' and I motion towards the camp, unsure of what exactly I'm getting at or exactly how to say it, '... this... is fucked. Parade me around as much as you want and make any type of fool out of me you like, but these people, let them be, let them play music if they want to, but never, ever, ask them to do something for me, or because I'm here. It's...' and I've lost it again and what is most surprising is I feel like I'm going to cry, and for once it's not because I feel shit for me. I can't remember the last time that happened and what surprises me even more is that I start walking and once I start I can't stop. I'm just heading out through the gates and along the road to town.

Eventually the charity woman stops shouting and they all get in the Jeeps and start just following me, slowly, a little way behind. I'm aware I must look fucking mental, but by this point I just don't care. I'm starting to get my breathing back and maybe because I'm caked in sweat the wind is actually cooling for a moment. When I look up again at the desert and red rock cliffs I realise finally that I'm glad Sam isn't here. Alone, apart from the Jeeps trailing behind me, I feel almost free or at least empty like I've been washed clean and wrung out and remade and the brick guy is laughing at me and telling me I'm a dick for having some sort of epiphany after seeing a refugee camp for five minutes. He's saying some pretty mean stuff about how I always manage to make everything about me, but I calm him down by ignoring him and turning away and for a moment it's just me, Barry, in the desert, living a life that feels real.

And then, before I know it, I'm being ordered to get back in the Jeep.

Back at the hotel I discover they got it all on camera and they're proud as fucking punch for capturing my performance, fuckers. The other journalist slinks off, saying nothing, and I get the feeling she's up to something, and I'd like to know what.

For now, I go to take a shower before I get the drink I'm longing for. In my room I wonder how many of those big tents you could fit inside of it. The bathroom looks ridiculous – it all does. I get in the shower cubicle, relieved it's only regular size, and stand there motionless, while the water pours over me, trying to feel normal – which I realise is, in itself, a problem. My normal for a long time has been a heavily medicated experience. The normal that's creeping in now is a sort of normal I haven't felt for years. The feeling is akin to waking up. I realise I've started to hum and my body's moving to the tune, which I can't place for a minute until I realise it's only the first number-bloody-one we ever had. Before I know it I'm singing along to the music in my head, and I tear up a little, but it's okay because the shower washes it all way. I finally get out and realise my skin is on fire from today's sun. I find another stash of tiny plastic bottles, cover myself in heavily floral body lotion, and put on whatever I find at the top of my suitcase, doesn't matter, as long as it gets me to the bar and a cold beer.

Downstairs the journos are pacing even more than they were yesterday and chattering away on their satellite phones, but the one who was with us all day still hasn't re-emerged. Two of them are arguing in a corner. They look like a couple, at least the sort that bang when they work together. One is saying they have to stay to cover the story. The other, that they have to leave.

The need for a drink is even more urgent than I realised. I walk to the bar, amazed that the barman is still in place, though he looks like he didn't sleep, and I wonder why my agent hasn't called to tell me to get the fuck out, or why Sam hasn't bothered to check on me once. But I guess places like this and the wars that run across them, backwards and forwards, over and over, aren't the sort that make the Evening Standard. I check my phone, which turned on with no annoying noises, because there's fuck-all reception in this place for my shitty network and the Wi-Fi doesn't function. I know Sam would say something about roaming and settings and such, but he's not here. I'm in a dead zone. I just have to survive one more day of filming and then we're done and I'm gone. Twenty-four little hours, and I'm free.

The barman smiles at me as I approach, and I can't be sure if it's because he's in shock that I'm still here or that the fact that I'm still here gives him comfort, because surely a cunt like me would fuck off as soon as there was real trouble. As he passes me my drink, I lean onto the bar and try again.

'What's really going on here, mate?'

And – as if he's finally taken pity on me and is willing to give me a chance to escape – he leans in too. 'We have English language newspapers here, mate, you should try reading them.'

Oh well, seems it's hard to make friends in this place. But he has a point, so I down my beer and make for the front door again. Tonight the sky is clear and the guard guy with the giant gun lets me past. I walk down the big road the hotel's on until I get to a smaller one, an alleyway really, with lights on a string running down the middle of it. Finally I find a newspaper guy, the dailies and weeklies all stacked along a long wooden table against the wall. It's now I realise I've got no bloody money – not the local stuff, anyway – and I seriously doubt they take cards, so instead I stand there on the street and read the only newspaper I can find in English. It turns out I'm in the middle of what looks to become a pretty serious civil war. Well fuck, I'm pretty sure the charity woman owes me an explanation, or at least a very large, very alcoholic drink, but as she's not here I head back to the bar and get my own.

With the clarity that often comes with the third double gin, I realise I might not get out of here. Twenty-four hours might be twenty-three too many. People call thoughts like this sobering. I've never understood it; thoughts like this always make me reach for the nearest alcoholic beverage.

Maybe the book will be written, but I won't be around to read it.

Maybe that's justice for all the shit I've done. When I'm gone, it'll be pretty easy to piece it all together. I send flowers to that girl's grave every month, for fuck's sake. I know perfectly well who she is.

44

THE NIGHT BEFORE THE END OF THE WORLD

ANA

I'm looking at my notes from the day, looking through the photos, my hands shaking, my heartbeat in my ears. I have not managed to maintain my wall of separation. I'm furious and sad at the same time. I feel the pain of these people in my bones, the bones my parents made for me. I try to focus again on my notes, to distance myself, but it's difficult. Luckily, I don't have to file anything until tomorrow, but I check my email and Pete's sent through a link to an interview from an American talk show in which the host accuses Barry of the hit-and-run. He's says they're still following up on other leads, but that it seems like this was leaked by someone pretty high up, and looks promising. I type a quick reply and close my laptop. It could be a big story but it could also detract from what's happening at the camp and the call for an evacuation. It's too much stuff all at once. Unsure what to do, and to take my mind off it, I call Callum just to hear his voice.

'I wasn't ready,' I say, and of course he already knew.

He tells me to come back, to come home, but I feel the responsibility to write about what I've seen, and let the world know what's happening. I want to dig deeper, to witness how this will all play out – or, better, to get these people to safety. He asks me why it has to be me, why now, and I explain the conversation I had with Amanda and the feeling I have about my birth parents. I say it's like I finally understand something about their lives, at least one small part of them, and that this might be one of the reasons why Catherine was looking into it in the first place. As a sort of justice, a thank-you for the daughter they gave her. She wanted to expose the systems and practices that lead to the persecution, and sometimes even death, of people seeking safety. I tell him how these people are trapped between states, between laws, with no chance of moving forwards or back, and finally he relents and says he understands.

'Just keep yourself safe,' he says, 'I've done a bit of research of my own, things aren't looking so great over there. Do what you need to and get out as soon as you can.'

'Of course,' I say, but even as I say it I no longer know how it will be possible to leave, if it means walking away from all the people stuck in the camp with no choice but to remain, regardless of what happens next; despite war and hunger, despite their rights as humans under various conventions. The evacuation has to work. It's the only way we're all walking out of here, but I don't say that. I don't want him freaking out any more than he already is.

'I met two girls today, Saleema and her friend Noor. They've written a list of questions for Barry Knight if you can believe it, they think he'll be able to answer them all,' I say, to change the topic.

'What did you tell them?'

'I didn't want to disappoint them, they're so young. I said they should try.'

'Maybe you could convince him to talk to them, seeing as you're staying in the same place.'

It's a complicated proposition given everything with Sol, but I don't think I can get into that right now.

'Yeah, maybe I'll try. I'll send you a picture of the list. They're pretty serious kids.'

We hang up and I leave my room to go downstairs to the bar. Barry's down there already. Where else would he be? But given what I want to discuss, I have no idea how to approach him. In the end, though ethically dubious in several different ways, I do it with gin, which I've noticed he's partial to, and open by asking him how he found going to the camp today, nice and friendly. It takes a few drinks for me to get to the point. There are some who would say that the art of heavy drinking while keeping a clear head is one of the most important skills a journalist can learn.

'So, was there anything to that accusation the TV host laid on you? Were you really involved in a hit-and-run? A pretty ballsy thing to get away with…' I try to keep my tone even, but he's obviously put on guard.

'How could I have been? I was at a party. Don't you people do any research?' It looks like he's going to get straight up and leave.

'Hey, stay for another drink. I'm only asking, I'm a journalist, it's my nature to be nosey. If you weren't there, you weren't there, end of.'

And he settles again, but I can see it playing on his mind, like he actually wants to talk about it after all.

'You should talk to Sam, he drove me there.'

'Where? The party?'

'Yeah, in the Cadillac.'

'You drive an American car in London? Parking must be a nightmare.' And I realise, as I say it, that this means it wasn't him, that even if he was in the car, he wasn't the one driving. Sol must have seen him as the passenger. It's definitely a story, just not the one I expected.

'And that's the car this Sam, your friend, was driving that night, you're sure?'

He nods, and as he does, I can see he looks confused.

'Is he a good friend, this Sam?' I ask, but he doesn't even try to respond and before I know it he's up and off, holding his phone up in the air like he's got no idea how network signal works.

I feel an immense sense of relief that this is not a story I have to cover after all, but it's soon quashed by the realisation that I forgot to ask him to talk to the girls I met, and the sense of failure descends once again. Sol's not anywhere to be seen and I don't know his room number, so I can't tell him about Barry. I wonder how he'll feel after believing for so long that it was him and after coming all this way.

45

OTHER, BETTER SELVES

AMANDA

Here's what I was actually thinking while I was supposed to be fawning over Barry the-rock-god Knight. I was thinking, I remember when I last felt free. I was thinking, it was a very long time ago. Even in the great expanse of the desert I didn't feel it, a place people have dedicated their lives to writing about; a place of wonder, of life-filled emptiness, of clarity. Well, not for me; at least, not anymore.

When I met the people I built this thing with, when I met Omar, it was like I had finally come home, after a lifetime of searching. But I'll admit it: this thing was always an adventure – done for all the right reasons, but an adventure, nonetheless. And in my blurred reflection in the window on the way to the camp, I could see that younger self. She had her head to the side, looking at me like she couldn't work me out, didn't even know who I was, and the only way to get rid of her was to close my eyes. But her voice in my head wouldn't shut up.

My first desert – our first desert, her first desert, the desert of my younger self – was not so far from here, only next-door, in fact. It was a simple enough job, handing out food packs to internally displaced people, as they're called, which makes it sound like they wandered too far from home, got lost, got stuck; it's not a phrase that has much of a punch, it doesn't scream war, rape and torture. I did it for three months, got home, and realised I no longer knew how to have a normal conversation with my lovely middle-class parents. Their bickering over who bought the wrong brand of breakfast cereal was worse than silence. Even my friends from university, who'd all studied the same thing as me, were either off out in the world doing something, making change, or were exactly where I'd left them, and I'd travelled too far from that place to find my way back.

It was Alex I met first. She was reading Development as Freedom, one of my course books, in the coffee shop I went to on the border of my parent's leafy suburb. I could tell immediately from her intense stare, her general presence, that she was a different type of person altogether from the people I'd studied with. She had the glow of someone who spent her life outdoors, yet here she was in a London coffee shop. I sat down at the table next to hers, and when she looked up for a moment from her reading, I asked her what she thought of it.

'I think I'd hate anyone to write a book about my development and freedom, but then the world's a fucked-up place and I've got a fucked-up life, so maybe someone should. Fancy it?'

I don't think I bothered answering, just laughed, feeling like I'd found a friend in a sea of strangers. That night we arranged to go to the pub together, and that's where I met the others: Ruhi, Jem, Omar and Catherine, the oldest, the grown-up. They were all sitting together when I arrived, a little older than me and a little cooler, a little further on their paths. They'd already started a project raising money through music gigs and extended family to go out to war-torn countries and build playgrounds; it was a few more years before Save the War Orphans was born. It was a response to what we found on our travels, to who we met, to the children we had to leave behind.

People have often asked me why I wanted to work in conflict zones in the first place. Was there something missing from my life, did I have a death wish, am I unusually brave? The answer is perhaps none and all of these things. The answer is it felt like the right thing to do at the time. The question is, do I still believe that?

Omar is in my head again, and while I'm dissecting the day, we're already arguing. I'm already wrong and he's already righteous. The tour of the camp, the music, went terribly, as he would have predicted. But we just wanted to show the skills these people have, form a connection with their would-be benefactor. We didn't build the place, we never would, but something about managing that camp day-in, day-out, makes it feel like we're responsible for its very birth, makes you forget the dirty deals that span the Mediterranean, the governments at play with people's lives. They're all so bloody far from here, so clean, so pristine, sometimes even I think it can't possibly be them, it must be us. Surely, no elected ruling body would impose these conditions on other humans, surely... but fuck it, if this life has taught me anything it is exactly the opposite. That they will do this time and time again as long as it is hidden, faraway and off the media agenda, and even then, they'll do it anyway and talk some bullshit about national security. The only thing that can cut through all this crap? The photo. I can't even say it again in my own head, but it's goddamn true, and you know exactly which photo I mean.

46

SOME THINGS, YOU CAN'T RUN FROM

OMAR

Amanda comes back into the room distraught, rambling about dead children, about fires and media strategies. She's teetering on the edge.

'There's a war,' she states, 'coming right to our front door and nobody is doing anything, nobody will be moved from that camp. What can I tell them? That a magic man, a rock star, for God's sake, will make it all alright? These people aren't stupid, they know what's coming. I see it in their eyes. I hear it in all their questions about any subject that doesn't directly point to the fact that everything they've run from, everything they've survived, is about to arrive smack bang in the middle of their lives again. I feel helpless, and they know it.'

I try to calm her down with words, but it has the opposite effect, so I pour her a drink instead.

'This isn't your fault,' I say.

'It's all of our fucking faults – you know that. It's your goddamn sermon.'

And it's true, this is exactly my argument.

'You've called everyone?'

'Of course, every commissioner, CEO, MP, MEP I know. I called them all. Nothing. Apparently there's no room anywhere else. Nowhere for these people to go.'

She almost spits the last bit, and, despite everything, her anger, which she has maintained throughout it all, inspires me, gives me hope.

'Have you told Susan?'

'No, I'll do it tomorrow after the filming. If it doesn't get any better we'll send them all home.'

'I'll come with you when you go to the camp,' I say, surprising myself. 'We'll do this bit together.'

47

FORGIVENESS

BARRY

The film crew are off setting up, arguing, mixing up their cables. I chase down one of them and suppress my ego long enough to ask him to fix my phone. He does it in seconds and grumpily hands it back to me. None of us have slept much. There was no night, just flashes on the horizon and far-off booms getting closer. I wonder how much the charity woman, Amanda, is paying everyone to stick around, how much she's lying to them. She's clearly not doing a very good job, they're all on eggshells, their minds already on the plane, in the sky, far away from this shithole.

I call Sam. I've had a bit of a realisation after my convo with the journo and it's not a pretty one.

'I know,' I say straight out when he answers.

'What, mate? What do you know?' he replies, all sheepish, which doesn't surprise me and I realise I don't really care.

'It was you that was driving that night, we were in the Cadillac.'

There's silence on the other end of the line.

'It's okay,' I say. 'I'm not going to rat you out.'

I don't care that he lied to me about who was driving that

night and I don't care why he didn't come. I don't care that he doesn't apologise immediately for any of it. It's all in the past. Stuff I based my previous life on. And that life, as of today, is over, and just in case this turns out to be literally the case, I have a back-up plan.

'One other thing,' I say. 'Call the lawyer, set up an appointment. I'm changing my will.'

'What?' he asks. 'What the fuck is going on over there?'

'Doesn't matter, mate, I'm going to leave everything to the war orphans.'

'Sometimes I just don't get you.'

'Just do it, do it as soon as you hang up.'

'Okay, look I'm sorry I didn't come and about...'

'It's okay, I get it, you've got a life. Don't worry about me, I'm fine and I love you okay, and I forgive you. You're my best fucking friend.'

And before he can say anything in response I hang up. I look up and for some reason that guy from the bar the other night is looking at me funny. Staring right at me like he knows something, like he's about to take me down, and I welcome it. Bring it the fuck on.

48

ESCAPE

AMANDA

Omar sat next to me all the way in the Jeep, gripping my hand tightly. I knew he'd be nervous about coming back into this situation; he only did it to keep me sane and to try and convince me to leave. When we passed a tank going in the opposite direction on the way here he tried one more time.

'Maybe we should head back,' he said, but I refused to even talk about it, so he turned to Ibrahim. 'I don't think you should come in with us. Drive back to town and you can pick us up later.'

Ibrahim agreed, his face grave in the rear-view mirror.

'Do you understand what might happen here?' Omar asked me.

'We still have time for an evacuation if we can just convince the world to care,' I said and he shook his head and kissed me swiftly on the lips.

Ibrahim drops us at the gate and drives away. The guards have left leaving only their tipped-up plastic chairs behind.

There's something in the air which makes me wish I'd listened to Omar earlier, but it's too late now, and my reasons remain. The people in the camp are all standing outside their shelters talking among themselves. They sense it too.

But I have to believe we have time.

Barry and the film crew are already here so I rush ahead while Omar walks so slowly it's as if he isn't moving, like he's trying to stop the clock. I get to the Portakabin first and sift through my bag for the keys. The lock is fiddly and when I finally get it to open I turn to watch him as he makes his way towards me, this man I have loved for so long, who I realise I still love. I think of how it would feel to let all this go, strip myself of responsibilities. There's an incredible lightness to the thought.

'Okay,' I say as he reaches me. 'After this, we'll do it.'

And I think, yes, we will find another way, but he takes my hands and shakes his head. He pulls me down to the floor with him and I don't understand what's happening until I see the French-made drone coming for us in the distance, and something in my gut tells me there is no other day, there is only now.

49

CONFRONTATION

SOL

Barry Knight's got here, and now, while everyone is distracted setting things up, is my chance. I spent all of yesterday, and every moment since Leila died, building up to this moment. I walk up to him and he doesn't flinch. Why would he? We shared a drink the other day.

'Do you recognise me?' I ask him, ignoring the shouting coming from somewhere else in the camp.

This is my only chance. I can feel it.

'Of course, from the bar the other night,' he says, but his tone suggests he understands this isn't what I meant.

'From the night you ran over a girl with your car. I saw you, I saw you see me.'

He takes a few steps back, not to run, but to take it in, like I shot him and he's reeling from the impact of it. He trips over a rock and falls backwards – he doesn't even cry out as it happens, it's like I've switched him off.

'Her name was Leila,' I say, speaking her name like a sentence.

'I know,' he says. 'I've always known, but look, it

wasn't...' and he is about to say something else but seems to think better of it. 'I'm so fucking sorry.'

I've spent what seems like my whole life imagining this moment, but Barry just looks crumpled and old, lying on the floor like that, his legs pulled up to his chest as he rights himself, his hands across his face. Life has already worked him over. I'm too fucking late to cause any damage. He's already done it to himself. I offer him a hand up, but he manages to get to his feet, only to be knocked down once more by a tremor that seems to shake the whole earth and a roaring sound bigger than the earth itself, bigger than everything. I'm on my back now too and as I look up, high above is a drone and from her belly stars are forming and I think of Ana, out there somewhere on her own.

'Barry,' I hold out my hand again, 'we've got to go.'

Together we stand up, using each other for stability as the woman from the charity screams at us to take cover.

'When did you last see the journalist?' I ask Barry.

He looks at me blankly.

'Ana, the one you were speaking to last night,' I say, aware that I'm losing precious time, but he shakes his head at me, he has no idea.

I run without looking back. The NGO office where the press team are based is not that far, but I can't see anything in the smoke, by the time I reach the site where they once stood there is only a crater and the lick of flames. I turn to see a young girl running towards Barry. Ana is cowering by a tent next to them. I get to her just in time. I think of Leila and Caspian and all the futures we could have had.

50

THE WITNESS

ANA

The militia guy I was about to interview is dead and only a few metres away from me. His gun is on the floor next to him and for a second I think about running to grab it, but what help would it be? I don't even know how to shoot.

Sol's got his arm around me, like he can shield me from all this. I wish he could. Amanda and a man are running towards us, motioning for us to get inside the container. She's still trying to organise things, just as Catherine would. I take out my phone, open up my messages to Pete and press the video icon. With one hand I hold it up, the seconds of footage ticking, with my other I search in my pocket and find the baby bomb cutting. I took it with me when I left. I hold it now, clutched to my chest. It's only now, in this moment, that I realise I wish I'd claimed them as my own when I had the chance. Banesh and Zemar, my parents, as real as Catherine, my mother. This last act is for all of them and for all of us in this camp.

I press send.

None of us expected this to happen so quickly.

I thought we had more time. I guess we always do.

50

THE MOST DIFFICULT QUESTION

SALEEMA

In the confusion of adults I finally see the famous man, Barry Knight; he's running towards the woman from the charity as if she'll save him, as if she could, so I chase after him. This is my moment. These people have never lived with war and so they can't stay calm in moments like this, but I can. I leave my mother's side without looking back. When I catch up with him, I scream his name above the noise and he turns, reaching his hand out to me as if he wants us to run together so I hold out my hand towards him in return. Let him take it if he wants, as long as I get my questions answered. There's panic in his eyes, but I have seen panic in the eyes of men before and I've survived. Before our fingers have touched I am already asking my first question: 'Why...?'

A noise louder than thunder, a noise I recognise from home, crashes around and above us. The famous man finally takes my hand and together we fly and for a second it is just like magic, but then, just as suddenly, we are falling and the magic is gone and so are we.

EPILOGUE

They carved us from the earth together, a diorama of our own making, frozen for eternity to the external and living eye. After the bombs stopped, when the next round of treaties had been signed, we were taken by heavy machinery, loaded and unloaded countless times until encased, to be dusted once a week and wiped down on weekends.

This museum, once thought out-of-date and struggling for funds, took us as their centre piece. The modern human, locked up with all the pain we caused each other, and indistinguishable when the flesh has fallen from our bodies. Though, of course, we're partly here for him, loudmouth that he is; for all he did in life, he is remembered as a saint in death.

The Bones of Barry Knight

So says the sign above us. The other names – our names, my name – are all extinct. And yet here we are, and here we will remain until remembered. Like the lion, cut in half and roaring for his mate through unblemished glass, we will not stop shouting our stories until we are heard.

ACKNOWLEDGEMENTS

For early readings and invaluable editing I would like to thank Jo McGain, Alice Bowley, Eeyun Purkins, Becka Wolfe, Claire Kohda Hazelton (who was very kind to a friend of a friend), Keira Dignan, Phillippa Metcalfe and Giulio D'Errico, always.

Free beds and good food have been provided by many, especial thanks, again, to those of the village of Verga. Further thanks to all my beloved friends in the UK – including those we've lost along the way – who know when I need to take a break and look in the other direction to see what's right in front of me. To Mani, a faithful four-legged friend, for the same reason. To the community that supports me every day in Greece, the friends that have offered me encouragement and given me time even when the world is hell-bent on making sure we have none.

A large chunk of this book was written while looking out over Loch Long at Cove Park and I don't think I would have managed it anywhere else. Thank you for giving me the space I needed.

To the wonderful team at Legend Press for their support and encouragement. To my family, for not thinking me too mad during the long years of writing that lead to this point, and to you, for reading.